TO SAVE A MATE

POPPY IRELAND

To all the readers who took a chance on this new pen name of ours. We're sorry for that thing we did to Corbin in this installment. Oh, who are we kidding? No, we're not. That guy totally deserved what was coming to him. Trust us, when you get to that chapter, you'll know. We hope you enjoy the ride as much as we enjoyed writing it.

Still wondering who we are? Well, that's a secret we'll never tell. Or maybe we will. Only time will tell, little witchlings... 😉

xoxo, Poppy

CHAPTER

ONE

Nicole

"Nicole! Nicole!" Corbin's voice was as sharp as a razor. His relentless pounding on my door and the sense of urgency in his tone *almost* convinced me to get out of bed and confront him, but I was still too raw from what had happened the night before.

Alexei's betrayal.

The complete humiliation.

My father's abduction.

Alpha Jones's sinister words.

Mace licked my arm, urging me out of bed with a whine. It embarrassed me to confess that I didn't *want* to leave my bed. Not because I was miserable and feeling defeated, but because these soft sheets smelled like Alexei.

His woodsy, masculine scent comforted me despite the pain he'd inflicted. If I stayed here and breathed him in, then I could almost forget the angry pang in my chest. The damn mate bond Alexei and I shared still drew me in with its deceptive pheromones.

If the mate bond was real, anyway. I wasn't so sure anymore. Maybe I was just dickmatized, as Bee liked to call it.

"I don't want to talk to him, Macey." My grumbling words didn't seem to bother her. My wolf was on a mission. She tugged at my sweatpants with her teeth, dragging me off the mattress. I gripped my comforter, but it was no use. I landed on the floor with a loud thud, the sound making Corbin stop shouting to listen.

"Nicole? Are you okay?" He twisted the locked door-knob, suddenly more desperate to get in.

Rage billowed within me. I didn't want to listen to him *pretend* to be concerned about me. "What the fuck do you care, Corbin?"

Maybe it would have been better to continue ignoring him, but I hated the sincerity in his tone. Everything had gone to shit, and I needed to remind myself that the only truth I could cling to was that I could trust *no one*. I brushed my fingers over my neck where I knew Alexei's bruising lips had left a hickey. The overwhelming longing I felt from the memory made my breath hitch.

Maybe I couldn't even trust myself.

"That's it!" I didn't have time to process Corbin's

muffled words through the protection of my dorm room door, because soon after he'd said them, he was kicking it down. Mace positioned herself in front of me, growling as wood splintered the frame, and Corbin strolled through the threshold, a concerned look on his face. "You've been crying."

I hated the way his gaze swept over me with pity.

"Are you crazy?!" I scrambled to stand up. "Did you really just kick my door down? And don't you dare stand there and look like you give a shit, Corbin. I heard the recording, remember?" I prayed he couldn't hear the way my voice wobbled.

Macey growled again, this time really showing her teeth.

Corbin held his palms out in surrender as he spoke to her. "Calm down, girl. I thought we were pals." His hazel eyes flickered to me. "And this whole mess isn't what it looks like, Nicky. Please let me explain."

To comfort me and to figure out what was going on, my familiar whimpered and nudged my leg with her wet nose. I could tell she was torn. She might have pissed on Corbin in the beginning, but like me, the annoying asshole had grown on her. We were both fooled.

"You lost the right to call me Nicky." I shook my head. "And I think it was pretty damn self-explanatory. I've never been more humiliated in my life."

He winced. "I know. And I'm sorry. Alexei's sorry. But—"

I pointed a stern finger at him. "Do *not* bring him into this. If Alexei was *really* sorry, he'd be here begging for my forgiveness instead of sending his lackey to do it for him."

Corbin released a heavy sigh, lowering his voice. "That's not true. We're trying to protect you. I give you my word."

"Like you protected my dad?" I scoffed, choking back a sob as the memory of my father being taken against his will flashed through my head. "Your word doesn't mean *shit*, Corbin. Neither does Alexei's. Now, *get out!*"

"Your dad?" Corbin frowned. "What does your dad have to do with this?"

Soft murmurs drew my attention to the hall where at least a dozen sleep-rumpled people were now gathered, watching the spectacle before them.

Fucking hell.

"Don't insult my intelligence by pretending you don't know exactly what I'm talking about," I snapped. "After what you guys did to me, you owe me a little honesty, don't you think? Although, let's be real; I'm not holding my breath. Fool me once and all that."

"I *am* being honest!" Corbin insisted. "I do not know why you're bringing up your father right now. This has nothing to do with him." The murmurs from our audience became louder, causing Corbin to turn toward them and yell, "Get the fuck out of here, assholes!"

Macey barked as they all scattered like cockroaches back to their rooms.

I folded my arms across my chest. "You should take your own advice. Also, someone had better be here within the hour to fix my damn door."

He huffed, pulling his cell out of his pocket. His thumbs ran over the screen for a bit before he said, "They're already on the way. Now tell me about your father."

Was it possible Corbin didn't actually know? Or was this a test? Was Corbin acting dumb to see if I would defy his alpha's order? I thought about what Alpha Jones said to me last night before leaving me to head back to my dorm.

"Before you get any stupid ideas, if you say a word to anyone about this, I will *know, and you* will *pay. I'll be watching you, Nicole. Never forget that."*

I needed to drop it. It wasn't worth the risk. My dad's safety was my top priority.

"My dad... I tried getting him to leave with me last night, but he wouldn't agree. This fucking school is the last place I want to be, but until I can convince my dad to come with me, I'm staying put."

"You were going to run away?" Corbin asked incredulously. "Nicky, you can't just run away. That would *destroy* Alexei."

Once more, I felt myself growing angry. "Destroy *Alexei*? What about *me*? I don't care what Alexei's reasoning is. He humiliated me. Made me feel worthless. All for what? Some cruel joke?"

"No!" he insisted. "It was *never* a joke. You're his mate. He would *never* do anything to hurt you."

"Bullshit." I swallowed the lump in my throat. "That's all Alexei's ever done! I may have fallen for his pretty lies once, but I sure as hell won't make that mistake again. Because my handy little built-in supernatural reference guide agrees with you on one thing. A shifter would *never* intentionally hurt their mate. It defies every part of an actual mating bond. I did *a lot* of thinking after I ran out of that sorority house last night, Corbin. And the fact of the matter is, if a guy looks like a lying asshole and talks like a lying asshole, then he's *a lying asshole*! I'm done. For good. Once I can convince my father to leave, I'm out. Fuck shifter politics. Fuck fake mating bonds. *Fuck all of you.*" I blinked rapidly, stubbornly willing my impending tears to go away.

Corbin's eyes widened. "Can you at least let me explain before you decide? I only need a few minutes."

"I've seen firsthand that I'm completely alone in all of this. I can't count on you. I can't count on Alexei." Mace nudged me with her nose, quietly reminding me *she* was still here for me. "Nothing you can say would make this okay."

"Alpha Jones was at Beta Phi last night, Nicole. If he knew you were mates—"

I was tired of all the fucking lies. Corbin thought he could just walk in and smooth things over for his future alpha, but I wasn't so easily fooled anymore.

"Enough. I don't care. I really, truly don't. I want nothing to do with this world, Corbin. I want nothing to do with *any of you.*"

"I'm just trying to help, Nicole." Corbin sighed, his eyes soft and full of sadness.

"And I just want all of you to leave me alone. If you feel such a strong need to help, help your future alpha understand that if he tries talking to me, I'll rip off his balls and feed them to Mace."

My wolf barked in agreement. *Good girl.*

Corbin lingered in my bedroom, opening and closing his mouth like a goldfish. It didn't matter what he said. I didn't trust him anymore.

"So, what's the plan? Do you think you're rejecting Alexei for real this time? I'd hate to point out the obvious here, but you've already slept together. The bond is more intense now. It can't just be erased."

"Stop talking about a fucking bond that doesn't exist!" I didn't care that I was screaming at that point. "I bet Alexei was just *thrilled* to—wait—what did you say? *Loosen me up with a few orgasms?*"

Corbin had the decency to look ashamed, but I didn't buy his act for one second.

"I'm just so glad it wasn't a *hardship* for Alexei. I guess being *hot as fuck* has its perks, right? Correct me if I am wrong. I'm just quoting you." I poked him in the chest with my index finger. "Maybe you should have joined in, Corbin. The three of us would have really taken that video to the next level, don't you think? Or do you prefer to ridicule me from the sidelines? I knew you dabbled in cuckolding, but I had no idea you got off watching your friend get humiliated, too. But I guess we weren't friends, were we? Because friends don't say shit like that about one another. Friends don't allow sex tapes to show up on a big-ass projector screen for a bunch of strangers to see." My voice was shrill. The more my words tumbled out of my mouth, the louder I got.

Corbin looked close to tears, and if I wasn't so pissed, I *almost* would have felt a little bad for him. "You *are* my friend, Nicky," he whispered. "Mara was trying to compel me. She doesn't know I've trained myself to resist her powers. I said what I said because I was trying to keep your secret."

"I don't believe you," I choked out, furious tears streaming down my cheeks. "Alexei was up there celebrating with Mara, like the three of you got exactly what you wanted. Well, you know what, Corbin? She can have him. And you can all go to hell."

"Nicole. Please. I'm begging you, just hear me out. I care about you so much—"

"Stop. Just stop." I held my hands up. I couldn't hear him anymore. Corbin wasn't my friend. None of them were.

Corbin's eyes widened, and he looked visibly shaken. Good.

I grabbed a sweatshirt and threw it over my pajamas, a

plan already forming in my mind. I just had to get to Juniper.

"Where are you going?" he asked as I walked out of my room.

"None of your business."

I didn't even care that I was leaving my room wide open for anyone to come take advantage of. I placed the only possessions that mattered to me in the trunk of my dad's car last night so we could run the moment I figured out where he was and freed him.

"You can't just leave, Nicky. We need to talk." He reached for my arm, but the moment his hand wrapped around my wrist, Mace snapped at him. "Shit, Mace!"

"Good girl," I said while continuing to march out of the dorm.

"Seriously. It's not a good idea. You're going to get yourself hurt."

I sniffled. "It's too fucking late, Corbin. I can't imagine anything hurting worse than this."

Macey dutifully took her place at my side, and we walked away without another word.

TWO

Alexei

I HAD A CRACKED RIB, a broken jaw, and couldn't feel my leg. There were bruises covering every inch of my body, yet my father was just getting started.

Everything fucking hurt. Each inhale was like a needle sinking deeper into my lungs. The pain I felt seeped deep down, splintering my bones and sending excruciating shockwaves through my nerves.

But it was nothing compared to the shame.

My quick healing pleased my father. Not only did it let him draw out my pain, but it also meant that I wouldn't look roughed up for the event tomorrow night. His fist slammed into my chest, nearly stopping my heart.

And I couldn't hit back.

I could *never* hit back.

If I did, then that would be taken as a formal challenge for alpha, and I wasn't sure I was ready for that. He'd been beating me within an inch of my life since I was old enough to take the hit, and there was nothing I could do about it.

"A sex tape with a *human*, Alexei! A filthy, worthless human." He punctuated each word with another punch to my chest. The distinct crack of another bone nearly made me puke. "What. The. Fuck. Were you thinking?! Do you have any idea what kind of PR nightmare you've caused?"

Bright red blood splattered the white marble flooring of my childhood home as his forceful blows returned to my face. He hadn't even made it past the mansion's foyer when he started wailing on me.

"I didn't make it," I wheezed, wiping sweat from my brow. Or was that blood?

I held my sticky, wet fingers in front of my face. *Yep, definitely blood.*

My father's clenched fist paused mid-air. "Bullshit. You were fucking bragging about it last night. Not so tough now, are you?"

"I swear!" I choked out.

"Then, who did?"

"Don't know yet." I had my suspicions but no solid proof. I sure as hell was going to make finding the responsible party a priority, though. "But I'll find out soon enough."

I prodded a loose molar with my tongue.

Fuck.

Teeth were a bitch to heal. Once they were knocked out entirely, they were a lost cause. I really hoped my gum tissue repaired itself before that happened.

"You have an entire pack full of female shifters ready to suck your cock, and you screwed a *human*?" He pulled away from me with a grunt and rolled up his sleeves. "I don't care who you use as a fuck toy, but broadcasting the evidence to the pack is unacceptable. Do you know how many calls and emails I've gotten today? It's shameful."

"I'm sorry, Alpha," I grunted.

"Sorry will not cut it." He kicked me in the stomach one last time, his hard boot colliding with my body and knocking the air out of me. "Now I have to smooth things over for you again. Our only saving grace is that you humiliated that girl. I'd rather people think you were playing a cruel joke than actually enjoying fucking that worthless cunt. We need to do damage control. I've decided your engagement to Mara Sullivan will be announced tomorrow night at the banquet."

My entire body halted. I went deathly still while processing his words. No. I couldn't. I fucking *refused.*

Mara was a terrible person, a disgusting user drunk off her own power. I'd rather stab myself in the eye than look at her, let alone *marry* her. "Engagement? Father, I—"

"Don't you *dare* argue with me. I'm saving your ass, Alexei. Mara comes from a respectable family, and she's one of the strongest she-wolves we have. Her compulsion skills will be a valuable asset as a future luna."

"Mara is probably the person who set up the camera!" I argued, knowing damn well I was practically begging my father to hit me again. "And she's *definitely* the one who broadcast it to the entire house knowing what was on it!"

All I wanted to do was get this over with so I could see my mate and try to explain. It didn't matter how much my father hit me; nothing compared to the pain of hurting Nicole. I knew I had my work cut out for me, though. The devastation on her face last night had gutted me. If my father hadn't summoned me back to Ridgeview, I would've gone to her immediately after she ran from the Beta Phi house.

But when my father summoned me, I was always forced to obey.

Going against him meant certain death, and I couldn't fix my relationship with Nicole if I was buried six feet under. I waited for his return all night, pacing the estate like a caged beast until sunrise, when he finally graced me with his presence and proceeded with the beatings.

"All the more the reason for her to suffer the consequences by marrying your weak, pathetic self. Believe me, boy, you're getting the better deal in this scenario." His smile was wicked as he unbuttoned his shirt and tossed it on the floor for the maid to clean up. "You should thank me. It's time to grow up, Alexei. I'm sick of fixing your screwups."

"Mara is untrustworthy. She—"

"I didn't say you had to *trust* her," he interrupted. "But you *will* marry her. If it's any consolation, at least you'll have some premium shifter pussy on tap. And she'll produce fine pups. You could do a lot worse than Mara Sullivan."

Doubtful.

I knew I had to try a different tactic. I could tell my father intended to stand firm on this decision, and there was no way I would *ever* marry that traitorous bitch.

I winced as I felt my ribs fusing back together. "Father. You're playing right into Mara's hand. Being my luna is *exactly* what she wants. She's dangerously ambitious and self-absorbed. You wouldn't be punishing her. You'd be *rewarding* her."

A villainous grin stretched across his face. "Well, then consider it *your* punishment, son, for being such a colossal disappointment to this family. This isn't up for negotiation, Alexei. You marry Mara, or you step down from your position as future alpha. Plain and simple."

A fleeting idea struck me. One that made my heart race with the possibilities. Maybe stepping down wouldn't be such a bad thing. Nicole and I could run away. We wouldn't have to deal with my father's rules or the pack politics.

"You like that idea, don't you?" Dad asked, his lip curled in a snarl. "You're thinking about walking away— giving up your birthright."

My chest constricted with fear. Was I really that transparent? "N-no, Alpha. That's not—"

"Don't lie to me, kid. From the moment you were born, I knew you weren't cut out for this world. You're too weak. Too emotional. But let me be clear." Dad crouched so that we were at eye level, a splatter of my blood on his neck. "If you shame this family by running away, I'll track you down. I'll kill you and everyone you love. I'll make a brutal, bloody example out of you for the entire world to see. Either you step up or you die a painful, humiliating death." He stood back up and rolled his neck. "As alpha, I know that I have to do what is necessary for the good of our pack. I'm not afraid to make the hard choices—the sacrifices. Last night is proof of that. Do you know what I was doing?"

I shook my head.

"Because you—or Mara, it doesn't really matter—thought it would be funny to share your human sex tape with the world, that stupid girl thought she would take her father and leave."

My stomach sank. "She left?"

"She *tried*. Her father is currently locked in a lab with three of my men guarding him."

Shit. This was bad. Really fucking bad.

"What about Nicole?"

"I made sure she knew who was in charge. She's on campus so I can watch her. There's something... different about her."

"Did you hurt her?" My voice sounded more confrontational than what was appropriate. But I felt nothing but murderous rage at the idea of my father harming my mate. My healing sped up because of the hard, furious adrenaline pumping through my veins.

"She's fine. *For now*. What happens next will depend on how compliant you two are. The human will move into the Beta Phi house as planned, and you will stay far away from her and focus on your proposal. Everyone at the banquet hall will watch you, waiting for you to screw up. If you know what's good for you, you'll do whatever it takes to make your engagement to Mara look authentic."

"Do you honestly think that the scientist will work with you if you kill the only leverage you have?" I gritted my teeth.

"I *think* you aren't strong enough *or* smart enough to provide any commentary on the decisions I make." His eyes flashed with anger. "And I believe Dr. Fairweather is wise enough to cooperate, especially now that the block has been removed from his mind. He is *well* aware of what we are and what we're capable of should he choose to resist."

I tried my best to hide my shock. "Your witches got past the block?"

His mouth curved into a sinister smile. "No. Interestingly enough, I believe his daughter accomplished that somehow. She's claiming ignorance, but I'm not convinced. Everything about that girl marks her as a human, but that's not possible if she's capable of wielding magic. I'm looking into her background a bit more thoroughly. Sadly, her father has already proven useless in that respect. He may know supernaturals exist now, but my mind-walker wasn't able to glean any useful memories that make Nicole extraordinary."

Fuck.

My father had the resources to dig deep. Dr. Fairweather may not have known his wife possibly belonged to the supernatural community—*thank God*—but there were at least two people in Nicole's life who did. I was sure it was only a matter of time before my dad's people connected the dots. I needed to figure this out before my dad did so I knew how to best protect my mate. And I had the advantage because, unlike my father, I knew exactly where to start.

The problem was, I knew my father would have men tailing my every move, and I was smart enough to take his threats seriously. I needed to stay away from Nicole, but I needed information from her as well, and time was of the essence. I knew Nicole's godmother and her friend were the key to uncovering whatever the late Mrs. Fairweather was hiding; the woman from the video chat admitted as much. But I didn't conveniently have access to their contact information. The only person I could trust was Corbin, but I was sure my dad's men would watch him, too. I couldn't possibly task him with hacking into Nicole's cloud server to get that information. It had to come directly from my mate or, at the very least, from one of her devices that stored that information. There had to be a solution, but I couldn't think of one. One thing I knew was I needed to throw my father off the scent.

I stood to my full height and lifted my chin. "Nicole Fairweather is utterly unremarkable in every way."

"Yet you bedded her anyway, and seemed rather taken with her during the act itself. If I didn't know better, I'd swear you actually *liked* the troublesome human." My father's stony gaze narrowed as he cocked his head to the side. "Why is that, I wonder?"

I swallowed back bile at the thought of this man watching that video. He saw Nicole naked. Emotionally vulnerable. Every instinct inside of me wanted to gouge out the eyeballs of anyone who witnessed such a private moment with my mate, but especially this man. I knew my father well enough to know he studied that video through a different lens than anyone else who was at Beta Phi last night. He was no doubt searching for anything he could use to his advantage, like my obvious feelings for Nicole as I worshiped her body. I needed to give one helluva performance to convince him otherwise.

"It was all part of the act. I don't think I've ever had to work that hard to get laid in my life." I laughed. "Hell, I had to convince her she was my *fated mate* before she finally gave it up. Talk about a tough sell."

I wanted to vomit as my father clapped me on the back with a boisterous laugh. "Losing your touch, are you?

Maybe I should give you a few pointers, eh? I may be twice your age, but bitches are still lining up every day to please their alpha."

I stiffened. My father's affairs were no secret, but it infuriated me when he disrespected my mother even further by shamelessly discussing his side pieces.

"I'll respectfully pass."

"Your loss." He shrugged his broad shoulders. "I'm still unclear why you went through the trouble, though. Explain."

"Corbin already explained that on the voice recording. I was trying to keep Nicole happy to ensure her father remained dedicated to his research. I did it for the pack. As their leader, I considered it my duty."

Suspicion was heavy in his gaze as he took a moment to think about that. "Hmm."

I raised a brow, meeting the challenge in his eyes head-on. "Hmm? What does that mean? Are you doubting my ability to lead the pack, Father?"

"I've doubted you since you came screaming out of your mother's cunt. I suppose time will tell. You have a *long way* to go to prove your worth before I'll be ready to hand over the reins. And you can start by publicly proposing to Mara. Now, clean yourself up. I'll tell the family jeweler to expect you within the hour. And remember, whatever ring you select reflects this family, so nothing less than five carats is acceptable. I want to see that goddamn diamond from space. Are we clear?"

I barely heard a word after *publicly proposing*, but I managed a stiff nod in reply.

"Good." He nodded. "I need to clean up myself before heading into the office. I'll see you tomorrow night. Don't fuck this up, Alexei."

"Yes, Alpha," I said, though I wanted to rebel with every fiber of my being. This was wrong. Not only would it destroy both of us, but I didn't want to give Mara any more influence than she already had. It would only make her more ruthless toward Nicole.

My father had backed me into a corner, but he forgot one thing.

I knew how to fight my way out of a shitty situation, and I'd fight for my mate—or die trying.

THREE

Nicole

I WAS STORMING through the quad, fury forcing every step. I kept looking over my shoulder, my gut swirling with anxiety as I scanned the coeds marching to class alongside me. My skin prickled with awareness, as if someone or *something* was watching me as I made my way toward the witchy sorority house. I didn't have time to weigh the consequences or determine whether I trusted Juniper. The only person I knew I could rely on at this damned university was myself, but she had the skills to handle a situation like this.

I had to break my bond with Alexei. If there even was a bond, that is. It was my only option for survival. Fighting for our relationship was no longer an option. My father was in danger—*I* was in danger. I couldn't wait for Alexei to fight for us—not that I was even sure I wanted him to. I had to fight for myself.

"Oh, *Nicole*!" a perky voice called out. The tone was smarmy.

I squeezed my eyes shut and tried to keep my breathing steady. Mara's voice was like needles stabbing my ear drums. She was the last person I wanted to talk to right then. I kept walking, shoving through people while I ignored her.

"Stop!" she called at my back, her compulsion washing over me and making my ears itch. Luckily, I still had the earrings Juniper gave me to block her commands, but I still didn't feel safe, especially after last night.

I took another step, prepared to run, but the she-wolf's manicured hand wrapped around my bicep, yanking me to a halt. Macey growled, and I had half a mind to tell my wolf companion to rip Mara's hair out, but I didn't have a death wish. I spun around to face her, my mouth fixed into a feral snarl. "What do you want?"

Mara had a wicked grin on her face. Not a single hair was out of place, and her hot pink outfit was a designer getup that was so over-accessorized that I was certain she'd topple over from the weight of her jewelry.

"What's wrong, Nicole? You look like you've been crying." A brutal grin stretched across her pretty face. I wanted to slam my fist into her glossy lips, maybe knock a couple of teeth out.

Fuck her. *Fuck all of them.*

"Leave me alone," I growled before jerking out of her grip.

Her eyes widened, as if surprised I could pull away from her shifter strength. The angry energy pumping through me was making my hands tremble.

"No can do, *human*," she said. The word *human* sounded like a curse word on her tongue. "I've got orders straight from Alpha Jones to make sure you get moved into the Beta Phi house today."

I gaped at her. "You can't be serious." There was no way in hell I'd move into that house. They all stood by and laughed while Alexei announced to the crowd that I was nothing more than a conquest. I'd always been a joke to them, but I was done letting them treat me like a punch-line to a terrible joke.

"I assure you, I am *quite* serious. If you would've stuck around last night, you would've received your formal invitation to join our sorority."

"You're fucking crazy if you think I'd *ever* want to move in with a bunch of cold, vindictive she-wolves."

Mara's green eyes rolled back in annoyance. "Well, we're not exactly thrilled about it either, but when Alpha Jones gives a direct order, you listen. Perks of being the top dog and all." Just thinking of Alpha Jones and his *direct orders* made a shiver travel down my spine.

I laughed mockingly. "You forgot one thing, Mara."

"What's that?" She raised a perfectly manicured brow.

"*I'm not a goddamn shifter,*" I sneered. "Therefore, he's not *my goddamn alpha*, and I don't have to follow his orders."

Sorta.

I would definitely do what I needed to until I could figure out how to rescue my father, but surely moving out of my dorm wasn't necessary.

What if he made me?

Would I have to sleep with one eye open? Pray they didn't kill me every hour of the day?

Her glossy lips curled upward. "Ah, but that's not exactly true, is it?"

"What's that supposed to mean?" I asked, frowning with confusion.

"Well, you see, Alpha Jones *personally* asked me to see that you were transferred into the Beta Phi house today. And I'd do *anything* to please my alpha." She studied her nails as she delivered her next words. "Don't play dumb, Nicole. Alpha Jones clearly warned you this was coming when you two had your brief *discussion* last night."

I stiffened. "*What* discussion?"

Was it possible Mara knew about my encounter with Alexei's father? Did she know *my* father was being held against his will?

Her chin lifted. "He told you to expect to hear from one of his representatives with further instructions, did he not? Well, *I'm* that representative, and your *instructions* are to *move your ass* into the Beta Phi house."

I stroked Macey's soft black fur as she growled in warning. If Mara was truly speaking on behalf of her psychotic alpha, having my familiar attack her would no doubt have consequences.

She took a step closer to me, her floral perfume striking me like a slap to the face. "I know you think you're tough and all because you had Alexei's attention for a hot minute, but the truth is, you're nobody. Nothing. You're a joke and an embarrassment. We laughed so hard after you left last night, and then Alexei worshiped my cunt like he was starving for it." Her words hit me hard, a strange pain surging in my chest. The idea of Alexei being with anyone but me hurt on a visceral level. It was more than just jealousy or heartbreak; it was something much deeper. "At the end of the day, you're on *our* turf. So you'll follow *our* laws. *Our* instructions. If Alpha Jones wants me to monitor you, then you'll do what I say."

I didn't feel safe moving in with Mara. She was spiteful. The more access she had to my life, the more turmoil she could cause. I had to do everything in my power to stay far away from her.

"I accepted a bid with the witches," I choked out. "It's too late."

She tilted her head back and laughed. "You think I give a fuck about the witches? You're moving in."

I looked around. Even though we were outside, I felt this sudden wave of claustrophobia, like I couldn't take a deep breath. Everything in my life was out of my control, and they wanted to lock me down even more.

"Is there a problem here?" a smooth, slightly husky voice said. Cristian slung his arm over my shoulders and stared at Mara. I stiffened under the vampire's touch, but he was better than Mara any day of the week. Even if he got on my nerves, at least he wasn't actively trying to humiliate—or worse, threaten—me.

Mara shifted her glare to him. "Mind your own business, Cristian. This doesn't concern your kind."

He offered a charming smile, but it was laced with warning. "Well, correct me if I'm wrong, but if this is a supernatural matter, it doesn't concern my friend, Nicole, here either. So if you'll excuse us, we're about to be late for class."

Was Cristian genuinely trying to help me? I didn't trust him one bit, but in this case, he was definitely the lesser of two evils.

I stood taller and cozied up to the vampire, despite the warnings in my head. "Yes, Mara. We've gotta run. Our fashion professor does not take kindly to tardiness." I looped my hand through Cristian's crooked elbow. "Shall we?"

He smiled down on me—this one without the malice he directed at Mara—and winked. "Let's go, beautiful."

"You're going to regret this!" Mara called behind our backs, followed by an exaggerated huff. I could hear her heels click, click, clicking on the pavement, but I refused to give her the satisfaction of looking back to see if she was walking away. I knew this was only a temporary reprieve. She'd be back, and I had to pray she didn't bring reinforcements. They'd have to drag me kicking and screaming to the shifter house.

As we approached the art building, Cristian leaned down to whisper in my ear. "She's gone now. You can relax."

"Thanks." I sighed in relief. My tense muscles all relaxed, and I practically leaned against Cristian as the adrenaline left my body. It all felt so hopeless. What was I going to do? "Now, care to tell me what your motive was behind that?"

Cristian chuckled darkly. "What makes you think I have a motive?"

I released his arm and took a step to the side. "Because a man like you *always* has a motive."

"A man like me?" he repeated, his blue eyes sparkling with mirth. "What's that supposed to mean?"

"The first time we met, you propositioned me," I reminded him.

"Because your blood smells so delectable. Mouthwatering." *Ew.* How could the coppery scent of blood ever smell appetizing? I noted the fact that vampires could apparently smell blood without any open wounds. "If Corbin hadn't claimed you that night, I would have seduced you."

I snorted. "You mean you would've *tried* seducing me."

"Whatever makes you feel better, Nicole." He winked. "It's unfortunate, really. You'd be *protected* if you were mine. The shifters wouldn't have any say on what you did. *Or where you live.*"

"You think you're so sly," I deadpanned.

"I'm simply stating a fact." He tossed me a sly smile. "If you were a feeder, that protection increases tenfold."

"How *protected* are we talking?" Of course, the asshole grinned like a kid who just won a prize at the arcade. "Spell it out for me, Cristian."

"Ironclad laws. No other supernaturals can touch our feeders. Once you're brought in, you are protected by our community." He led me toward the building and opened the door for me. "Humans think vampires want to use them, but that's not the case. We *worship* our blood donors. We're fiercely protective, and many develop intense emotional bonds."

Hmm. That didn't sound so bad, but there had to be a catch. "But you feed from them," I whispered. "You drink their blood."

"Yes. But never too much. Just enough to sustain us."

"Can a feeder leave at any time?" I raised a brow. "And what's the difference between an official feeder and a... snack?"

I worried I inadvertently offended his species when Cristian's spine stiffened. "It's rare for a human to leave once a blood oath is made. My father's feeder, Bernadette Bright, has been with him for over sixty years. They're very close, but even without an emotional bond, regular feeders are well paid and want for nothing. You could say they live in... extreme comfort. There are many perks, so to speak. Bernie takes vacations in the Maldives regularly, or at least, she used to. She started getting sick a couple of years ago, so she had to cut back. Bernadette raised me, actually. I think the world of her. Feeders are *family*, Nicole, not food. We don't blindly make blood oaths with just anyone."

It was strange to hear him speak so fondly of this woman. "Sick?"

He scratched the back of his neck. "Dementia. She's eighty-seven now, so it's not exactly unusual. Dad offered to turn her when she was first diagnosed, but she declined. He's kind of king, so—"

"Your dad is a king?!" I exclaimed, probably louder than I should have. A few coeds turned to look at us.

Cristian laughed. "Yep. He gives final approval on all vampire changelings, but immortality doesn't appeal to everyone, I suppose. It's... hard... watching Bernie age. I'm not really used to the concept. Everyone I care for will live forever, provided they don't die by some kind of attack or freak accident. Except her."

I waited for a moment to let him gather his thoughts. His blue eyes looked off for a moment, as if he were lost in a memory.

"It's hard losing people you love," I whispered.

Cristian swallowed. "It is."

I cleared my throat. "I'm assuming you're telling me all of this because you... might... possibly..."

"Want to offer you an official feeder position? Absolutely. Ten thousand percent. Can we start now? Maybe a trial run? I promise you'll *enjoy* it." He waggled his eyebrows playfully.

I rolled my eyes. "Quite frankly, Cristian, you barely know me. If vampires *don't make blood oaths with just anyone*, why me?"

He thought about it for a moment. "Honestly? I don't know. There's just something about you that draws me in. And it has *nothing* to do with your blood."

I told myself to ignore the warm and fuzzy feeling his declaration sparked.

"Well, since you're being so honest, I should probably tell you that the whole fangs-piercing-my-skin-blood-sucking-thing freaks me out. And it sounds like an enormous commitment. I need time to think. Consider all my options."

He nodded as if he understood. "What if you watched me feed? It might help you see what you'd be getting yourself into? Besides, traditionally, asking someone to make a blood oath requires a bit of... fanfare. I'm supposed to court you and make an official request with my father. You'd have to meet him and—"

"Is this a marriage proposal or a business transaction?" I laughed.

"A bit of both. Vampires only mate with other

vampires. Like shifters, we're expected to continue the bloodline. But feeders are kind of like the partner we *choose*. Some are friends. Others are lovers. My mother and father meet up for public events and get together when she's in heat to produce heirs. But when he's with Bernadette, it's just them. They live together. They travel together. It's very intimate, despite her age."

I swallowed. "I'm not sure my heart can handle something... intimate." Even though I didn't trust Alexei, I still felt this strange pang in my chest for him. "Besides, you live in a fraternity house, don't you? I'm not living with a bunch of smelly dudes."

Cristian laughed. "I can assure you, there's nothing *smelly* about me or my Rho Eta Theta brothers."

I inhaled, getting lost in his spicy cologne for a moment. "Regardless, I'm not living in a frat house."

"You wouldn't have to." He lowered his voice and pulled me to a stop outside our classroom. "I've heard rumors... about what happened. Alexei doesn't *deserve* you, Nicole. I'm a patient man. I've got all of eternity. Even if I seem cocky or cavalier at times, I know when to be serious. I can offer you protection. It would be a mutually beneficial relationship." He leaned forward and took a deep inhale, punctuating his point with a raspy breath. "Fuck, I want to taste you unlike anyone I've ever met. And you want to be as far away from the shifters as possible, do you not? I can help with that."

I swallowed, thinking about his offer. "I'm not saying yes."

He quirked a brow. "But?"

"But... I'm not saying no. I have more questions, but we really don't have the time now. I have no desire to get on Professor Hankey's shit list, unlike you."

Maybe I shouldn't be worried about what my professors thought of me, because I had no intention of staying at Redwood University, but this particular class—Intro to Fashion Design—was one of my favorites. Despite our professor being one of the biggest hardasses I'd ever met, she knew what she was doing. I'd learned so much from her over the last month, and I'd like that to continue for however long I was forced to stay here. Frankly, *any* kind of future seemed so far-fetched right then, but I refused to allow shifter politics to ruin my chances of living my dream as a fashion designer.

Cristian laughed again. "I don't particularly enjoy being on anyone's *shit list*, as you put it, but I have much more important things to worry about than being a good student."

Like what? I wondered. On our first day of classes, Professor Hankey had mentioned this was Cristian's fifth year at Redwood U. She implied he was rather flighty, which I couldn't exactly disagree with because I didn't know him much at all, but I had a feeling there was much more to Cristian Luca than he allowed the general population to see.

Just like Alexei.

Ugh. I shook my head, refusing to deal with that can of worms. Cristian was right about one thing. Alexei *didn't* deserve me. And his father may have had me in a proverbial chokehold at the moment, but there was *no way* I could move into the Beta Phi house so Mara could be his little watchdog. If aligning myself with a vampire was my way out of that, I was going to seriously consider it.

FOUR

Nicole

"I'VE BEEN CALLING you all freaking morning," Juniper said the moment I walked out of the classroom. Macey stood from her position outside the classroom door and greeted Juniper by licking her hand. "Well, hello to you, too, pretty girl."

Cristian, who was practically attached to my hip during the entire class, smiled as he saw the witch. "Hello, Juniper," he purred before I could answer her. "How's Ivan doing? I haven't seen him flying around recently."

Juniper's pearly teeth contrasted beautifully against her golden brown skin as she beamed at him. Literally *beamed*. "Ivan is visiting Brazil this week with his family for the festival. He loves confusing everyone and flying around with the parrot pack."

Cristian laughed good-naturedly. "Well, you know the two of you are welcome over anytime. I always enjoy hanging out with you."

My stomach dropped. "Wait. Are you two..." I wasn't sure how I felt about knowing someone *else* who was involved in Juniper and Ivan's unique relationship.

Cristian and Juniper laughed. He quickly explained. "Oh, no. Although I'd imagine a night with them would be fun, we have more of a professional arrangement. Juniper occasionally needs vampire blood for spells, and in exchange, sometimes I need magic."

Juniper gave him a look of admiration and respect. "Cristian has the *best* blood for charisma spells. My friend Alice has terrible anxiety but aced a job interview thanks to him."

Oh, wow. That was nice.

"Stop it. *You* have the best magic in the country. I still can't believe you managed to make an entire town forget about my bloody streaking incident." He winked.

Bloody streaking incident? I wasn't even sure I wanted to know.

"Anyway." Juniper's expression looked practically feral as she turned to me. "I've been calling and calling, even ordered every witch on campus to look for you. I tried a location spell, but it didn't work." She moved to place a hand on my shoulder. "I heard what happened, are you okay?"

I blushed. It was embarrassing to talk about my sex tape fiasco, and I didn't really want to take a trip down trauma road in a public hallway. "I'm fine. I mean, Alexei was using me as a huge joke and we're not actually ma— meant for one another." I wasn't sure I could talk about the whole *mate* situation in front of Cristian.

My familiar whimpered, as if she could sense my inner turmoil.

"It's bullshit he tricked you into believing you're fated," Cristian said, his mouth twisted in disgust. "I wish you would have told me. *Everyone* knows humans and shifters can't mate. I could have warned you."

I gave him a curious look. "How do *you* know what Alexei did?"

He sucked in a deep breath. "Well, I didn't want to freak you out, but that video has kind-of-sort-of-maybe traveled all over campus. And there's a video of Alexei's speech, too." He rushed out his words like they were fire on his tongue. "On the bright side, I have a feeling a *lot* of supes are about to ask you out. I'm just glad I got to you before any other vamps could start courting you."

I gasped. "You watched it?"

"If it makes you feel any better, I was a perfect gentleman and didn't jack off during," he promised, though I still wanted to kick his immortal ass. "Though I can't say the same for anyone else. Thanks to my super hearing, I heard you screaming Alexei's name on cell phones everywhere last night."

"You're not helping, Cristian," Juniper said while giving him a stern look.

"Sorry." Cristian winced. Around us, I noticed a few students giggling and looking my way. Just what I needed. "Either way, it's bullshit. Telling you that you're mates so he can get in your pants is low."

It really was low. The sad thing was, I probably would have slept with him, regardless. Alexei and I had sexual tension that made my toes curl. Why go through all the trouble of lying about what we were if I was just a quick fuck?

"I feel stupid," I said softly, tears gathering in my eyes. "How could I believe that we were mates?"

Juniper scoffed, interrupting my pity party. "Of course you're mates. I can sense the mate magic from a mile away."

I looked around. "Mate magic?"

"At its core, a mate bond is pure magic. Natural magic that doesn't need intervention or direction from a witch. It leaves a very specific residue higher ranking witches can sense. You're mates, Nicole. No question about it."

Cristian shook his head. "No way, no how. Shifters don't mate with humans. Your senses must be off."

I ignored him. "What about that spell we talked about, the one that could end the bond? Could you still do it?" I felt a rush of excitement. Maybe there was a way out of this after all.

Juniper gave me a sad smile. "I'm sorry, Nicole. But your bond is already halfway formed. When you and Alexei—"

"Bumped uglies?" Cristian offered.

Juniper gave him a sour look. "Had sex, you started solidifying your mate bond. There's not a spell or charm in existence that could sever that. I'm sorry."

My spirit seemed to deflate. "Are you sure?"

"Trust me, Nicole. I know what I'm talking about," June said with a wave of her hand.

"I'm struggling to trust... *anyone* right now." Even if what June shared with Corbin was pure fun, I wasn't sure where her allegiance truly lay. Plus, Alexei's threat about his father killing me if he discovered we were mates wouldn't leave my head. I didn't think June understood the threat it potentially posed, but I couldn't risk continuing this conversation in front of Cristian.

She gazed at me with her golden, knowing eyes. "I bet it's hard to trust a lot of things right now. A lot of people. It's why I was so anxious to find you. I think you should move into the Kappa Zeta house."

My brows raised. "What? Why?"

She grabbed my arm and started easing me down the hall, Mace and Cristian following close behind us. "Well, we had your formal invitation to join the sorority last night, but you never showed, though I could guess why after I heard about what went down at that damn shifter house. But in addition to that, I'm not sure you're safe at the dorms. The Kappa Zeta house is already warded against threats. You'd be protected within those walls."

Why did these two suddenly want to protect me? Was this a trick? Were they both working for Alpha Jones?

"I don't..." I shook my head, not quite sure how to finish that sentence.

Juniper gave me a sad smile as she brushed her purple corkscrew curls away from her face. "Look, Nicole. I know you're hurt. I know you're guarded, and with good reason. But I swear to my favorite goddess, I am being one hundred percent honest with you. If I'm lying, may she forever curse me with bad luck. I *am* your friend, if you'll have me."

"But... what about Corbin?" My eyes filled with tears as I heard the clear conviction in her statement.

She frowned. "What about him?"

"You two were... close. Wouldn't you feel some sort of obligation to him? I don't want a connection to Alexei, or any shifter for that matter. Corbin showed up at my dorm first thing this morning pleading their case. Begging for a chance to explain, but I wasn't interested in being duped again, which I told him. It's not fair of me to put you in the middle of my drama."

"For the record," Cristian interjected, "I will *gladly* place myself in the middle of a little shifter drama. Especially if it pisses off the future alpha or his conniving fangirl."

Crap. I had almost forgotten he was even there.

"Wait, a second..." I started, remembering a conversation between Mara and Cristian on the day we all met. "Didn't you and Mara have a thing once? If I recall correctly, you were more than interested in hooking up again?"

Cristian's canine teeth extended as he smiled. "Do I detect a little jealousy, or is that simply wishful thinking on my end?"

"Uh, *no*." My face scrunched up. "Definitely not jealous. Just trying to make sense of your sudden disdain."

"Pity." His full lips turned into an exaggerated pout. "But to answer your question, yes, Mara and I had a one-time thing, which was decent enough to warrant a repeat, but after I found out what she did to you, I wouldn't touch that bitch if she were the last blood donor in this realm. That woman has some kind of ulterior motive in play, and I am not interested in being her pawn. As for shifters in general, I have no allegiance to any of them, especially not the Ridgeview pack. Ask anyone on campus, there is no love lost between me and Alexei Koenig. One might even go as far as to say we're rivals."

"Why is that?" Alexei always spoke of vampires as if they were a plague on this earth, but he never really explained why he felt that way. And he definitely didn't like this vampire in particular.

"My best guess is they're threatened by us. *All* vampires have the power of compulsion. Humans love us. Witches ally with us. Alpha Jones has alienated his people, while the vampires formed powerful alliances. Nothing specific happened, but Alexei was raised to hate anything that didn't piss on fire hydrants or sniff asses."

I snorted. "It's all just so complicated. Alpha Jones is a bad man."

Juniper nodded. "Which is exactly why you need to move in with us. He doesn't have jurisdiction over the witches—"

"Or the vampires," Cristian added. "In fact, between the two of us, you'd be practically *untouchable*."

Juniper looked between us. "Are you considering being a feeder, Nicole?"

"I... don't know."

There was a mischievous glint in her eyes. "Have you ever *seen* a vampire feed?"

"Well, no. But Cristian offered to let me watch."

She looked at the towering vampire and smirked. "Oh, I bet he was thrilled by the idea of you watching."

"I feel like I'm missing something." My encyclopedia simply said that feeding could be enjoyable for humans, but what the hell did that mean?

"I think it's a marvelous idea. You'll see." Juniper slung her arm over my shoulder and started walking me toward the doors. "Let's get you moved into Kappa Zeta. We can throw a party to celebrate tomorrow after you're settled.

Oh, shit, we have that Greek fundraising banquet. Perhaps we can save the festivities for later?"

"What banquet?"

"Basically, it's a fancy banquet for all the Greek houses to get together and brag about how much money they've raised. It's all one big dick-measuring contest. Witches might not raise the most money, but our spells help the most people. That should count for something. You'll see what I'm talking about tomorrow night."

Cristian coughed. "Are we sure it's a good idea for Nicole to attend? After last night, I'm not sure..."

I opened my mouth to respond, but Juniper cut me off. "Of course she should. She needs to walk into that room with her head held high and on the arm of the most powerful witch on campus."

"I thought she'd be on *my* arm in this scenario." Cristian frowned.

"I have two arms, guys." *And I'd need all the support I could get.* "But maybe Cristian is right. I'm not sure if I should go. I'm not ready to see Alexei or Mara again."

Juniper stopped walking, jerking me to a halt with her surprisingly strong hold. "That's exactly why you're going. We're going to show Alexei and all those other assholes who's boss."

I chewed on my lip. All of this sounded great, but there was still a huge problem. If I pissed off Alpha Jones, there was a chance he would hurt my father in retaliation. I couldn't risk it.

Cristian pulled me to look at him. "Why do you look so scared? Do you think we can't protect you?"

Tears started streaming down my cheeks. I wanted to tell them, but I was so damn terrified for my father. It was all hitting me at once, and I wasn't sure what the right answer was. "They... Alpha Jones..." I paused and looked for a private place to tell them. Spotting an alcove beside the building, I marched over to it while furiously wiping at my eyes. I wasn't going to save my father by letting my emotions get the best of me. I needed to be strong.

"What's going on, Nicole?" Juniper asked.

I let out a shaky breath. "Alpha Jones has my dad."

Both Cristian's and Juniper's eyes widened as they said, "What?!"

I knew I was risking everything by telling them this, but I really fucking needed someone on my side. I just hoped I didn't regret it.

"Yeah." I nodded. "He, uh, last night... we were going to leave Redwood. But Alpha Jones showed up with members of his pack and stopped us. His henchmen threw my dad into the back of a car and drove off. Alexei's dad told me if I didn't cooperate, my dad would... suffer." I hiccuped a sob on the last word.

Cristian's dark brows furrowed. "Cooperate how? What *exactly* does he want from you?"

"For starters, he wants me to move into the Beta Phi house."

"Why?" Juniper frowned.

I shrugged. "I don't know. I know my dad's research is important to their pack. Maybe he just wants to make sure I don't try running again."

Even though I desperately wanted someone to confide in, my gut was telling me to keep my mouth shut for now about the real reason I suspected Alpha Jones wanted to keep tabs on me. I thought about the overwhelming rush of power I had last night when I was trying to shake my dad out of that weird trance. I had never felt anything like it. It was the greatest high—pure adrenaline injected into my veins—but afterward, I felt... empty, as if it never happened. No matter how hard I tried, I couldn't replicate it. Not even Macey could show me the answer using her gift.

I needed to figure out what my mom was hiding. I knew she was the key to figuring out what I was capable of and why I hadn't been able to harness that kind of energy before last night. After Alpha Jones's henchmen dragged my father off, I went back into his apartment and called my godmother, Jade, hysterically letting her know what happened at the frat house. I had to be careful not to mention what happened with Alpha Jones and my father, as I wasn't willing to risk his safety or hers. She could tell something was seriously wrong, though, when she asked if I had gone to tell my father what had happened and I brushed her off.

Once I was able to calm down a bit, she promised me that she and Hannah would find a way to circumvent the secrecy spell they were bound by. But they needed time, a luxury I didn't exactly have. I had to promise her I would lie low until I heard back from them, and not do something crazy like hunt for my dad's whereabouts or antagonize Alpha Jones. As difficult as it was to do nothing, I knew they were right. But that didn't mean I had zero control over this situation.

My mother and her two best friends went to great lengths to hide her identity. Until I understood what I was dealing with, I had to remain silent. Juniper knew something was off, because of what happened at the Kappa Zeta house when she tried giving me that protection charm, but I couldn't risk telling her what I discovered after the fact.

I gasped as I thought about one huge problem.

"What?" Juniper asked, clearly picking up on my anxiety.

"Nothing," I lied.

Fuck.

Alexei was *right there* when I learned about my mother having a life-or-death secret. Who knew how many people he'd told by now?

"I need Jade and Hannah," I said, mostly to myself.

"Who?"

"They were friends with my mom. They will know what to do."

Juniper eyed me. "One of them is the witch that gave you the protection charm, right? It couldn't hurt to have some more supes here. Ones who are undoubtedly on your side."

Cristian was typing on his phone. "My father is coming to the banquet," he said before pocketing his cell.

"What?" My mind was overwhelmed by everything.

"Alpha Jones won't touch you if my father is there. It'll make it clear you're under our protection."

I scowled. "I haven't agreed to being your feeder, Cristian."

He shrugged. "Alpha Jones doesn't know that. My father has some sway, and holding a human hostage goes against every rule we have. Your father is protected by extension."

Juniper sighed. "I'll invite my mother. It'll be good to have her on our side for this because she's very influential in the community."

"Reach out to your mom's friends, Nicole," Cristian added. "I can use the family jet to get them here in no time. We'll be a united front, and I promise we'll get your father back, okay? Alpha Jones knows it would be foolish to go up against the vampires *and* the witches."

I still felt a rush of anxiety about attending that banquet. I wasn't sure if I could trust Cristian and Juniper with my father's safety. Juniper grabbed my hand and gave me a reassuring squeeze. "We got you, girl. You don't have to do this alone."

With a shaky breath, I sealed my fate. "Okay. Let's do this."

CHAPTER
FIVE

Alexei

MY NECKTIE WAS too tight. I felt a burning sensation spread through my body as my wolf tried to get closer to Nicole, but I wasn't willing to risk it. I kept myself rooted to the floor by sheer stubborn will.

"Nicole refused to move into Beta Phi. Mara is pissed," Corbin said under his breath. "Apparently, Cristian has something to do with it. This is going to make protecting her a lot harder."

Fury stabbed me in the chest. What the fuck did Cristian have to do with this mess we were in? I groaned. Beta Phi wasn't an ideal situation for Nicole, but at least Corbin had access to the building so he could keep an eye on her there. I was worried about my father's reaction when he learned Nicole defied his command.

"Have you seen her since yesterday?" I asked softly.

We were surrounded by people, and we had to be careful not to let anyone hear us. The only reason I felt safe even discussing this now was because my father hadn't arrived yet and Mara was likely still trying to squeeze her breasts into a dress three sizes too small for her.

Corbin smoothed a hand over his dark blond hair. "I tried, but I spotted one of your father's enforcers following me. Since Pack Daddy tasked my sister with getting Nicole moved into Beta Phi, I didn't really have a valid reason to seek Nicole out. I figured it was best to stay away until I had a chance to talk to you, especially after I caused such a scene at the dorms."

"Yeah, not to mention what I learned while my father was kicking the shit out of me."

"Right." Corbin swallowed. "How are you doing, by the way?"

I shrugged. "I'm almost fully healed. I'll go for a run after this and I should be good."

I was a fast healer, but nothing worked better than running under the light of the moon in my wolf form.

"You want some company?" Corbin's eyes pleaded with me to accept. It was in his nature as my beta to ensure I was content, and the best way he could monitor that was by my side.

"Yeah, sure. But just the two of us."

He smiled. "You got it, boss."

I scrubbed my hands down my face. "I hope Nicole doesn't show up to this thing. I don't want her to witness this joke of a proposal."

I was livid with my father for forcing me to go through with this. Every cell in my body rebelled at the idea of hurting our mate like that. But I had to play along until I got the upper hand, so I had the most ostentatious ring I could find burning a hole in my pocket.

"Why would Nicole show up at a Greek event if she didn't accept the invitation to join Beta Phi?" Corbin's greenish-gold eyes widened, and he cursed under his breath as something over my shoulder caught his attention. "Oh, man, Pack Daddy is gonna lose his shit."

I followed my best friend's gaze to find the Kappa Zeta sisters entering the banquet hall as one unified front. Juniper Hale took the lead, purple curls bouncing as she strutted into the room like she owned it. My beautiful mate was right beside her, looking equally proud as she scanned the room, icy blue irises pausing briefly as she spotted me before moving on as if I were completely insignificant.

My inner wolf whined.

Out of the corner of my eye, I saw Cristian-fucking-Luca crossing the room with a devious smile. My fists clenched as he approached Nicole, bowing like a goddamn Victorian gentleman before kissing the back of her hand.

My enhanced hearing allowed her responding girlish giggle to travel to my ears.

"What. The. Fuck?"

Corbin placed a hand over my forearm and whispered, "Chill, dude. This is the last place you want to cause a scene."

I knew my beta was right, but that didn't quell the urge to break every bone in that smug-ass vampire's body. Nicole hooked her arm through his and gave the asshole a bashful smile, her cheeks blazing a beautiful red hue.

All eyes were on my mate. I knew that our sex tape had spread like wildfire through campus. It didn't matter how many threats I made, Mara made sure there wasn't a person at Redwood University who didn't see the way Nicole arched her back and writhed beneath me. The sound of our skin slapping haunted me wherever I went. If I could destroy every cell phone on campus, I would.

It surprised me that Nicole would willingly show up to something where she knew there'd be gossip. But that's who she was. Fearless, determined. A true luna. Someone who looked a challenge in the eye and laughed at it.

And not only that, she dressed to stand out. Her short blue dress, the same color as her eyes, was like a second skin. She wore her brown hair in curls down her back and had on sky-high heels that had me worrying she'd topple over with one misstep. Not only was every guy jacking off to the sound of her breathy moans in the video last night, she showed up here looking like a wet dream, practically daring everyone to look at her.

She took my breath away.

I scanned the room, noting all the wolves that eyed her with hunger. Cristian leaned in to whisper in Nicole's ear, his lips brushing against her skin as he did. She bit her lip. He curled closer to her.

I wanted to know what he said.

I wanted to cut his tongue off and roast it over an open fire.

"You're about to wolf out. Take calming breaths," Corbin murmured under his breath.

"Get Cristian away from her," I growled.

Corbin slapped me on the back hard enough to jar me out of my stare down. "No can do. It appears all the supes wanted to show up tonight. Look." Corbin nodded at the door just as Vasile Luca walked into the room with an entourage of twelve vamps following after him. His tailored suit had faded fabric, as if he'd bought it a century ago—which he probably did. He looked a lot like his son. Same brown hair and pale skin. Same assuming grin on his angular face.

"What the fuck is the vampire king doing here?"

Corbin gulped. "No idea. That's not all."

Behind Vasile's vampy crew, a woman with bright yellow hair, piercing gray eyes, and brown skin walked through the doors. She wore a diamond cloak that glimmered in the light.

Juniper ran to her with a grin on her face. "Mom! You made it!"

I scowled. "Did I miss the memo that this event was doubling as a family reunion?"

"Guess so," Corbin murmured, jerking his head to the head table where my parents sat next to his parents. "Although, considering the Lucas and Hales are alumni, it's not that weird, I suppose."

"This feels like more than a coincidence," I grumbled, watching Nicole take the seat Cristian pulled out for her at the Kappa Zeta table. Her back was to me, but I swear I could feel her smile as he leaned down to whisper something in her ear before moving to his own table.

My best friend sighed. "Just keep calm, bro. I know that's easier said than done, but you need to think about the endgame here. Think about Nicole's safety and her father's safety."

My reply was cut off by his sister's arrival. I stiffened as Mara approached our table with a cunning smile plastered across her face. As predicted, she was wearing a skintight mini dress and fuck-me heels, but unlike Nicole, Mara's fashion statement was tacky. The difference was in the way they carried themselves. My mate held her head high in pure confidence, whereas Mara reeked of desperation.

"Alexei," she practically purred. "I'm looking forward to our announcement later."

"I'm sure you are," I grumbled.

"I'm assuming your father told you what kind of jewelry I prefer? I really don't want to be embarrassed with a modest ring."

I hadn't even really looked at the rings when I met with the jeweler. I simply told him to give me the most obnoxious piece he had. If it were Nicole, I would have spent weeks agonizing over the perfect design, the perfect cut. I'd select something timeless that accentuated her unique style, tastes, and preferences.

Mara got whatever they had in stock with the highest price tag.

The fact that she didn't want to be *embarrassed* was fucked up, considering she had no problem doing the same to my mate.

"I wouldn't dream of embarrassing you," I gritted sarcastically, even though my dreams featured my wolf tearing out her throat.

Her smile grew, seemingly oblivious to the bitterness in my tone. "Perfect. Well, if you'll excuse me, I should take a seat. I found a spot with great lighting for the photographers. Every magazine and newspaper is going to want a copy. We can show our pups how beautiful their mother looked." She winked at me, and the idea of having babies with this cruel, insane woman made me sick to my stomach. "The speeches should be starting in ten minutes or so."

Mara disappeared, swaying her hips with every step as she went to her table.

"She's a piece of work," Corbin muttered under his breath. "Shit. Pack Daddy is coming."

I followed Corbin's gaze to see my father storming over to me, a determined look on his face. I took a moment to mentally prepare myself for his anger as he approached, my injuries from yesterday morning flaring with awareness at his proximity. My wolf wanted to fight back, but I knew that would do much more harm than good.

"What the *fuck* is Vasile Luca doing here?" he hissed the moment he was close enough.

I scanned the room, looking once more at the table where Nicole sat. Both Luca men had pulled up chairs to join the Kappa Zetas instead of sitting at their designated frat table. There was obviously something going on, but I had no idea what. "I'm not sure."

My father seethed with anger. "That fucking vampire. Is he trying to challenge me?"

I cleared my throat. "Perhaps he's here to support his son."

Dad tore his eyes from the vampires and back to me. "Everyone always has an ulterior motive. He's sitting with that pathetic human. Vasile Luca is up to something, and I want you to find out what."

I sighed. "As you wish, Father."

He straightened his tie and scanned the room, checking to see if anyone saw his little temper tantrum. "I'm going backstage to prepare for my speech. Meet me there in five minutes."

I stood from my chair, buttoning my suit jacket. "I'll be back."

Corbin stood with me. "I'll come with you."

"No need," I assured him. "I'm not going to make a scene. I simply want to welcome the vampire king to our territory."

"Alexei." Corbin shook his head. "I don't think—"

I braced a hand on his shoulder, subtly applying pressure until he took the cue to sit. "It'll be fine."

Corbin reluctantly took his seat, but I could feel his stare as I crossed the room toward the Kappa Zeta table. Unfortunately, his eyes weren't the only ones following my approach. I'd wager nearly everyone in this room was currently watching, waiting for the drama to unfold. As I got closer, I had to focus on taking deep breaths as Cristian casually looped his arm behind Nicole's back, as if he had every right to touch her like that.

"I feel like Nicole would make a wonderful candidate, Father," Cristian said.

Candidate? Candidate for *what?*

My mate stiffened as I approached. As much as my inner wolf hated her discomfort, part of me preened she had such a heightened awareness of my proximity like I had with her.

I cleared my throat. "Excuse me."

Cristian and his father both twisted in their chairs to face me, but Nicole made a concerted effort to not do the same. She simply picked up her water glass and took a measured sip.

The vampire king gave me a practiced smile as he stood and offered his hand. "Alexei. Nice to see you again. It's been a while."

I shook his hand. "Please, make yourself comfortable. I just wanted to stop by to say hello on my way backstage. How are things up north? Are you in town for a visit?"

Mr. Luca quirked his head in curiosity as he took a seat. Probably because I'd never really sought him out like this before. It was an alpha's job to nurture relationships with the leaders of other factions, so hopefully, he assumed I was acting on behalf of my pack since I was their future leader.

"Partially." He inclined his head toward Nicole. "Mostly, I wanted to meet this lovely lady."

"Oh?" I had to make a conscious effort not to clench my fists as Cristian's finger looped around a piece of Nicole's long hair. "Why's that?"

Cristian grinned. "Because I'd like to bring Nicole on as a feeder, and as is customary, I needed my father's approval to do that."

My nostrils flared as I growled, "That's *never* going to happen. She belongs to my pack."

Nicole whipped around, glaring at me with the force of a thousand suns. "The hell I do."

She was careful to keep her voice low, but there was no disguising the sudden tension between the four of us.

Vasile Luca looked between me, his son, and my mate. "Really? The lady seems to disagree."

"*The lady is wrong*," I seethed.

"Interesting," Cristian's father mused. "I suppose I'll need to speak with your father before making my decision then, since *he's* the current alpha."

The implication in his tone was clear. This man had no intention of continuing this discussion, because he considered me irrelevant as I wasn't officially in a position of power like my father was. I may have run things at this university, but when it came to interfaction politics, the current alpha was the only person capable of making decisions on behalf of his pack.

Nicole tilted her chin higher. "Why don't you run along then, Alexei? Didn't you say you had to get backstage?"

It took every ounce of willpower I possessed not to throw her over my shoulder and spank her for mouthing off. "We need to talk, Nicole."

She laughed breezily, but I could see the pain hidden behind the mask she donned. "I think you said *everything* I needed to hear the other night, don't you?"

"Alexei." Corbin was suddenly beside me, tugging on my arm. "Your father is requesting your assistance backstage."

It burned me to see her chest heaving and her eyes staring me down. She was obviously trying to hold up a strong facade, but Nicole's pain was practically bleeding through our bond. I'd hurt my mate, and our bond was suffering because of it.

Shit. And things were only going to get worse. Nicole was about to see me propose to Mara.

"Juniper," I said while turning to her. I prayed she'd recognize the desperation in my tone. "Why don't you and Nicole go for a walk?" I peered at her, begging her to see my true intentions.

"We're comfortable here," Nicole interjected with a wave of her hand.

Cristian grinned. "Yes, we are." The purr that vibrated in his chest punctuated the fury I felt.

"I really think you should leave," I growled.

Nicole rolled her shoulders back and glared at me. "I'm enjoying a night with my friends."

"Leave, Nicole." I paused to lower my voice. "I'm *begging* you. I don't want you here."

Her eyes widened for a fraction of a second, but she let out a huff and tilted her chin confidently.

Vasile Luca cleared his throat. "I was under the impression this event was for every Greek house, which Nicole is now a part of. I knew your father was discriminatory, but this is a bit excessive."

I wasn't trying to kick her out because she was a human, I was trying to spare her from what was about to happen.

"Alexei, we have to go," Corbin urged me.

I stared at my mate for a lingering moment, soaking in

the flash of defiance in her eyes and wishing things could be different.

"Fine," I grunted before turning to leave.

Every step that carried me farther from Nicole was like a knife digging into my chest. I wanted nothing more than to wrap her up in my arms and explain what was going on with my father. Protecting her was more important than my desires, though. I may not have known what the future held, but I knew I didn't want one without her. And if I didn't go through with this proposal, my father would see to it that Nicole wouldn't have a future. This proposal was simply a matter of buying myself some time. I just had to hope my mate could find a way to forgive me once I figured shit out.

CHAPTER
SIX

Nicole

Once Alexei's thundering form disappeared behind a thick curtain covering the stage, I sighed in relief. Seeing him again, hearing his gruff tone made my heart pang with sadness.

"You did great, beautiful. So strong. So brave," Cristian whispered seductively in my ear.

I was comforted by the charming vampire and thankful to have him on my side, but there was a small part of me that compared this interaction to the passion I felt with Alexei. I was seriously fucked in the head, because despite all the hurt, I couldn't help but trail my gaze over the way Alexei's suit fit his bulky frame or inhale his warm scent.

"I can't believe he demanded I leave." The way my voice wavered now made me feel pathetic.

Juniper's eyes were trained on the stage. "Do you think he was trying to warn us about something? That's definitely the vibe I was getting."

Juniper's mother, Eve, chewed on her lip. "I'm pretty good at reading a person's intentions. I felt as though he was sincere."

Vasile's nostrils flared. "I disagree. Alexei's like every other power-hungry alpha. Just wants to push people around because he can. I'm glad you called me, Cristian. It's obvious this human is important to the pack."

As everyone spoke around me, I slipped deeper into sadness. I knew I'd run into Alexei sooner rather than later, but I wasn't prepared for the strange feeling that now resided in my chest. I needed to focus on finding my father, needed to lean into this alliance Cristian was offering, but that didn't stop my stupid heart from getting excited the moment I saw Alexei sitting at the Alpha Nu table. It was another layer added to the pile of betrayal, except this time, it was my own body working against me.

Maybe Juniper was right. Maybe Alexei wasn't lying about us being fated mates. Why else would I feel such an intrinsic pull to a man who'd gone out of his way to tear me down? But even if that were true, it didn't matter. I wasn't a shifter. I wasn't ruled by the same code. The one thing I was sure about was that I couldn't allow myself to get sucked into his orbit ever again.

What Alexei and Mara did the other night was unequivocally unforgivable. They took a private moment —as much as I hated to admit, one of the best moments of my life—and turned it into something ugly. Cristian wasn't exaggerating earlier. That video *had* made it all throughout campus. The soundtrack our bodies made was running on a constant loop through my head. I'd lost count of how many leers I'd been on the receiving end of during my classes. How many lewd gestures and propositions were tossed my way, as if this were all one big joke. The entire student body was talking about me. Most of them hadn't even cared enough to try to hide their cruel remarks.

Oh, look, it's that slut Alexei fucked!

I can't believe someone like her thought she was actually mated to the future alpha.

Poor Alexei. I can't believe he had to screw someone so unworthy for the sake of his pack. He's going to be the best leader.

Do you think she'd suck my cock if I told her we were fated?

And then there was my personal favorite.

Why is she still here? She should save us all the trouble and just kill herself.

"Hey, you okay?" Cristian asked while nudging me.

I made an effort to seem controlled and focused, refusing to allow Alexei to steal my peace. I was determined to save my father and escape this place, and already had a plan to do so. I had to lean on the people supporting me and hold my head up high. Alexei had hurt me for the last time.

"I'm fine," I replied briskly.

Cristian offered me a sad smile. "It's okay if you aren't."

I needed to change the subject and focus on the plan. "Are my mom's friends coming?"

"They'll be here in two days," he answered. "Jade wanted to get some protection spells before showing up. I told her it wasn't necessary, but they both seemed a little... *anxious* about coming here."

I felt a smidge bad about bringing them back to the supernatural world they ran away from all those years ago, but if I was going to get out of this mess, then I needed them.

"Thank you, Cristian."

"Anytime, beautiful."

The curtains opened up and Alpha Jones walked out wearing a fitted suit and a malicious smile. He stepped up to the podium with purposeful strides, flashing his sharp teeth for the flickering cameras at the base of the stage. "Welcome, everyone. I'm thrilled to see so many dignitaries in attendance tonight."

The crowd applauded as Vasile raised a flute of champagne and Eve pressed her palms together and bowed.

"It is such an important night for many of you. Redwood University houses the top minds in the country, and many future leaders are sitting amongst you tonight. My own son, Alexei, is president of Alpha Nu and is proud to share that they have raised over three million dollars for their charity so far this year, putting them in the lead." He waved at someone offstage. "Come out here, son. This is your moment, too."

A round of applause surged through the crowd as Alexei joined his father. Meanwhile, I gripped my glass so tightly I feared it would break, but holding onto something was the only thing keeping me from fleeing the room.

"All of our houses have made significant contributions to their individual charities," Alpha Jones continued. "Rho Eta Theta is currently in second place with an impressive two-point-two million dollars raised." His cold gaze scanned the room, landing on our table. "I'm pleased to see one of our most reputable alums here tonight to support Rho Eta's current president, who also happens to be his son." He chuckled darkly. "Though I think they got their seating assignments mixed up and are sitting with our witches, who came in *last* this year."

The crowd laughed uncomfortably. One look at Cristian's father confirmed he was *not* amused by Alpha Jones's antics. Cristian's fingers curled around my shoulder as Alexei stared at us with murderous intent.

There was a clear power struggle in play, which I seemed to be directly in the middle of. I suspected this would happen if I showed up tonight with the witches and vampires, but it felt even more dangerous in practice than theory.

"I have great hopes for Redwood University this year." Alpha Jones patted Alexei on the back. "I have great hopes for the future of my family. You see, my son asked for a little stage time tonight so he could ask one lucky lady in this crowd a very important question."

What was he talking about?

Whispers scattered throughout the room.

"He'd better not do what I think he's about to do," Juniper murmured.

I leaned forward to get her attention. "What do you think is about to happen?"

Cristian's hand moved to my thigh as he held me in a punishing grip. "Do *not* show weakness, Nicole."

"Ow," I complained. "What is your problem?"

Cristian lightened his grip but didn't release me. "You're about to find out."

"Mara Sullivan." Alpha Jones looked toward the Beta Phi table. "Sweetheart, could you please join us?"

Mara made a *who me?* gesture, only rising from her seat when Alexei's father nodded encouragingly.

I felt like everything was happening in slow motion as she headed toward the stage, clearly loving the fact that she was in the proverbial spotlight. Her long blonde hair swished in time with her hips as her glossy red lips curved into the fakest smile I had ever seen. Alpha Jones extended his hand to assist her up the few stairs until she was standing directly in front of Alexei, who was in the process of dropping to one knee.

Oh, hell no.

Was this seriously happening?

Cristian's earlier words suddenly made sense.

"Asshole," Juniper said under her breath.

"Mara Sullivan, will you be my luna?" Alexei said, his voice booming throughout the banquet hall.

My heart cracked, fizzled, and popped when she squealed with excitement and said an exuberant *yes*.

Mara grabbed the ring and slipped it onto her finger, the dazzling diamond glimmering in the light as she did.

I didn't think it was possible to hurt any more than I already did. Any doubt I had was squashed the moment he stood up and she slammed her lips to his.

But I didn't cry.

I didn't crumble at the sight of Alexei proving how little I meant to him.

I rolled my shoulders back and drank in the sight of them together, letting fury burn any lingering feelings I had for the future alpha. I was done.

"Whew. Your aura is intense." Eve fanned herself. "If you were a witch, the power would go out with all that rage thumping through you."

"Mom," Juniper hissed. "Be kind."

The lights flickered overhead, making everyone at our table freeze.

"Nicole? Do you want to leave?" Cristian had a worried look on his face.

I shook my head. "And give Alexei the satisfaction? Never."

"I like her a lot," Vasile murmured. "Wise choice, son."

Suddenly, the music began to play, and out of the corner of my eye, I saw Mara pulling Alexei toward the dance floor where other couples had already begun to dance. God, they really were the perfect match. Both ruthless and heartless to their cores.

"Would you care to dance?" Cristian held his hand out for me. I knew this wasn't him seeking out a romantic connection. He was helping me channel the revenge roaring in my gut into something productive.

"I'd *love* to." My tone sounded sickly sweet.

Cristian guided me to the dance floor, his hand on my lower back and his lips brushing against my ears as he sang along with the music. I smiled despite the anger swelling within me and forced myself to feel confident. He pulled me close, molding his firm body against mine as we started to sway to the music.

"I'm not a good dancer," I whispered.

Cristian let out a sultry laugh before spinning me around and pulling me against his chest. "Dancing is a lot like sex. Just move your body with mine, beautiful. I can do the rest."

I locked eyes with Cristian, determined not to let my gaze wander to where Alexei and Mara were embraced on the dance floor, though it was hard to ignore her annoying voice.

"The ring is amazing, Alexei. Everyone is going to be so jealous."

I rolled my eyes as a fresh pang of agony tore at my soul.

"Is it bad that I feel a little sorry for him?" Cristian asked. "Marrying that she-wolf would be a punishment any way you look at it." I tensed as he moved us closer to the newly engaged couple. "How much do you want him to hurt, beautiful?"

I lifted up on my toes, our lips inches apart. "What did you have in mind?"

"Alexei keeps sneaking glances at us. I think the wolf is feeling a bit possessive, although I'd say he's lost that right, wouldn't you? We could give him something worthwhile to look at, if you're up for it."

It would have been easy for me to close the remaining distance between Cristian and me, but there was something still holding me back. "I'm not ready... I don't want people to talk... with the video... kissing you would feel wrong."

Cristian smiled. "Although I'm disappointed, that's not what I had in mind."

He pulled away, and all eyes fell on us as he dropped to one knee.

Oh my God. No. This wasn't happening.

"Nicole Fairweather, you are the most stunning, brave,

beautiful woman I've ever laid eyes on." Cameras started flashing as Cristian began his speech.

I debated on fleeing. Panic fluttered in my chest as I realized what he was doing.

"Cristian, this is not what—"

Whispers throughout the crowd cut me off. *Is that the vampire prince? What is Cristian Luca doing with that slut?*

"Nicole, I have been searching for a feeder for years, someone worthy, someone to be my companion in *all* ways. Will you do me the profound honor of making a blood oath with me?"

All around us, people gasped. From what I understood, blood oaths between feeders and their vampires were perfectly normal, but since Cristian was vamp royalty, it made his proposition a pretty big deal.

Before I had the chance to answer the vampire prince's question, Alpha Jones stormed up to us, seething.

"What do you think you're doing?" His hazel eyes were darting between me and Cristian so fast I couldn't tell which one of us he was asking.

"Is there a problem here?" Mr. Luca interjected, nodding to his son before Cristian positioned himself in front of me, not so subtly shielding me from the angry wolf.

There was a bit of a scuttle before yet another intrusive ass joined us.

"Dad, not here." Alexei briefly glanced at me before directing his attention back toward his father.

Alpha Jones pointed at me. "I warned you, girl, yet you dare to make a fool of my family with this absurd display of..." He shook his head. "I don't even know what the hell is going on right now."

"What's *going on*..." Cristian's father stood tall, not allowing the alpha to intimidate him in the least. "Is that my son petitioned my court to make Nicole his primary feeder, which I approved."

He did? When did that happen?

An honest-to-God growl erupted from deep within Alexei's chest.

I glared in response, while Cristian couldn't possibly have looked more pleased with himself.

Jesus Christ, I was surrounded by stifling levels of testosterone. I was glad Juniper arranged for my familiar to have a playdate with her younger sister, Kate. I had a feeling Macey wouldn't have taken all this alpha-macho bullshit very well when a lot of their anger was directed at me.

"Nicole is *shifter* property," Alpha Jones seethed.

Mr. Luca's spine straightened. "Oh? Has one of your wolves claimed her as their mate? How progressive of you."

Alpha Jones's face turned a bright shade of angry red. "Disgusting. No one in my pack would dare mate a filthy *human*." His lip curled, and I felt myself growing even angrier at his words. No wonder Alexei humiliated me. This was the man who raised him. No matter what I felt for him, Alexei would always view me as an unworthy human.

"Well then, according to shifter law, she is *not* your property. A mate bond is the only reason you'd have to claim her. Section five of the accords states that by default, a human brought into the supernatural world is the property of the faction that enlightened her. And according to my records, that responsibility falls on the witches."

Juniper slid into the fold, a wicked smile on her face. "It's true. My brother, Antonio, gave her a reveal spell."

Mr. Luca grinned at her before continuing. "And I just spoke with High Priestess Hale. She was happy to approve a transfer of allegiance to the vampires as long as Nicole consented to it." He paused to look at me. "Do you accept my son's proposal?"

I opened my mouth for a moment, feeling like a ton of bricks was just dropped on my chest. I thought I'd have more time to think about this. "I... I... um."

"Don't answer that," Alexei blurted out, forcing everyone to turn and look at him. Straightening his spine, he fiddled with his cufflink before letting out a forced sigh, as if he wanted to seem unaffected, though the throbbing vein in his temple said otherwise. "The law states that we have a right to contest."

"On what grounds?" June's mom, also known as the high priestess, asked. She'd floated over to the group, polishing her nails on her dress as she arched her brow.

Alpha Jones grew increasingly angry, and I worried there would be a fight. "I have a right to contest this."

"It's curious you care about a little human, Jones. She's a pretty little thing, but hardly your type. You prefer creatures with fleas." Mr. Luca laughed at his own joke, his face twisted in mockery.

Alpha Jones looked around the room, noting the crowd with smirks on their faces. "Shall we discuss this in a more private forum?"

The priestess rolled her eyes, and with a wave of her hand, a shimmery, purple bubble surrounded us.

"What's happening?" I gasped.

"Shit, love. Hold your breath." Cristian grabbed my hand and took a deep inhale.

I followed his instruction as the bubble closed in on us. Smaller and smaller, it molded around Alexei first, then Alpha Jones. When it closed around Mr. Luca, he was nonchalantly checking his watch, as if this were an everyday occurrence for him. And finally, when it closed on Cristian and me, my bones went rigid as a tingling magic traveled down my spine. My lungs felt like they were burning, and then, my entire body faded into nothing. I wanted to scream, but just as quickly as I disappeared, I reappeared in what was presumably an office. Landing on shaky feet, I let out a yelp as my legs wobbled.

Though my vision was bleary from the bizarre experience, I could see Alexei taking a step toward me. Luckily, Cristian grabbed my arm and pulled me against his muscular chest, steadying me while I figured out what the hell had just happened.

"Is this a better venue for you, Jones?" the priestess asked. "Have you redecorated? I love the art above your desk."

"I don't want to exchange pleasantries," Alpha Jones snapped.

Mr. Luca shook his head. "So uncivilized."

The alpha glared at the vampire king. "I claimed her father first! When I hired him to work for the university, I paid to have a reveal spell performed. He couldn't conduct his research properly without knowing about our people. And according to the law you've so helpfully cited, immediate family members of claimed humans are automatically under our jurisdiction."

My jaw dropped in outrage, finally feeling normal again after the strange magic that carried us here had worn off. "You're lying! You did *nothing* to enlighten my father!"

I could've sworn everyone in the room stiffened as if they could feel the danger in the air.

"Nicole..." Alexei started.

"No!" I pointed at him. "You stay out of this. This has *nothing* to do with you!"

"This has *everything* to do with me," he growled.

Alpha Jones's nostrils flared as he casually straightened his tie. "You're treading on paper-thin ice, young lady. I would choose your next words very carefully, considering what's at stake. Or have you forgotten about the leverage I have over you?"

I could feel the heat rising to my face. "I most certainly have *not* forgotten."

"What leverage?" Cristian asked, challenging Alpha Jones to admit what he'd done with my father.

Alpha Jones tipped his nose up. "It's shifter business."

Silence stretched between everyone, the tension so thick I was suffocating on it.

"There's an easy solution to this. We simply need to figure out who was given a reveal spell first." The high priestess's voice was smooth and slightly condescending, as if she couldn't be bothered with these silly games. "I'll schedule a council meeting and perform a timeline spell."

"That won't be necessary," Alpha Jones stammered. "*I* was first."

"Forgive me for not wanting to take your word for it, Jones." Mr. Luca chuckled condescendingly. "I think a timeline spell would be perfect, Eve. And we'll need to meet with the girl's father. Our human protection board will want to make sure the shifters are following all appropriate standards of care." He raised a brow. "Which I'm assuming won't be a problem. Didn't your father pioneer that initiative, Jones?"

"The human protection board isn't legally required by any supernatural faction," Alpha Jones choked out.

"Ah, but it's considered best practice. What's the matter? Do you have something to hide? You're not torturing the poor man, are you?" Mr. Luca gave him a challenging glare, and my stomach dropped.

My imagination ran wild, visions of my father chained up and beaten ran rampant through my mind.

"Of course not," Alpha Jones snapped. "That man is my *asset*. Why would I torture the one person I've found who could potentially find a cure for my people?"

I sighed in relief as I heard the truth in the alpha's words. I didn't believe he was treating my father well for one moment, considering he wasn't above kidnapping him, but it was good to know my dad wasn't in any physical danger.

At least for now. I hadn't forgotten Alexei's warning about how dangerous this man was.

"I'm inclined to temporarily grant the vampires custody of Nicole. We can have a formal hearing where you can present your case to the council, and my coven will perform a timeline spell to verify who revealed the supernatural world to her first. As high priestess and an unbiased judge on the immediate problem at hand, I have the authority to approve this, and you know it."

Alpha Jones's eyes flashed a vibrant shade of red, and fine hair started sprouting on his arms. He was close to shifting, and I didn't want to be anywhere near him when that happened. Alexei took a step forward, his eyes darting between Cristian and me.

"Was there something you wanted to say?" My voice sounded braver than I felt. I wanted him to shout from the rooftops what we were, to finally claim me in front of his father and make everything we shared feel real, if only so I could stop feeling so pathetic for trusting him.

We shared a meaningful look, him pleading me with his gaze and me staring at him with icy eyes. "No," he choked out reluctantly.

The high priestess smirked. "You sure? You seem... off, Alexei." She sniffed the air, and I wondered if like her daughter, she could sense the magic of our mate bond.

"I'm sure," Alexei gritted.

"Well, then..." Juniper's mom smiled. "I suppose all that's left is to arrange a time for Nicole to visit her father, to see that he's okay with her own eyes." She turned to Alpha Jones. "That won't be a problem, will it?"

Alpha Jones tilted his chin up in indignation. "Of course not. Like I said, I have nothing to hide."

I resisted the urge to snort vehemently. *Nothing to hide, my ass.*

But I wasn't going to look a gift horse in the mouth, so I said, "That'd be great. Where is he? I'd like to visit him now."

Alpha Jones shook his head. "It's late. You can meet with him tomorrow in his lab. Say noon?"

I didn't like that option one bit, but I knew I had to tread carefully. "Noon is fine."

"Great!" Mr. Luca said. "It's settled then. Nicole, I'm sure my son would be more than happy to accompany you. Isn't that right, Cristian?"

Cristian smiled as he took my arm, placing a gentle kiss on the back of my hand. "I'd do anything for you, Nicole."

I didn't miss the way Alexei's fists clenched by his sides, but he was wise enough not to say anything.

"Thank you." I returned the vampire's smile. "I appreciate the offer, Cristian. I wouldn't want to get eaten by the big, bad wolves after all."

Everyone but Alexei and his father chuckled at my terrible joke. I knew I shouldn't have been antagonizing them, but I couldn't seem to help myself. Fuck them and their pack. Supposed mate bond or not, I wasn't going to let them scare me. I had allies now—protection. I wanted Alexei to step up, but I didn't need him to rescue me from this hell.

I could save my father.

I could save *myself.*

Alexei

My FATHER's mood was like a raging storm, growing with power every passing moment. After everyone left, he sat at his desk in brutal silence, staring off in the distance while thinking. I learned to fear the moments my father was quiet. It meant he was scheming. Even though I wanted to excuse myself and run as far away from his anger as possible, I was worried what he would do if given the opportunity to sit and stew.

"Bring me Percy Zats."

I was caught off guard by his command; I had expected that he would retaliate against Nicole's father. However, it seemed that was just *too* obvious. He couldn't hurt the person who was working to find a cure, and because Nicole was under the vampire's care, he couldn't go after her either—for now.

"Percy?" I asked.

I watched my father roll up his sleeves as he nodded. "Two weeks ago, one of my informers told me that he had been visiting one of the blood lounges. I refuse to have a vampire spy in my pack. Bring me Percy Zats."

I tried not to squirm. Percy Zats was one of the lower-ranking shifters in our pack. My father gave him a job as a custodian at his office, and I knew he was struggling to make ends meet. My father didn't think Percy was worthy of anything meaningful in the pack because two of his sons were born without wolves. The poor man was probably going to the blood lounge to make a little extra cash to provide for his family. Vampires paid their donors well.

"There are no laws against shifters going to the blood lounge, Father." I forced myself to sound as submissive as possible. "He hasn't made a blood oath. He's just a casual donor making ends meet. Again, it's not prohibited. Only blood oaths are forbidden."

My father rolled his neck, as if preparing for a fight. "Perhaps there *should* be laws against it. And who's to say he *hasn't* made an oath? Perhaps the vampires have been building an army of loyal shifters right under my nose. I won't stand for it! We have to cut off the head of the snake, Alexei." He glared at me challengingly, as if daring me to tell him no. "I want to have a little talk with Percy."

My feet were cemented to the floor. I didn't want to

get this innocent man and bring him to my bloodthirsty father. "Why don't we focus on the vampire king. *He* is who you are mad at—"

My father slammed his fist on the top of his desk with the growl. "I will burn every vampire, witch, and fae to the ground. For now, my main goal is to ensure the loyalty of my pack members. Percy is letting those nasty vamps feed from him, and that is unacceptable!"

I knew that I would regret it, but still I challenged my father. "Percy is harmless."

My father stood up and stalked over to me, his fist clenched at his side. "If I can't control even the weakest members of my pack, then how am I supposed to lead the shifters to victory when we go to war?"

War?

What in the hell was he talking about? We worked well with the other supernatural factions—despite our various differences. The witches provided us with magic, the vampires were our allies, and the fae traded goods with us from their realm.

"Why would we go to war over a simple custody dispute?"

My father stared at me with his menacing eyes while he pulled out his cell phone and typed something. I had a feeling that he was making someone else summon Percy. "This isn't about the custody dispute. I don't give two shits who that fucking human spreads her legs for." Jealousy sliced through my chest at his words as he took a step closer to me. "This is about *obedience*. This is about being respected in our community. If the witches and vampires think that they can go against me, then I will show them that they are wrong for messing with our pack. I am in charge. I am the *motherfucking alpha*. And you're either with me or against me, son."

A cold sweat broke out on my brow as his veins bulged in anger. "Of course I'm with you, Father. I'm just trying to understand."

My father looked at me as if I were an old piece of gum beneath his boot. "Don't you get it? I'm trying to increase our numbers for a reason. Shifters deserve to be at the top of this food chain. I'm tired of letting the witches, vampires, and fae make decisions for us. It's time they all learned to submit to me as their alpha."

My father was talking about ruining the delicate balance our world maintained. I had always considered him to be a fair leader, but lately he had grown crazy with power. That's why he brought Nicole's dad in. It's why he exercised his control every chance he got. Every year, our influence grew and grew. When would it stop?

"There are lots of shifters who won't want that," I insisted. "Our communities are happy—they're thriving."

My father unbuttoned the top of his dress shirt. "If they aren't with me, then they are against me."

His words were like a weight on my chest. I saw my father through clear eyes for the first time in my life. Even though he had beaten me for as long as I could remember,

I never thought he was this cruel, this dangerous. I didn't know what to say to him. It wasn't like he respected my opinions, and I definitely couldn't challenge him without facing the repercussions. I had so much more to lose now that I had found my mate.

The door to my father's office was kicked open, and two of his enforcers dragged Percy inside the room. The poor man was pale from terror, his eyes wide as he looked at me and my father.

"Alpha!" he exclaimed in shock before the burly enforcers dropped him on the ground. He fell to his knees with a thud and bowed before my father. "Whatever this is about, I can explain." The poor old man was groveling already, and my father hadn't even started.

My father gave a stern look to his hired muscle. "Leave us." His demand left no room for objections.

He then turned to me. "Stay. You're about to learn a valuable lesson, Alexei."

Percy was trembling on the ground, his eyes wide with fear. He had a smaller stature and malnourished look. The years of grueling work had not been kind to him, but he had only served our pack faithfully. Percy never complained when my father gave him terrible jobs. He loved his mate, cherished his children, and he was an honorable man who didn't deserve my father's wrath.

"Is it true that you have been frequently visiting the blood lounges belonging to the vampire king?" my father asked, his ruthless tone pulsing with alpha influence.

Percy's already pale skin went ashen. "Y-yes, Alpha. But—"

"Did I ask for your excuses?!" my father roared.

The terrified shifter's graying hair fell into his eyes as he lowered his head in submission. "No, Alpha. My apologies."

I tensed, not liking where this was going one bit. Whatever was about to happen, my father was clearly trying to make a statement, and I had a feeling Percy Zats was about to be collateral damage.

"Father..." I interjected, unable to stand here and do nothing. "Maybe we should—"

"You're either with me or against me, Alexei!" he repeated. "So, which will it be? Are you going to prove that you're too weak to lead this pack after I retire? Or are you going to finally fucking prove you're worthy of leading the strongest pack in existence?!"

My nostrils flared with anger. I was fucking tired of my father telling me that I wasn't good enough. "I *am* worthy. I've been training for this my entire life."

"*Prove it.*" My father sneered.

"How?"

He ran a hand through his dark hair as he looked down on a man who had dedicated his life to our pack.

"Show this pathetic excuse for a shifter how kindly his alpha takes to betrayal!" He threw his arm out, gesturing to the man kneeling on the floor.

Percy whimpered at the menace in my father's tone, shoulders shaking in fear.

"Just so I'm clear..." A muscle in my cheek jumped. "What *exactly* are you asking me to do, Father?"

"Only the strongest shifters deserve a place in this pack," he began. "Do you think Mr. Zats here fits that description? Do you think he's loyal? Or do you think it's time to drain the vampires' blood bag?"

"I think he adds value to this pack," I replied. "He's a hardworking man, and he's doing his part to help grow our population. His wife, Teresa, is due to deliver their twins any day."

"*Both* of his current children were born without wolves!" my dad yelled. "You can't get better proof as to how weak he is. Why should I have any hope the new pups will be any different?"

"The children's bloodlines are pure," I reminded him. "The genetic mutation that's causing the missing wolves is plaguing the entire shifter community, not just our pack."

"*There is no room for weakness in my pack!*" My father's voice was so loud it echoed throughout the room, but his next words were delivered so calmly and quietly, it was disconcerting. "Men like Percy Zats are holding us back. You must eliminate that weakness at the source."

"You want Percy ousted from the pack?" I asked.

"I want him ousted from the *world!*" my father

corrected. "And I want *you* to be the one to make that happen! Right here. Right now, Alexei. Make your choice."

I chanced a glance at Percy, whose green eyes were looking back at me with a sad sort of acceptance. He was silently pleading with me to have mercy on him, to make it swift. I knew my father had evil inside of him, but until this moment, I had no idea he was capable of taking someone's life who posed no threat to him. Maybe I was naïve in thinking he had hard limits. Maybe I was looking for a good inside of him that never really existed at all. I was more convinced than ever that my father needed to be taken down.

I sucked in a fortifying breath as my head slowly sliced to the left, then the right. "No. I will not hurt an innocent man. The only thing Percy is guilty of is trying to support his family in a *perfectly legal* manner. Would you really like to be held responsible for the death of this man, Father?"

"Fucking useless," my father spat. "Fine. If you won't do it, I'll show you how a *real* alpha handles his pack."

Before I could even blink, my father had lunged forward, his giant black and silver wolf bursting from his clothes before I could even blink. In the next moment, he was viciously attacking the man on the ground. With his sharp teeth, my father clamped down on Percy's arm, tearing apart his muscle meat. Blood splattered onto the carpet fibers, staining every inch of space with crimson, and as my father pulled at Percy's stretched tendons and bones, I watched in horror as he effectively severed the limb while Percy screamed in agony.

I took a step toward him, wanting to intervene, but my father turned to look at me. I knew if I challenged him now, it would be a fight to the death, and whoever won would remain alpha.

No one challenged my father.

No one survived his wrath.

Percy's eyes rolled back in his head from the pain and blood loss, his bloodcurdling screams turning raspy and weak.

Once my father was sure that I wouldn't challenge him, he went back to Percy's body, working out his anger on the poor man's innocent flesh. He tore a hole in his gut and pulled out his intestines. He punctured his stomach with his claw, and a foul smell filled the air.

Percy Zats was dead.

All because of an angry whim. Alpha Jones wanted to feel powerful for a moment, so he picked one of the weakest members of his pack to kill.

My chest tightened in disgust. It wasn't the first time I'd seen my father brutally murder someone, but it *was* the first time I'd seen him kill an innocent. I wondered how many victims he had in secret. How many disappearances could be explained by my father's judgments.

And worst of all, for a moment, I pictured Nicole's limp body on the floor in front of me. Her beautiful brown hair coated in blood. Her lifeless eyes. Limbs bent at odd angles as my father turned her precious body to ground meat.

Rage and fear swirled inside of me.

I couldn't let this man hurt her, but was I strong enough to stand against him?

My father picked at Percy's bones with his sharp teeth, reveling in his kill as I watched in horror.

Alpha Jones was a fucking monster. At that moment, I knew without a doubt that if I didn't take him down, we were all doomed.

Nicole

CRISTIAN STOOD with me outside of the Kappa Zeta house, both of us waiting in awkward anticipation for Jade and Hannah to arrive. The eager vampire wasn't kidding when he said that feeders were cherished in his community. I hadn't even made the oath, and he brought me breakfast this morning, gathered notes for the class I'd be missing today, and had Jade and Hannah flown in on a private jet. He was kind, attentive, and protective. I knew it was smart to make him an ally, but I was still intimidated by the idea of a blood oath. He was showing me through his actions that he was willing to support me, something I craved from Alexei from the start and never truly got.

So why couldn't I feel anything other than friendliness

for the man? Was it my supposed mate bond with Alexei holding me back, or was my heart too battered?

"Why do you look so nervous?" Cristian asked while nudging me. "I thought these women were allies."

Jade and Hannah had been like surrogate aunts to me since I was born, and even though I'd come to terms with all the secrets, I still wondered if things would be different between us now that I knew they'd been hiding a whole world from me.

I sighed. "They are. It just feels different now. I'm also worried about bringing them here."

"Why?"

"They ran away from the supernatural world, and now I'm dragging them back. Isn't that selfish of me?" I knew I needed all the support I could get, but I still felt wrong for forcing them to confront the past they'd so desperately left behind.

"From my very limited interactions with them, it's obvious they love you. Love makes you capable of incredible things. Stronger. Braver."

"Stupider," I grunted.

Cristian's eyebrows lifted in surprise. "I understand the mate bond can make you feel connected in a profound way, but I didn't realize you *loved* Alexei."

I cleared my throat. "I *don't* love him."

My response was a little too rushed, a little too transparent. I wasn't sure what I felt for Alexei. So much had been against us right from the start, and this confusing bond we supposedly shared made deciphering what was real difficult.

"Are you trying to convince me… or yourself?"

Both? Neither. Ugh. I didn't freaking know.

I shook my head. "It doesn't matter how I do or do *not* feel about Alexei."

His blue eyes softened. "Nicole… we don't know each other well, but I really hope you know you can talk to me. It can't be easy keeping everything bottled up all the time. We didn't exactly get off to the best start, but I'd like to think my recent actions have made up for that."

"One thing I've learned in my time at Redwood, Cristian, is that the only person I can trust is *myself*." My familiar barked at my side. "And Mace."

Macey nudged my leg with her snout as her tail wagged. She stood at attention when a black town car pulled up in front of the house. The window tint made it impossible for me to see its occupants, but I could *feel* Jade and Heather's presence. The vehicle had barely come to a stop before they were both bounding out of the back seat.

Jade's thick black locks bounced as she ran toward me with open arms. Hannah's blonde ponytail swished back and forth as she picked up the pace, seemingly determined to get to me first. I could no longer stand still, so I ran toward them as well, suddenly feeling overwhelmed with emotion. As the three of us collided in a series of oomphs and laughter, the front passenger door opened and a man stepped out, dressed in a smart suit. The guy had *lawyer* written all over him—or maybe a mortician—as he stood to his full height. His wiry frame towered over the car, and he scowled at us as we squealed and hugged. I was instantly wary of his pompous demeanor.

"Who's the suit?" I whispered in Hannah's ear as she squeezed me so hard my back cracked.

"Who?" She sniffed my hair and whined, seemingly in a daze.

"The man frowning at everything?"

She reluctantly pulled away and turned to look. "Oh! That's Thad. Don't worry about him, he's just naturally grumpy, as far as I can tell."

I nodded, like that somehow explained his presence. "And why is Thad here?"

Straightening his tie, the man waltzed up to us with purposeful strides. "Thad Harris. I'm the Luca clan's attorney. They've asked me to be present to document your father's condition for the council."

"Document his condition?" I frowned. "What does that mean?"

Jade smiled encouragingly. "We just want to have all our ducks in a row, sweetie. If they hurt a single hair on David's head, we'll ruin them." At the mention of *ruining* someone, she got a wicked look in her eyes.

"We'll prosecute to the full extent of the law," Thad amended, giving Jade a scolding look. "Please refrain from making any threats while there."

Jade shrugged. "A little threat never hurt anybody."

"As your legal counsel, I disagree."

I let out a whoosh of air and stared at the two women that had taken care of me since I was born. I tried to sense if I noticed anything different about them. Jade seemed the same. There had always been an ethereal beauty about her. I still remembered the time she saged our new house when we moved across town. She'd been in tune with the moon phases and always gave me crystals when she went on trips. Now that I knew what she was, it all made sense.

When I turned to look at Hannah, my mental encyclo-pedia went haywire, as if glitching. My stream of consciousness was jumbled, like it was trying to say two things at once.

"Ouch." I rubbed my temples while trying to make sense of the words flowing across my mind.

"You okay, babe?" Jade asked while rubbing my back. Cristian took a step forward, drawing everyone's attention while I winced in pain. "Ooh, is this the hunk that got us private jet service?" Jade wiggled her eyebrows. "Nice!"

Cristian ignored her, all his focus pinned on me. "Are you okay, Nicole?"

I groaned. "My mind-fuck is going haywire."

"Your *what?*" Thad asked while pressing his palm to his chest, seemingly scandalized by my cursing.

I groaned as the pain started to dim. "The reveal spell. It's trying to tell me what Hannah is, but it's freaking out."

At my words, Hannah's face fell, a shadow of shame

crossing her features. "Oh, Nicole. I'm so sorry." Her bottom lip quivered.

I shook my head. "You have nothing to be sorry for. I just don't understand what's going on."

After a few more moments, my mental encyclopedia went silent, done with its spiel.

"I guess now's a good time to tell you what I am." Hannah gulped.

I didn't want her to feel pressured into telling me, but I was still curious. "It's okay if you aren't comfortable—"

"I can leave," Cristian added, sensing her discomfort.

Thad huffed. "It's nothing to be ashamed of. Half-breeds are increasingly common and are now recognized as a protected entity by the council."

Jade reared back and slapped his arm hard. "Jeez, Thad. You need some serious people skills."

"Half-breed?" I asked, feeling sick at that term; it felt derogatory.

Hannah looked at the ground. "Half wolf shifter, half fae."

If my eyes could have popped out of my head in surprise, they would have. "Seriously? So you can turn into a wolf *and* you have magic?"

"Not exactly." She shook her head. "You'd think you'd be more powerful when bloodlines are mixed, but that's not how it works. It's why all the strongest factions are so big on the whole purity-when-breeding thing. When you dilute the blood, you lose some of the best benefits.

Like for me, I have predatory instincts, which have saved my ass on more than one occasion, but no ability to shift, which makes me a leper in the shifter community. For the fae half, technically, I possess magic, but it only works in Faerie, so I can't even open my own portal to get there."

Cristian stared at her in awe. "I've never met a half-breed from such powerful factions before."

Her eyes thinned to slits. "Well, now you have. Good for you."

He held his hands up in mock surrender. "Whoa, I wasn't trying to offend you. It's curiosity, nothing more."

"Sorry. I was teased my whole life for what I was. I'm a bit defensive about it." She sighed. "Being here brings up a lot of bad memories. Neither community accepted me. Not even the two people who gave me life. There wasn't a day I could remember from my childhood where someone wasn't reminding me how inadequate I was."

"I can imagine," Cristian said. "Kids are cruel, especially the predatory factions."

"You can say that again," Hannah muttered before clapping her hands together and pasting a smile on her face. "Enough trauma dumping for the day. Let's focus on the task at hand, shall we? What's on our agenda?"

Ah, there was the girl boss we all knew and loved. Hannah didn't get her book box company to the level she had by standing there and looking pretty. She was the most organized and driven person I'd ever met. Now that I knew she'd basically been living her entire life in survival mode, it made sense.

I let out a shaky sigh. "First, we're going to see Dad at the lab. At some point, I need to finish unpacking my room at Kappa Zeta, and I guess I need to recite some sort of blood oath, too."

Jade's eyebrows shot up. "A blood oath? Do you know what that entails?"

Cristian interrupted me before I could answer. "We don't have to do the blood oath right away." He paused to turn to Jade and Hannah. "I was planning to... um... take Nicole to a feeder party so she could see what it's like before committing to anything."

I looked at Jade and Hannah, who were both wearing equal smirks. "Want to come with us?" It might be nice to have them with me while I learn how to be a feeder.

Hannah let out a single laugh before covering her mouth. Jade, however, managed to keep her cool. "I don't think that's something you'll want us to be present for..."

"Why not?"

Cristian cleared his throat. Hannah bit her lip.

Thad didn't beat around the bush. "Vampire bites are known to cause spontaneous orgasms. For many, it's an extremely sexual experience."

I gaped at them. "Oh."

Why the hell didn't my mental encyclopedia warn me? I'd basically just asked my mother's best friends if they wanted to watch me get off. *Gross.*

Jade patted me on the shoulder. "Get it, girl."

I glared at Cristian. "You probably should have told me about that."

Scratching the back of his neck, Cristian fought a smile. "I probably should have. In my defense, you would've figured it out soon enough."

I tried really hard not to blush, but my face felt like it was on fire. I thought back to the first time I'd met Cristian. The disturbingly sexual vibe he instantly gave off. I was drawn to him, my body responding to his presence in a primal way. It wasn't anything close to what I'd felt with Alexei, but now that I thought about it, everything about Cristian was carnal. Maybe my... *whatever* with Alexei muted that for a bit, but imagining Cristian's bite and the possible effect it could have on me was... intriguing.

"She's totally thinking about it." Hannah elbowed Jade affectionately.

Jade smirked. "She takes after her Auntie Jade and Aunt Hannah."

They both erupted into a fit of giggles.

Rubbing my temples, I tried not to slump away in embarrassment. "Can we stop talking about this, please?"

Thad tugged at the collar of his shirt. "I charge by the hour. Perhaps we should table this conversation for later and get to the biology lab?"

Saved by the stodgy lawyer.

I cleared my throat. "Yes, please."

"So you've verified that's where Dr. Fairweather will be?" Cristian asked.

"Yes." Thad nodded. "I confirmed with Alpha Jones's secretary on the drive here. She assured me Dr. Fairweather would be expecting us."

I was practically bouncing on my heels, the need to see my father overwhelming. "What are we waiting for then?"

"After you." Cristian fanned his arm out.

I started walking down Greek Row, heading toward the science building with my impromptu entourage by my side. The closer I got, the quicker my strides grew, until I was practically running toward the tall building where my father was.

Two shifters were posted outside the front doors, both wearing expensive suits and scowls on their rugged faces. I slowed my pace and stared at them, frustration building in my chest at the idea of these guards watching over my father like he was some kind of prisoner.

"I'm here to see my father," I said when they didn't step aside.

The one on the left popped his neck and kept his gaze focused ahead, not even bothering to look at me.

What the fuck?

I took a step closer, and a low growl poured out of the man on the right. I opened my mouth to argue with them, but Thad stepped between us. "I truly hope you aren't poised here to intimidate my client. I'd hate to share this unfortunate interaction with the council."

One of the men looked at my scrawny, frigid lawyer. "A representative from the pack will be accompanying you. Alexei will be here in a moment to escort you inside. You can wait here until he arrives."

Thad rolled his shoulders back. "We weren't informed that we needed an escort."

"Take it up with Alpha Jones," the one on the right said.

I was equally infuriated and nauseated at the thought of being near Alexei again. As much as I wanted to wipe the memory from existence, I couldn't stop thinking about his proposal at the banquet last night. As if broadcasting our sex tape to the entire university wasn't bad enough. I didn't understand how anyone could be so cruel. To Mara of all people? It was like he pulled the knife from my back just to jam it right back between my ribs.

Part of me couldn't stop trying to piece the puzzle together to justify Alexei's actions. And the irony in this whole situation was that I'd always lived by the motto "Actions speak louder than words," yet when it came to the bossy future alpha, it didn't seem to matter. One second in his presence, and I wanted to forget the rest of the world existed. I wanted him to tell me the last few days had all been a horrible nightmare. But then logic would kick in, and I'd feel his betrayal down to my marrow. I hated the control he had over me. I was sick of feeling so conflicted about this man. I wasn't this girl. I didn't let a guy dump all over me and get away with it.

Juniper's insistence that Alexei and I were in fact mates was the only explanation, but I didn't want that to be true. Because if it was, did that mean I would never stop feeling so conflicted all the time?

"I'm excited to meet the asshole that broke my baby's heart." Jade cracked her knuckles.

Hannah gleamed. "I'm going to neuter him."

"Nobody is getting violent," Thad demanded.

"Damn lawyers. They take the fun out of everything." Jade huffed.

A few awkward minutes passed, but a strange awareness washed over me, a buzzing in my skin I couldn't ignore. I didn't even have to look up to know that Alexei was approaching. I could feel him in my bones, a deep part of my soul awakening the closer he got.

I hated my body's response to him. How could I possibly move on when I felt like this?

"Hello, everyone," Alexei said stiffly the moment he approached. He gave Cristian an icy stare before looking at me. I swear my heart cracked right down the middle when his gaze roamed my exposed shoulders and trembling lips. "Dr. Fairweather is just inside. Alpha Jones has requested that only a select few enter the building because of the proprietary information."

"Why wasn't that disclosed earlier?" Thad asked.

Alexei's brown eyes never left mine as he answered the lawyer's question. "Does it matter? You asked for verification that Dr. Fairweather is in good health. You'll be able to ascertain that whether one person or your entire group is allowed inside." He briefly glanced at Hannah and Jade, obviously recognizing Jade from our recent video call. It probably wasn't difficult for him to figure out who the blonde at her side was. "Ladies, I'm sorry, but I cannot allow you to come inside." He glared at Cristian. "And you're *definitely* not coming."

Cristian took a menacing step forward, but I placed my hand on his chest to stop him. "It's okay, Cristian. Thad will be with me." I narrowed my gaze on Alexei. "That won't be a problem, will it?"

He gave Thad a cruel look. "Our lawyers sent over an NDA for you to sign this morning. Did you get it notarized and returned to us?"

Thad was already naturally pale, but what little color he had in his cheeks vanished. "I didn't receive anything." He quickly pulled out his cell phone and started frantically scrolling. "It must have arrived while we were on the plane."

"That's bullshit!" Jade shouted.

"Agreed!" Hannah added.

"It's not really up for discussion." Alexei puffed his chest out. "I have my instructions, and under no circumstances will I be deviating from the plan. No NDA, no entry. The research conducted in this lab is protected by law."

"I didn't sign an NDA. Does that mean you won't let *me* enter?"

Alexei's lip twitched. "You signed an NDA when you were admitted to this school, since you are close with your father. It's on page seven of your admission packet."

"I'd like to see that packet!" Thad demanded.

"I'll have a copy forwarded to your email," Alexei replied coolly. "Be sure to check your inbox this time."

Jade folded her arms over her chest and scoffed. "Wow, you're a real piece of work, aren't you, Shifter Boy? Lemme guess. Daddy Dearest told you to be a giant prick. Am I right? If so, you're doing a bang-up job!"

"I'm simply following the rules," Alexei insisted.

Jade grabbed my arm. "I don't feel comfortable with you going in there alone."

Part of me agreed with her, but I wasn't about to miss out on a chance to visit with my father.

"I'll be fine. I've got my protection spell," I assured Jade before pinning a glare on Alexei. "Macey can come, right? She's a wolf, so it's not like she'll be sharing any of your important super secrets."

Alexei looked down at my wolf, who was glaring right back at him. "She's welcome to come."

I lifted my chin. "Great."

Alexei turned to the guards. "Stay here and keep an eye on them. Don't let anyone else inside."

"Sir, your father wanted one of us to go in with you."

Alexei sized him up. "And *I* am telling you that those orders have changed and you're to stand out here. I don't want *anyone* waltzing through these doors, do you understand me?"

"But—" Alexei snarled threateningly, cutting off the man's excuses. "Yes, sir."

With a simple nod, Alexei stormed toward the front door, leaving Mace and me to follow after him.

I side-eyed the jerky shifter. "What happened to not deviating from the plan?"

Mace growled when Alexei grabbed my elbow. "Just get inside, Nicole."

I jerked out of his hold. "I don't think your fiancée would appreciate you manhandling me."

He opened the door with a frown. "Inside."

I stepped over the threshold with my familiar trailing closely behind. I gave Alexei a questioning look when he locked the doors behind us.

"Don't your father's men have keys?"

"They did. But I had Corbin change the locks this morning."

"What are you doing?" My breath hitched as he stopped walking and gave me a look that promised all sorts of dirty things.

"What I wanted to do last night." He opened the door beside us, giving me a solid shove.

"What the hell?!" I yelped as I stumbled into the dark room.

Were we in a closet?

I heard the door close behind me, followed by a loud

bark. Mace howled and scratched the door, trying to get inside.

Fear traveled up my throat and burned my tongue. Even though Alexei had hurt me emotionally, I never thought he was capable of harming me physically. Was this it? Was he going to make me obey? He closed the short distance between us, his chest heaving as his eyes flashed in the dark. I could feel his imposing presence crowding my body, sending my feet backward until my calves hit a shelf.

"Are you going to hurt me?" I croaked.

"Baby," Alexei rasped. "I'm trying to *save* you. Can't you see that? Hurting you is the *last* thing I want to do."

"Yet you continuously do so anyway," I snapped. "Let me out of here."

Macey continued to bark and growl from the other side of the door.

"Tell her to stand down," Alexei commanded. "She's going to draw attention, and trust me when I say we do *not* want anyone to find us here alone in the dark."

My eyes had adjusted enough for me to make out his shadowed jawline. "I don't want to be alone with you in the dark! I want to see my father!" I stepped forward, but Alexei's big body blocked my way.

"Nicole. Please. Just give me a few minutes. Tell Macey to stand down."

"Why?"

Mace was stepping up her efforts. The door rattled.

"Just do it."

I blew out a breath, hoping I didn't regret this. "Mace. I'm okay, girl. Stand down."

The racket she was making instantly ceased. I could hear my familiar whimpering on the other side of the door as she stilled.

"Thank you."

"Get to the point," I hissed, crossing my arms.

"Nicole," Alexei whispered.

I flinched as his hand cupped the side of my neck. "I told you not to touch me."

His fingers flexed against my skin, but he made no move to release me. I had to remind my stupid body that he hurt us and didn't deserve a reaction. "I'm so sorry it has to be like this. This is the last thing I wanted."

"Then why did you do it? You're the one who put us in this position, Alexei. *Not* me!"

"My father can't know we're *really* mates. He was at Beta Phi that night. Mara must've invited him. I *panicked* when I saw him. I had to make it seem like—"

I cut him off. "Fuck you, Alexei." I wasn't about to sit here and listen to his excuses. "You humiliated me in front of everyone. We've been playing this game of push and pull since the moment we met."

"It's complicated, Nicole. There are so many things you don't know. My father is losing his shit. I'm afraid of what he might do to you. I can't let him hurt you."

"*You* hurt me!" I roared, shoving his chest. "You *keep*

hurting me. Over and over again. You tell me I'm not good enough because I'm human. You dangle Mara in front of me to push me away. And then worst of all, you draw me back in like a dirty little secret so you can get off behind closed doors, then turn me into a joke in public. It's fucked up."

"I'm trying—"

"You're *not* trying, Alexei. Because if you were, you would have stood up to your father. Jesus fucking Christ, you're engaged!"

"The engagement was staged! I don't want Mara." Alexei reached for me, but I slapped his hand away. "But my father is incredibly connected and impossibly strong. If I challenged him, he could kill me, and he'd *definitely* kill you for being the reason I stood up to him. It's not an easy choice, Nicole."

"You could have fooled me. You sure as hell seemed convincing when you dropped down on one knee in front of everyone."

"It's not real!" he roared.

"*It was real to me, Alexei!* You made all these promises and still picked her." I swallowed the emotions lodged in my throat.

His eyes turned tender, and he responded in a soft voice. "You're the only real thing in my life, Nicole. My feelings for you are genuine. I'm sorry, okay? I'm so fucking sorry. I hate that I hurt you. I can feel your pain like it's my own."

Though he sounded remorseful, I didn't trust him enough to believe him. "If you cared about me, you wouldn't have proposed to her." I poked him in the chest with my index finger. A shiver traveled down my spine the moment we touched. "Actions speak louder than words, Alexei."

"I *know* that," he insisted. "But it doesn't change how I *feel*. Nicole, I... I *love* you."

I let out a bitter laugh. Of course he would say that in the middle of our fight. I'd hoped the first time a boy declared his love for me would have been a beautiful moment, but all the pain shared between us made his words feel hollow. This wasn't love. This was toxic. It was destroying my confidence and breaking my heart.

"Oh, yeah? Prove it. End your engagement."

"I will. When the timing is right."

Yeah, right. Alexei would never stand up to his father. He'd never turn his back on his pack.

Alexei would never *choose me*, and I couldn't just wait around for him to figure his shit out.

"I suppose Mara is the perfect girl for you. A ruthless she-wolf your father can be proud of. What exactly is your plan? Put a rock on her finger and fuck me in private until you're strong enough to challenge your father?"

He was silent for a moment as if he were considering it.

My fists clenched. "Oh my God, you ass! That wasn't a serious question. I'm not going to be your mistress!"

Alexei shook his head. "I would never ask you to be."

My stupid eyeballs were filling with tears. "Really? Because to me, that's exactly what you've been doing. I'm done being your dirty little secret, Alexei. Now take me to my father."

"Nicole, please. I'm begging you. Just give me a chance to explain. Don't make a blood oath and become Cristian's feeder. We can fix this."

"Is that what this is about? You won't have me, but no one else can either?" A wildfire of rage tore through me. "Listen here, Alexei. Right now, you're going to unlock that door and silently take me to see my father. Later, I'm going to make a blood oath to Cristian Luca, because unlike you, he knows what he wants and isn't afraid to admit it. Years from now, when you're married to that bitch and miserable with life, I hope you look back on this and know that right here—*right now*—was the moment you lost me for good."

CHAPTER
NINE

Alexei

My skin was buzzing. Standing this close to my mate, feeling her pain, and knowing I was the cause of it was tearing me up inside. Nicole deserved grand gestures and groveling and action. But I had to be smart about this. My father's unhinged mental state was dangerous for everyone.

"Take me to my father," Nicole demanded. My heart clenched at her brisk tone, her commanding words like barbwire wrapped around my wolf. It was my job to be the leader. My job was to take care of her. And once again, I'd failed.

I lingered just a moment longer to breathe her in. It

was on the tip of my tongue to beg her not to complete the blood oath with Cristian again. I understood why she felt safer with the bloodsucking asshole, but because we'd halfway completed our bond, I'd *feel* her with him. Her pleasure would ripple through the thin tether that tied our souls together, and if that happened, I feared I would become just like my father. I would rip that bloodsucker's throat out with my teeth for touching what's mine.

It's why I'd avoided Mara almost entirely. Kept my bedroom door locked at all times. I wouldn't put it past that cunning she-wolf to try waking me up with her mouth one morning, and I didn't want Nicole to feel my pleasure before I awoke enough to realize what was happening. It took some creative liberties. I had to send Corbin out with my credit card today to fill up her schedule. My plan was to keep Mara so busy with massage appointments, spa days, and brunch outings with friends that she didn't have time to focus on me. It pissed me off to reward the bitch with things I wanted to give my mate —my *true* mate—but I had to keep doing this until I could publicly end this farce.

I opened the door, and the moment I did, Macey launched at me. Nicole's familiar was a massive wolf, but I was bigger. When she threw her black paws into my shoulders, I stumbled back a few steps, but remained standing. Her fangs dripped with saliva as she snarled at me, trying to lock her jaws around my carotid.

"A little help here?" I grunted with the effort it took to not get my throat ripped out.

Nicole sighed, as if she was inconvenienced by asking her dog not to murder me. "Mace. Down, girl."

The wolf's front paws hit the ground with a thump before she hurried to my mate's side.

I brushed some loose dirt off my white T-shirt. "Familiars are supposed to recognize a person's true intentions. She should inherently know I'd never hurt you."

I wanted to kiss the smirk off her beautiful face. "Maybe that should tell you something. Maybe she can recognize your true intent before *you* can."

Ouch. That fucking stung. I'd deserved that though. "Let's just go check on your father."

"Great."

As we walked the long hallway that led to the laboratory, Macey was practically cemented to Nicole's side, as if daring me to close the distance between us and get my head snapped off. I was leery of the wolf, but at least she would keep Nicole safe when I couldn't.

I stopped outside a double door. "He's just in here."

Nicole pushed past me and flung the door open before waltzing through them like she owned the place. The determined look on her face was yet another reminder of how fucking perfect she was for me. She was fierce and protective despite the fear I knew she felt inside.

"Dad?" she croaked before running across the tiled

floor to Dr. Fairweather. The doctor spun around and sighed in relief the moment he saw her, and then they collided into a harsh hug as Nicole shook with emotion. "I was so worried about you."

He held the back of her head, murmuring something too quietly for me to hear. Nicole nodded in reply, sniffling as she pulled out of their embrace. Her hands roamed his face, fingertips lightly brushing over the fading bruise on his cheek.

"Hello, Nicole." Dr. Cammie Viden offered my mate a sad smile.

Nicole gasped as she stopped fussing over her dad. "*You're* in on this?! What are you? His official jailer?"

Her father shook his head. "No, honey. I swear. Cammie... uh, Dr. Viden is assisting me with my research. She doesn't like this anymore than I do." He glanced at me, eyes widening as if he just realized I was in the room. "I mean..."

I held a hand up. "You have nothing to fear from me, Dr. Fairweather. I'm not happy about this situation either."

My mate snorted. "Right."

Her dad looked between me and his daughter, frowning, before clearing his throat. "Yes... well, if that's true, then I suppose you won't blame me for being a bit skeptical."

"Feel free to be downright distrusting, Dad," Nicole grunted, her tone full of malice.

My wolf scratched at my soul. This was so wrong. How would I ever fix this?

Dr. Fairweather pushed his reading glasses up the bridge of his nose. "Right. Well…" He gulped in a large breath and eyed me warily. "I'm perfectly safe. Nothing to worry about. Alpha Jones is… uh… a lovely host. Truly. I don't have any complaints." The more he spoke, the louder he got, like he wanted the bugs we set up in his lab to catch the blatant lie.

"Dr. Fairweather," I said, stopping his awkward rambling. "Is there anything you need?"

He blinked twice as if not comprehending what I asked. "Oh, no, the oatmeal and sandwiches are… delicious. My cot gets a bit cold at night, but they gave me a change of clothes, so that's nice."

Nicole bit her fist and hot tears streamed down her cheeks. "Oh, Dad."

"I'll fix this," I promised them. "The least we can do in thanks for your hard work is provide good meals and a comfortable place to sleep when you rest."

"Alexei the Magnanimous," Nicole muttered.

I fought the urge to growl. Couldn't she see I was making an effort?

"We also need some test subjects for our research," Dr. Viden said, drawing our attention to her. "I have a… close friend whose son is wolfless. The boy would make a great candidate, but your father is refusing my request to bring him here. Maybe you can convince him to… reconsider."

I squinted at Dr. Viden speculatively. Her wording was... careful, and I wondered if she was insinuating something. I really fucking hoped her friend wasn't a pregnant widow.

"Who's the guy with the missing wolf?"

"Hunter Kline. Do you know him?"

I scratched my jaw. The name sounded familiar.

"I know him," Nicole piped up. "He actually seems like a really nice guy."

Oh, fuck.

I knew exactly who they were talking about. It wasn't Percy Zats's son, but it *was* the asshole who was hitting on Nicole during the river float during a rush event. A rush of possessiveness ran through me at the reminder.

"You almost drowned because of that guy," I reminded her. "What's so *nice* about that?"

Her blue eyes narrowed. "Actually, Hunter *saved* me from drowning that day. But you were probably too busy with your fan club to register that very important fact."

"Really?" I challenged. "Remind me again who came to your aid, cleansed your wounds, and took you back to your dorm?"

She huffed.

Dr. Viden cleared her throat. "Perhaps this conversation would best be had elsewhere?" She flicked her gaze to the camera in the corner of the room, making her point with that simple gesture.

Right. My father was watching. I had to be careful. He didn't know I took care of Nicole that day, and I didn't need another reason for him to punish me.

Holy shit, did that mean the fae was actually on my side? Or was she simply trying to protect Nicole and her father? She seemed to have a fondness for the scientist. I needed to speak with her when we didn't have witnesses.

Dr. Fairweather checked his watch. "I don't want you staying here for long, sweetie."

"Dad…" Nicole's voice cracked as she stared at him. "I'm going to get you out of here."

He held a finger up to his lips, wordlessly telling her to keep quiet. "I'm *aware* of all the dangers we face. Right now, you need to keep your head down, okay?" He then looked at me, his eyes stern with unspoken words, and I wished I could read his mind.

"I'll be fine. Jade and Hannah are here."

Dr. Fairweather's eyes widened. "They're here?"

"Yes. Came as soon as I called."

Dr. Viden cleared her throat. "I'm sorry, did you say Jade and Hannah are here? I'd like to speak with them."

Nicole blanched, and I felt myself stiffen.

"Do you know them?" I asked, trying not to sound accusatory.

Dr. Viden smiled politely. "Only what David has told me. They sound like lovely people. If you'd like, I can accompany you out of here and introduce myself?"

Nicole eyed the fae woman warily. "I want to spend more time with Da—"

"You must leave," Dr. Fairweather interrupted her before grabbing both her hands and squeezing. "Nicole, I don't want you to come back to this lab. Distance yourself as far away as you can for the time being. Alpha Jones is here daily requesting updates, and I... don't want him to think I'm being distracted from my work."

Nicole shook her head, tears shimmering in her eyes. "Dad. I can't leave you here—"

"You can. And you *will*." The old man trembled with fear, but he held firm. "You're so important to me, Nicole. The light of my life. My world was so bleak when your mother died..." He paused to stroke her cheek affectionately. "But you were like this full moon on a dark night, giving me hope and the courage to pull myself back up. I would be miserable if anything happened to you."

"David," Dr. Viden said. "We should get back to work. I'll walk them out."

The fae's anxiety rolled off her in waves, and I wanted to get to the bottom of it. I had a feeling she knew more than I originally gave her credit for.

Nicole lingered, obviously distressed by the idea of leaving her father, but he was right. We needed to keep her as far away from here as possible. I respected him for having a clear head about things and wanting to protect her.

Nicole hung her head, her familiar glued to her side, as

Dr. Viden escorted us out of the building. I was perfectly capable of seeing to the task myself, but I had a feeling the fae had a reason for accompanying us. She gave me a questioning look when I needed to unlock the front door, but I didn't bother explaining. She would find out as soon as I had Corbin deliver her new set of keys later this afternoon. My father claimed there was a flood in this building, so all science classes were temporarily housed in the anthropology building. The forensics lab had some equipment, but there were plenty of furious chemistry majors and professors. Dad didn't care who he pissed off, though. He wanted to keep David's work under lock and key. The only way he could sell the cure to the highest bidder was if no one else had access to the doctor's research.

"It's about damn time," Jade huffed as the three of us stepped outside. She pulled Nicole into a hug. "Are you okay, honey?"

"I'm fine." Nicole sniffled.

The blonde woman—presumably Hannah—eyed Dr. Viden with curiosity. "Who's this?"

Dr. Viden pulled her shoulders back and offered the group a warm smile. "I'm Cammie Viden. I work with David." She glanced at my mate. "I'm also one of Nicole's professors."

Hannah didn't look impressed. "You're fae."

"I am," Dr. Viden confirmed. "As are you. At least partially."

"Unfortunately," Hannah grumbled.

"Yes, I can certainly understand your grievances, considering your... status within the fae community. But as I once told Nicole, not all fae are bad. I'd be happy to demonstrate if you gave me the chance." Dr. Viden extended her hand in a gesture of peace. "What do you say?"

Hannah glanced between the professor's hand and Nicole. When my mate gave her a subtle nod, Hannah closed the distance and shook hands with Dr. Viden.

"This doesn't mean I trust you." Hannah glared.

"Understood." Dr. Viden's lips twitched. "I can see why she was so fond of you."

"You can see why *who* was so fond of me?" Hannah questioned.

Dr. Viden's eyes rounded. "Oh. Um... Nicole's mother. David mentioned you were close, and that you and your friend stepped in when his wife passed."

Jade squeezed Nicole into her side. "There isn't *anything* we wouldn't do for Nicole." Her dark brown eyes shifted to me before narrowing. "Got that, Shifter Boy? I am not above causing bodily harm to protect my girl."

My father's guards, who were stationed at the doors, stepped forward, but I held up a hand to stop them. My wolf's hackles instantly rose at the woman's threat, but I managed to keep my cool by reminding myself she was acting in my mate's best interest.

"Why must you always threaten violence?" the vampire's attorney asked. "Are you so dense you cannot comprehend the possible legal ramifications, or are you simply unhinged?"

"I'll show you unhinged," Jade promised him.

Cristian chuckled. "On that note, we should be going. Nicole didn't you mention you had to finish unpacking?"

Why the fuck was he still here?

Her full lips curved. "Yes, I did. Thanks for the reminder."

My fists clenched as she moved toward the bloodsucker and looped her hand around his arm. "Would you mind walking us back?"

His fangs lengthened as he smiled back at her. "I'd be honored."

Nicole, Cristian, and the rest of their group then turned their backs on me and began walking away.

Yep, goodbye to you, too.

My nostrils flared as I forced my feet to stay glued to the ground rather than marching after them and tossing Nicole over my shoulder like I wanted to. I knew my mate well enough to know how poorly that would work in my favor. An involuntary growl spilled from my throat as Luca pressed his hand to the small of Nicole's back, leading her toward Greek Row. The cocky shit looked over his shoulder as he did it, to ensure I was watching. Even though I hated giving him the satisfaction, I couldn't look away until they were out of sight. I didn't know what I was going to do if Nicole went through with this blood oath bullshit. My inner animal wanted to murder the vampire at the mere thought of it. Nicole was *mine*. She had no business completing *any* kind of bond with another. But how the fuck was I going to convince her of that before it was too late?

Because one thing I knew for sure was that time was *not* on my side.

Nicole

Jade was fluffing pillows on my bed while Hannah looked at my wardrobe with envy. "You have the cutest clothes, Nicole."

Settling into my new room at the Kappa Zeta house was such a mundane task, especially since my world had fallen apart. Even though the witch sorority was a better option than Beta Phi, I didn't want to be anywhere near this university. When I saw my father, all I wanted was to grab him and escape. Dad seemed terrified, and I wasn't thrilled about his living conditions. Alexei had promised to fix things, but it wasn't like I could trust my wishy-washy supposed mate.

"It's so nice of them to put you on the ground floor so Macey can get out and run." Jade patted my familiar on the head.

My room had double doors leading to the woods behind the Kappa Zeta house. Macey spent most of the last two days outside running. Juniper spelled her collar so when I called her name, she could hear it no matter how far she ran.

"Macey seems to love it too." After we got back from visiting my father, she spent all afternoon jumping and playing.

"This feels like a good fit for you. The members are so welcoming and inclusive. I'm glad you found a home." Hannah smiled at me encouragingly, her eyes kind and warm.

I grumbled. It was strange how much I once wanted this, but now I couldn't stand the thought of belonging to *any* sorority at Redwood. I just wanted to get away from here. "This *isn't* my home. The first chance I get, I'm leaving Redwood University for good. It's not safe here— for anyone."

Jade and Hannah exchanged a look. "We want you out of here, too. But maybe being here and learning about *your* supernatural community while you can isn't so bad..." Jade started furiously scratching her neck, her long nails leaving angry red marks.

"Too close, Jade," Hannah murmured.

I looked at them. "What do you mean?"

Jade started scratching harder, nearly drawing blood. "Curse this fucking secrecy spell. Can't even hint without my skin feeling like it's on fire!"

Hint? What hint? My mind scraped over what she'd just said. *Learn about the supernatural community while you can...*

No. That wasn't what she said. Jade had said *your* supernatural community.

"Do I belong to one of the factions here?" I asked.

Hannah grabbed her neck, a choking sound escaping her lips. Jade cradled her head in her hands. Shit. I stared at them with my eyes wide in shock. The pain flashing across their expressions made me feel guilty. I didn't want to hurt them.

A knocking sound on the door interrupted us, and with eyes still trained on Jade and Hannah, I went to open it. "You really can't say anything, can you?"

"Even *thinking* about telling you makes my head hurt," Jade replied with a wince. "It's infuriating."

How was I supposed to get answers when the truth literally hurt the people I loved?

"Whew!" Juniper fanned the air with her hand the moment I opened the door. "This room reeks of secret magic. Who's trying to torture themselves?" She walked into the room, sniffing the air. "I found a friend of yours wandering your old dorm, Nicole. Bee? She's in the sitting room if you want me to bring her here. She has a beautiful aura perfect for kindness spells."

"Bee?!" My stomach dropped. "Bee is here? Right now?"

Juniper shrugged. "She's human, so I didn't think she was a threat, but wanted to make sure you knew her before bringing her up here."

I reached into my pocket and pulled out my cell phone. The screen was black because I'd powered it down the night Mara showed my sex tape to everyone. I didn't want to deal with the nasty text messages from other supernaturals wanting a turn to fuck me, too. Cristian had coordinated Jade and Hannah's visit, so I didn't really need it back on since.

But still, Bee was *here*?

"Bee is here? God, I *love* her. Such a devoted friend." Hannah clapped her hands excitedly. "Let's not keep her waiting."

I held up my hand to stop them. My pulse started to race with anxiety. It was one thing to bring Jade and Hannah here, but Bee was human and therefore vulnerable. "It's not safe for Bee at Redwood. We need to get her out of here as quickly as possible."

"Already trying to get rid of me, Nicole?" my best friend's voice echoed as she walked through the open door and into my room, her boots scuffing along the floor. "Sorry to invite myself in, but I've been worried sick, and you were taking too long."

Bee's wild mane of black curls was tied up on top of her head, and the oversized glasses she wore were sliding down the bridge of her nose. With her camera bag slung over her shoulder, she wore sleek jeans and a button-up blouse. She cocked her head to the side and glared challengingly at me.

I sputtered. "Bee! What are you doing here?"

My best friend crossed her arms over her chest. "What am *I* doing? I haven't heard from you in three days, Nicole. *Three freaking days.* Your dad wasn't answering me, and Hannah and Jade told me they were visiting to help you with something." I felt a sudden urge to shove her out the door and plop her on the first plane out of here. "Are you going to hug me or what?"

With a sigh, I closed the distance between us and wrapped my trembling arms around her curvy frame. She smelled like expensive perfume, and my soul felt lighter the moment we embraced. "I missed you."

She pulled away. "Missed you too. Now tell me what's going on at this damn supernatural university. My father was *not* thrilled about me coming here."

Jade laughed. "I'm surprised your father didn't follow you. That man is a helicopter parent if I ever saw one. I'm glad you know about the supernatural community, though. Really streamlines things. I wasn't sure if your father ever told you what he was, and it wasn't my place to pry."

I squeezed my eyes shut, then opened them again.

With everything going on, I hadn't had time to talk to Bee about what Jade had told me. But evidently, I didn't need to. Something Jade said that night suddenly made a lot more sense.

The military is more involved with the supernatural community than you might think.

I had to admit, it did make things easier, though. If Bee already knew about the supernatural community, she would be immune to the containment spell that was cast over the campus. I felt slightly better about her safety if she knew what we were up against.

Bee let out a sigh. "Yes. I know. Kind of hard to ignore your father wolfing out on occasion. You know as well as I do that there are very intense laws regarding keeping the supernatural secret. For the record, I'm thrilled that you now know, Nicole, so I can finally talk to someone. Dad took me to meet the fucking Loch Ness monster one time, and I couldn't say shit. He photographs well, though."

Juniper gasped. "I hear their scales turn humans into mermaids."

Bee shrugged. "I dunno about that. I just remember the smell. Like rotten fish." She gagged for emphasis.

"Great. Everyone in my life has been lying to me for years. I'm trapped at this fucking school, my dad is locked up, and my supposed mate is an asshole." I knew in my gut I sounded like a toddler throwing a temper tantrum, but I'd met my threshold for the day.

Bee's eyes widened. Jade covered her mouth, as if

trying to suppress a smirk. Hannah moved to pat me on the back affectionately.

"You need some Xanax," Juniper suggested.

"What, no magic spell to calm me down?" The way my voice kept climbing close to hysteria made Macey whine.

"I mean... I have that too, but sometimes humans are pretty effective with their pharmaceuticals. I can get you some if you'd like."

I threw my hands up and walked over to my bed, collapsing on the mattress. "Everything has gone to shit."

Bee moved to sit beside me, her soft hand stroking my forehead. "That's why I'm here, babe. You're not alone. Everyone in this room just wants to help you." She lay down, her hair scattering around her as she pulled her hair tie out.

I turned my head and stared into my best friend's eyes. I heard the door click, the others likely giving us privacy while I had a meltdown. "So your dad is a shifter, huh? Have you always known?"

"Sorta. You know I was two years old when he adopted me from the foster care system. Right? Looking back, I always knew there was something larger than life about him, but he waited until I was old enough to understand the importance of discretion to formally explain the supernatural world. Around age eleven, I think."

I nodded. "Now that I know about shifters, his intense personality makes sense. He's so damn protective of you."

She smiled fondly. "He always wanted a family but

never connected with anyone after his fated mate died early into their relationship, so he took the single dad route. My dad has been a lone wolf my whole life. He joined the military so he could have the feeling of a pack without joining one. Climbed the ranks like a true alpha, and he didn't even have to shift for it."

"You sound proud of him."

"I am," she mused. "He wants to talk to you, Nicole. Told me to have you call him once we're settled. He wanted to tell you everything before you came to Redwood, but was worried about drawing more attention to himself. He's an alpha, and a really powerful one at that. There are lots of wolves that want to eliminate him because they're worried he'll challenge them for their pack. Luckily, we've always been on the move, and the higher he ranks in the military, the more untouchable he's become. But Redwood is a whole 'nother world. He'd be here if he didn't think Jones would kill him on the spot."

I nodded. Bee had to protect her father, and considering my *own* dad was locked up by Alpha Jones, I couldn't blame her for that. She was human tossed into the supernatural world. "Thanks for telling me, Bee. I won't lie and say it doesn't sting that you kept this from me all this time, but I understand why you had to do it."

"I just hate that you were going through all of this alone. I knew something had happened, but I couldn't outright ask without exposing myself first. When I called

Jade, she told me you knew about the world. But then you stopped answering my calls, and I got really worried."

"I've been avoiding my phone. Something pretty embarrassing happened, and I was tired of the texts I was getting."

"What happened?"

I chewed on my lip for a moment. Even though rehashing everything sounded worse than plucking my nails from my fingers, Bee was my best friend. Maybe a little girl talk would relieve some tension.

"We need tequila if we're going to talk about it."

She popped up off the mattress with a giggle and started digging through her camera bag. "Good thing I always come prepared."

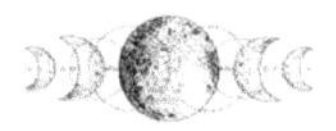

"WHAT AN ASSHOLE. To get engaged right in front of you? To *her*? I might not be a shifter, but I'm scrappy. I'll beat both of their asses."

I took another swig from the liquor bottle, then laughed, a warm buzz flowing through my veins as the hot liquid swirled in my belly.

"Get in line," Jade said from her chair, watching us with a giggle. "I feel like I should be discouraging underage drinking, but this reminds me so much of when we'd hang out in our room, Hannah."

Hannah was sitting on the floor, painting her nails. "I know! It's like reliving the glory days, though the drama with George was nothing compared to Alexei."

I wiped my lips with the back of my hand. "Who is George?"

Hannah smiled affectionately before inspecting her pinky. "Just a guy at a frat that I hooked up with once. I met him during rush week. He didn't tell me he had a girlfriend. She stormed into the room while he was balls deep inside of me."

Everyone gasped.

"Please tell me you both teamed up to kick his ass!" Bee exclaimed.

Jade cleared her throat, answering for Hannah. "The girl ended up taking him back. But Hannah and I put rotten anchovies in his room."

The two of them started cackling, and after a moment of processing, Bee and I joined them. "No way!"

"I bet his room smelled like the Loch Ness monster," Bee added, making us all laugh even harder, our drunkenness seemingly making the whole story even funnier.

"We were so mischievous. It's more fun when you're living like a human to get revenge. Everyone wants to spell one another when they're wronged, but when you don't use magic, you get to be creative."

Jade groaned. "And then we did the stupidest thing ever and performed a secrecy spell."

Bee took the tequila out of my hands and stole a sip, hissing as it went down. "But if we figure out what Nicole is without you, then you can tell us, right?"

"Correct."

Macey jumped up on my bed and curled in my lap. I reached out to pet her, an idea suddenly hitting me. "Mace? Can you show me more of my mom?"

I swear the wolf had a twinkle in her eye, as if she'd been waiting for me to ask her. Or maybe the tequila was just really starting to hit me.

"Wait. Can we all see these visions or just you?" Jade asked, she was practically frothing at the mouth.

I looked at Macey. "I'm not sure. Maybe if we all put our hands on her head at the same time?"

Jade and Hannah jumped up immediately, swaying a bit as they did, while Bee leaned closer on the mattress. The four of us hovered our hands over my familiar like we were in a race to see who would pet her first. Mace looked like she was in heaven to have so much attention on her, her bushy tail wagging.

"Okay. Let's try. One," I said.

Bee's pinky shook. "Two."

"Three," Hannah and Jade said together. We all touched Macey, and immediately a vision slammed into me, but it wasn't like the other times.

Jade, Hannah, and Bee were standing beside me, all of us like transparent ghosts in a crowded room.

"Where are we?" Bee asked, her voice echoing and deeper than usual.

"I know this place," Hannah replied. "It's a coffee-house near Cambridge University. We used to come here for our caffeine fix all the time."

The shop had a wall of windows so I could see that it was long past sunset, but the place was packed with coeds sitting at tables with open books and giant mugs of steaming liquid. Most of the guys were wearing popped collars and cargo pants, and most girls were dressed in tight shirts and ultra-low-rise jeans. It was definitely the late nineties based on the attire.

"Oh my God, it's George." Hannah was eyeballing a guy with spiky bleach-streaked hair leaning on the coffee bar, seemingly flirting with a barista.

"I heard he's bald now," Jade said gleefully.

"Why would Macey show us this—" My question was immediately cut off when I saw her. "Mom?"

It was evident from the look on her face that she was nervous. In the next moment, I saw why. A younger and, though this seemed impossible, an even *nerdier* version of my father approached the table she was sitting at, clumsily setting down two mugs that sloshed from his uncoordinated movements. My mother's bright blue eyes lit up as he took his first sip and immediately started sputtering as hot coffee spilled down the front of his button-up shirt.

"Aw, I almost forgot how adorable David was back then." Despite her ghostly form, Hannah had tears misting her eyes. "This was the first night they met. We had been there for hours studying for finals. This must've been shortly after Jade and I went back to the dorms. We didn't want to leave without Celena, but she insisted on staying, saying she couldn't shake the feeling she was right where she needed to be."

"Lena fell so hard, so fast," Jade added. "Your mom had her pick of any guy in Massachusetts, but when she met your dad, he was all she could see. The funny thing is, David wasn't really a *study in public* kind of guy. He'd much rather be tinkering in the lab at MIT or holed up in a quiet section of the library. Celena said he had originally planned to get his java to go. But when their eyes locked across the room as he stood in line, the rest was history. I used to tell Celena that her *feeling* was proof they were supposed to meet that night. Your mom was really attuned to the fates like that."

My eyes were misting as well. The four of us watched in silence as my parents talked to one another. I couldn't hear what they were saying, but their body language told me everything I needed to know. My mom leaned into him more and more as the night wore on. She laughed with her entire body as he undoubtedly cracked painfully awkward jokes. When she reached across the table and placed her hand on his forearm, my dad's nervous fidgeting instantly bloomed into confidence. He stared at her with awe, like the world began and ended with her. As they left the coffeehouse hand-in-hand a short while later, the bond between them was practically tangible. I had never seen two people more enamored with each other.

It made me realize how I never knew this side of my father. He was always the brilliant scientist or my nerdy pops, but I hadn't experienced David Fairweather, the *man*. My entire life, he threw himself into his work, which I had assumed was because parenting didn't come naturally to him, but now I wondered if it was because he was trying to fill the cracks in his broken heart by keeping busy. He never dated, as far as I knew. Never even had many friends outside of colleagues. I thought it was due to his extreme lack of social skills, but seeing him so at ease with my mother, a woman he'd just met, made me wonder how much he'd closed himself off from the rest of the world since she died.

It made me even more determined to get him as far away from this university as possible so he'd have the chance to experience life like that again.

As the vision faded, I tried not to feel a little disappointed. Seeing my parents together was something I'd cherish for a lifetime, but we were still no closer to figuring out what my mother was. I needed to know what supernatural faction she belonged to so I had a better understanding of my own existence in this strange world.

When the fog faded, Jade was wiping a stray tear. "I miss her so much."

Hannah reached out to hug her. "Me too. She had this way of brightening up a room, yeah?"

I sniffled. "Dad seemed so happy."

"He's still happy—and so dang proud of you, Nicole. She was the love of his life, but you're his whole world."

And his world would come crashing down if we didn't find a way to fight Alpha Jones and get all of us out of here.

CHAPTER

ELEVEN

Nicole

I woke up with a massive hangover, but Juniper had a tray of greasy food and coffee set outside our door to help ease our pounding heads. Hannah, Jade, Bee and I slept on my queen-size bed, all snuggling on top of one another, our sheets tangled as we snoozed. It was like the sleepovers we used to have when I was in high school, all of us together, laughing and enjoying each other's company.

Even though I woke up feeling exhausted, my cup was full. I felt a new sense of purpose and was ready to tackle the problems of my day.

"What's on the agenda?" Jade asked.

I popped a piece of French toast into my mouth. "I

have class. I don't really want to go, but I'm not going to let Alpha Jones ruin my GPA, too."

Bee rolled her eyes. "Always so studious. Are your professors hot? Can I sit in on class with you?"

"I'm sure I could sneak you in." I laughed at her. "I can't exactly help you out on the hot professor end, though."

"And what about tonight? Should we do anything?" Jade asked before snapping her fingers as if she'd had an epiphany. "We could check out the building where they're keeping your father? Maybe get an idea of when the guards change and see if we can catch any weaknesses in their security?"

Hannah high-fived her bestie. "Look at you being a super spy. Don't let Thad know we're breaking the rules, though."

I nodded. "I suppose that's a good idea." I sat back in my chair and mused over the possibilities. "I feel stuck. I can't go see my father, and whatever vision Mace gave us last night seemed to wear her out."

When I tried to get her to show us more, she fell asleep in her doggy bed. I didn't want to push her if it was draining.

Jade patted my knee reassuringly. "I think maybe the spy mission would be a job better suited for Hannah and me. We need to be stealthy, and you couldn't walk quietly if you tried."

"Thanks a lot." I knew my pout probably made me

look pathetic, but I was so tired of feeling like I was on a ride at the amusement park with no way to get off. "I want to help, though."

Bee cleared her throat. "We could work on solidifying your alliances. From what you said, this Cristian guy seems genuinely concerned about protecting you. You're living with the witches, but we need the vampires on your side if we're going against Alpha Jones."

Hannah and Jade exchanged smirks. "What a fabulous idea. You should go to the vampire house for a feeding party, girls. Seal the deal with the vampires so you'll have more protection."

"A little *Thirsty Thursday* action?" Jade nudged Hannah. "The vampires coined that phrase for a reason, you know."

"Huh?" I frowned in confusion. "What do you mean the *vampires coined that phrase*?"

"It's true." My bestie laughed. "Your supernatural reference guide didn't cover that?"

My jaw dropped. "Uh... nope. Can't say that it did."

Hannah beamed. "I heard bite-gasms are *intense*. Like an earthquake in your clit."

I flushed. Now that I knew exactly what a feeding party entailed, I wasn't sure that was something I was up for.

"I think a *Thirsty Thursday* party sounds like an *excellent* idea, Nicole," Bee stated. "I'd bet my new telephoto lens that the vampire frat is hosting one tonight. You should text Cristian and ask."

I shook my head. "I don't know…"

Bee held up a hand, cutting me off. "Look. I'm not saying you need to *participate*. But what harm could come from watching?" She gave me a wry smile. "If these feeding parties are as sensual as they're portrayed to be, it could be fun. There's nothing wrong with a little live porn."

Hannah and Jade howled in laughter while I was blushing so profusely I probably resembled a beet.

"Bee," I gritted, eyeing my surrogate aunts pointedly. *"Ixnay alkingtay aboutyay exsay inyay esentpray ompanycay."*

"Oh, please, Nicole." Jade waved her hand breezily. "You're a legal adult. And Han and I are certainly no strangers to casual sex. There's nothing wrong with a woman being sex positive."

"I didn't say there was," I assured her.

"And secondly, do you remember who taught you the rules of Pig Latin?" she reminded me.

Crap.

I supposed the whole thing was pointless when everyone else in the room also understood the language game.

"It's just…" Everyone leaned forward while I struggled to articulate what I wanted to say. "That video is still circulating campus, and I'm not sure showing up at this kind of party would send the right message. I'm certainly not about to jump from one supe's bed to another, and I worry my presence would imply that. I just want *protection*. I want to make sure I have people on my team so I can get my dad out of this mess."

Bee nodded understandingly. "I get it, babe. I know this has been really hard on you. But no one is asking you to whore yourself out for some vampire protection."

"Absolutely not," Jade agreed.

Bee smiled tentatively before continuing. "We're just gathering intel, so to speak. Cristian's offer seemed pretty low-pressure, don't you think? I doubt he'd turn you down if you *did* want to participate, but I don't think he expects that either. If you want, we can just pop in for a few minutes, then leave. Just be honest with him about what you're looking to get out of this."

"And let's remember, there's currently a lot of tension between the shifters and vampires. They're bound to help out of pure spite," Jade added. "But if you did decide to become an official feeder, you would have legal protection in the council's eyes."

"Text him," Bee encouraged.

I sighed, grabbing my phone off the nightstand and opening my message thread to Cristian.

Nicole: Hey.

It was still early, but he read my message immediately.

Cristian: Good morning, beautiful. Did you sleep well?

Nicole: Uh… yeah, thanks. I have a question.

God, why was this so awkward?

Cristian: Shoot.

Nicole: Does your offer still stand?

Cristian: Yes. But just so I'm clear, which offer are we talking about exactly? ;)

The wink emoji at the end of his message and his flirtatious tone made me smile.

Nicole: I think I'd like to see what these feeder parties are all about.

Cristian: Well, damn. That woke me up faster than a quad shot.

Nicole: Cristian… I didn't say I wanted you to feed FROM me. I just want to see it in action. Think of it as an information gathering session.

Cristian: You'll get there in time.

Bee, who was reading over my shoulder, giggled. "Damn, that's one smooth vampire."

"Aren't they all?" I rolled my eyes.

"Uh... I think Thad-the-lawyer-with-a-giant-dildo-up-his-butt proves otherwise," Jade argued.

Hannah laughed, while Bee and I made a *good point* face.

"I don't know..." Hannah mused. "I bet Thad is a closeted *freak* in bed. *And* he's tall, so you know odds are he's blessed with a long schlong."

Bee's and my expressions instantly morphed into *ew* faces. Jade's however was... intrigued, if I wasn't mistaken.

Well, okay then.

I was startled when my phone vibrated with an incoming text.

Cristian: Too far?

Oh, shit.

Nicole: No... sorry. I got distracted by the crazy-but-awesome women in my life.
So... are there by chance any upcoming parties?

Cristian: As a matter of fact... Thursday nights are pretty special at the RET house. But we don't usually get started until after nine. Does tonight work for you?

"Hey!" I shouted when Bee grabbed my phone out of my hands.

Her thumbs flew across the screen faster than I could track them, and before I had any hopes of stopping her, she hit the send button. My nerves flared when I took my phone back and read the reply that she sent to the vampire on my behalf.

Nicole: Tonight is PERFECT. I'll meet you there and FYI, I'm bringing Bee with me. See you then! ;)

"Bee!"

She shrugged, as if it were no big deal she just posed as me and accepted an invitation to a literal bloodsucking orgy. "That's what besties are for, bish."

"What the hell?!"

"I think the more important question is, what are we going to wear?" She stood up with a smirk, walked over to my closet, and began pulling out half my wardrobe at a furious pace.

I knew Bee would support me if I wanted to back out, but that wasn't going to happen. As my best friend, she knew I needed a little push to force me out of my funk. And when I really thought about it, maybe this was exactly what I needed to bring my formerly extroverted self back into action. I had no plans to hook up with anyone—the thought alone was pretty damn abhorrent —but that didn't mean I couldn't have a little fun to get my mind off all the shitty stuff surrounding me right then.

And what better place to do that than a *Thirsty Thursday* party hosted by a vampire frat?

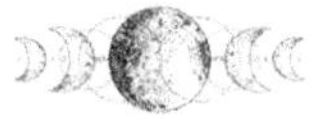

BEE CONVINCED me to wear the skimpiest outfit I owned. The bright red minidress was already so short I *knew* someone would see my black lace thong underneath at some point tonight. The midsection was sheer, showing off my stomach in a demure sort of way. It was strapless and pushed my chest up so high my boobs were like a cushioned shelf for vampires to rest their cheeks on.

I felt ridiculous but at the same time, really freaking sexy.

"You look *hot*," Bee said as I tugged at the hem. I'd rather not flash my ass cheeks to anyone attending the party, but it kept rolling up higher and higher, so I knew my odds weren't great.

"I shouldn't have let you talk me into the heels. What if I'm overdressed?!"

Bee laughed. "Odds are you'll be the only one *dressed* at this party. By the way, we should go over girl code rules. I turned off my location on my cell phone because my father would pop a blood vessel if he knew I was hanging out with vampires—"

"For good reason. Are we sure this is a smart idea?" My

voice sounded whiney, and I wished I could gather some confidence. I just wanted to feel like *me* again. My leaked tape and Alexei's dismissal of me had rocked my self-assuredness.

"This is a *great* idea. Let's go over the rules."

I rolled my eyes and ticked my fingers as we continued to walk. "No going off alone without talking to the other first. No accepting drinks from strangers. Wear condoms. If we want to leave at any time for any reason—we go together."

I wished I'd brought Macey with me, but bringing my familiar to an orgy felt... weird. So she joined Jade and Hannah on their spy mission. They'd worn all black and kept rolling on the floor to practice their James Bond moves before leaving. I felt good knowing Mace would keep them safe should they get too cocky with their skills.

"Good. Safety first. Think my dad will get mad if *I* make a blood oath to a sexy vampire prince? I asked around about him, and his family has a vacation home in Greece, Nicole. *Greece.*"

"Hey now, don't go stealing my vampire prince," I teased.

Bee nudged me. "I'm just saying we should have a backup plan if you can't pull the trigger. I volunteer as tribute."

We both cackled while walking up to the frat house. It was a gothic structure with black bars on the window and people forming a line out the door. We could hear the music bumping from inside, and I was surprised to see the number of shifters, humans, witches, and fae here.

"Wow. This place is popular."

"I wish June didn't have to do the full moon ritual," I whispered. My witchy friend had said potions brewed under a full moon were more potent, so she couldn't miss out on the opportunity.

Bee interrupted my thoughts. "Hey, did she ask you for a jar of pee, too? She said she needed it for a spell."

I gave Bee a horrified look. "You gave her a jar of your *pee?*"

Bee shrugged. "Seemed important. I hope she's not going to drink it or anything, though. To get over the ick factor, I just pretended she was a nurse at my gynecologist."

I shook my head in disgust. Witches had strange potions, and I wanted nothing to do with any of it. Considering I lived in the witchy sorority, it made things difficult.

I was about to tell Bee not to give Juniper any more bodily fluids when a smooth voice whispered in my ear. "Why are you waiting in line, beautiful?"

I spun around and was greeted with a shirtless Cristian towering over me. He had beads of sweat dripping down his abs and an impossibly white smile in the moonlight.

"Hey," I practically hiccuped. Something about Cristian made me nervous.

"The prince's feeder doesn't wait in lines."

"I'm *not* the prince's feeder," I reminded him.

"Not *yet*." He winked.

"Oh, you *are* smooth." Bee giggled, and then pointed to herself. "I'm Bee, by the way. Nicole's bestie. Which means you need to pass *my* inspection if you want my girl to be your blood donor."

Cristian grinned as he held his arms out wide. "Well? Don't keep me in suspense. Do I pass?"

Bee tapped her lower lip in thought, giving him a good once over. "Physically? Abso-fucking-lutely. But it's too soon for me to figure out if your personality is up to par."

He released the most seductive laugh I'd ever heard in my life, drawing all the women around us into some odd trance. "I like you."

Clearly, even my best friend wasn't immune to Cristian's charms, because it took her a moment to blink out of the haze. When she did, her smartassery was in full effect as she curtsied and said, "Why, thank you."

He held his arm out for me. "Nicole, shall we?"

I felt kind of ridiculous letting him guide us past the line of impatient people wanting to get in. Some of them sneered at Bee and me, while others looked at Cristian with longing. I tried my best to ignore all the catty whispers around us, but I wasn't doing such a great job.

"Did you lose your shirt?" I may not have been as susceptible as others to the sexual energy he radiated, but

I wasn't blind. Cristian Luca really was something to look at.

The vampire chuckled. "Not at all. It's all part of the process. You'll see."

In the next moment, we stepped through the front doors of Cristian's frat, Rho Eta Theta, and his words made a lot of sense. It seemed nearly everyone had lost their shirts, and then some, but there wasn't anything too scandalous going on at that moment. The temperature was significantly warmer than outside—likely thanks to all the bodies crammed into this space—so I couldn't exactly blame them for removing a few layers. Some people were dancing; others were getting cozy with one another in one of the many seating areas. A few were rounding second base, but it wasn't anything I hadn't seen at any other party I'd been to before. I was thankful my eyeballs weren't immediately accosted with couples going at it like I had assumed, but there were telltale noises echoing through the house, indicating we weren't too far from the real action.

"Would you ladies like a drink?" Cristian offered, leading us toward the back end of the first level, into a spacious kitchen.

"No thank you," I said, a little too quickly. I wanted to keep a clear head while I was here and not make any bad decisions.

Cristian seemed to understand where my mind was at. "We have water and soda, too."

"Water, please," Bee and I said simultaneously.

Cristian handed each of us a bottle. When I unscrewed the lid and took a sip, the refreshing water helped soothe my nerves a bit.

"So..." I cleared my throat. "What now?"

Cristian placed a steadying hand on my shoulder, his calling gaze striking a chord within me. "I can tell you're nervous. How about I find a spot away from the chaos that gives you a good view of everything we do here? And if at any moment you want to leave, just say the word and I will walk you out and take you home. You are in complete control here. That said... I think it's important for you to see what it's like when *I* feed from someone. If you're up for it."

I shook my head. "Cristian, I thought I made myself clear earlier. I don't think I'm ready for that."

He dropped his hand from my shoulder and laced our fingers together. "I wasn't talking about feeding from *you*, Nicole. I was referring to one of our regular donors. I think it will help you understand how much we respect the people we feed from. Feeding doesn't always have to be intimidating and overtly sexual, though it can be pretty fun when it is."

I nodded, though I still felt a smidge unnerved.

Bee and I eyed a handsome-looking witch that was walking toward us. He had neon green hair and bright white eyes. The guy was tall and lean, but his clearly defined jaw could cut glass.

"Hello, Cristian. Are you ready?"

Cristian smiled at him. "Nicole and Bee, this is Marcus. He's going to be my donor for the night."

Marcus slung a casual arm around Cristian and bumped his fist. "I'm a regular here." Marcus winked at Bee. "Cristian says it's your first time? I'll be sure to put on a good show."

I swallowed as Cristian leaned closer to Marcus, tilting his head. "I thought it was a..."

"Orgasmic experience?" Marcus finished my question for me. "Absolutely. I'm here every *Thirsty Thursday*. Cristian is the best vampire at Rho Eta. The more powerful they are, the better it feels."

I looked at Cristian as he spoke. "And the better it feels for them, the more *delicious* the blood. The endorphins. The pounding pulse." His fangs lengthened as he spoke.

My chest flushed. "Do you always eat right from the source?"

Bee gave me a teasing nudge.

"Not always," Cristian answered. "We have licensed nurses on staff to take donations. Some married and monogamous individuals prefer that. But..."

Marcus laughed. "But most prefer the *full experience*."

Bee clapped her hands together. "Enough with the foreplay, let's get this show on the road."

Marcus smirked and started walking over to what looked like a gothic throne. He waited for Cristian to take a seat before perching on his lap and tilting his head to the side to expose his neck.

"Oh, *hello*." Bee rubbed her hands together excitedly. "I'm *so* here for this. They look hot together."

They did, but I could see what Cristian meant about feeding not always being overtly sexual. Sure, he had a fang boner on full display, but I got the impression any arousal on his end was purely bloodlust. It seemed rather... clinical as he placed his hand on Marcus's jaw, tilting his head just right. I jumped a little as Cristian's pointed teeth pierced the witch's skin, but I wasn't nearly as put off as I'd expected. I was mesmerized as Cristian's mouth tugged on his donor's neck, watching his Adam's apple bob with each swallow.

Marcus's eyes rolled back in obvious pleasure as he white-knuckled his kneecaps. I was guessing he was trying to respect Cristian's boundaries by not touching him in a sexual manner without his consent. When Marcus released a lengthy groan, there was no doubt in my mind he had just made a mess of his pants. I should've probably been embarrassed witnessing this whole thing, but strangely, I wasn't. After one more tug, Cristian pulled back, swiping his tongue over the puncture marks. I watched with great fascination as the witch's skin knitted back together right before my eyes.

Marcus stood with a sleepy, satisfied smile. "Thanks, man. Always a pleasure."

Cristian simply nodded in reply.

"Damn. I think I need some fresh air." Bee fanned herself dramatically.

"Me too," Marcus said. "I'm heading out back. Care to join me?"

She looked to me in question. "You okay, Nicole?"

I gave Cristian a *is she safe with this guy* look. When he nodded again, I said, "Sure, Bee. But don't be gone long, okay?"

"'Kay," she agreed.

I waited until Bee and Marcus left before speaking to Cristian. "So that was…"

He leaned closer, and I saw a tiny bit of blood on the corner of his mouth. He licked his lips and grinned. "Was… *what?*"

"It was *something*. Definitely hot. You and Marcus have a good thing going. Why not have him make a blood oath with you?"

Cristian grinned. "He's delicious and fun. And more importantly, we have mutual respect for one another. I like that he doesn't pressure me to do anything, despite the fact that I know he swings both ways. It's why I selected him for tonight. I wanted you to see that we take consent very seriously."

I shook my head playfully. "Don't take this the wrong way… but I never would have pegged you as being so… decent. You didn't exactly make the best first impression in that regard."

He had the grace to look ashamed, the flush on his

cheeks hinting at a touch of embarrassment. "I was in rare form that night. I wanted to piss Mara off, and you smelled so fucking good. You *still* smell so fucking good. I can't explain it. My mouth waters whenever you're near."

I looked around the room, noting a few vampires eyeing me with interest. "Do, uh, other vampires think I smell good too?"

Did this have something to do with my mother's supernatural affiliation?

He reached for my chin and turned my attention back to him. "No one would dare touch you while I'm at your side. Not a vampire. Not a witch or fae. And definitely not a *shifter*." He chuckled. "Not unless you *wanted* them to touch you, of course. I'm an equal opportunity player. Shifters are possessive, but I don't mind sharing. It's *your* pleasure I care about, in whatever form it takes."

There was something about his words that made my pulse race. Cristian was so different from Alexei. He was confident and respectful, yet caring and attentive. Most notably, I didn't feel like he was hiding things from me at every turn. Why couldn't I just try things with Cristian? What the hell was holding me back? Alexei had proven over and over he wasn't worthy of my loyalty. Yet, I knew he was the reason I couldn't commit to this alliance.

"Can we do a trial run?" I whispered, wanting to defy my traitorous heart for a moment. "Like... a donor situation. Not the full blood oath."

He grinned. "It would be my honor."

"Where are we going?" I asked, trembling as we headed down a long hallway.

"I figured you wouldn't want an audience. Was that the wrong assumption? Some people enjoy being watched. *I'm* one of those people, so you'll get no judgment from me."

A little thrill shot through me. Would I enjoy something like that? The entire campus had already seen me on that damn sex tape. Maybe this time, it could be on *my* terms. I could steal a bit of my power back.

"How about right here? I don't necessarily want to sit on the throne, but..."

Cristian looked like I'd just given him candy. "Absolutely." He pushed me against the wall and whispered in my ear. "Is this what you had in mind? If anyone turns this way, they'll see you with my fangs in your neck and your entire body trembling with pleasure. They'll hear you moan. They'll see you toss your head back in rapture. I can smell how turned on you are." My mouth popped open, arousal flooding me as he dragged the tip of his nose along my neck and inhaled. "It's driving me crazy. Don't worry; I won't take much. Just enough to make you feel good. You can touch me if you'd like. And if you want *me* to touch *you*, grab my hand and put it wherever you want. Remember, you're in control here, Nicole. *Complete control.*"

Oh God, I couldn't believe I was doing this, but I couldn't seem to make myself stop. I truly felt empowered as the sharp tip of Cristian's fangs rested against my skin. I knew he was giving me one last chance to back out, but I didn't want that. My life was spiraling so out of control I *needed* something that I was completely in charge of. With that decided, I firmly grabbed the back of Cristian's head, pushing him closer.

I gasped the moment his teeth pierced my flesh. It stung, but it wasn't unpleasant by any means.

Cristian groaned, pulling harder on my vein. It was only a matter of seconds before I felt pressure building low in my belly. The more he drank, the headier the effect. My fingers twisted in Cristian's short strands, and my toes curled. I was straight-up writhing against the wall as he fed from me, so much so, that I knew my dress had ridden up to indecent levels. Modesty was the last thing on my mind though as a volcano raged inside of me, ready to blow. Just as I was about to reach the precipice of no return, the thumping bass blasting through the sound system cut off. Partygoers griped as a booming voice rang through the air, calling my name.

I froze the moment I recognized the source.

"Of course," Cristian muttered against my neck as he retracted his fangs. I shivered as his tongue swiped over my skin, sealing the wound.

I hastily tugged my dress back down over my ass as the vampire prince took a slight step back. I'd noticed he was still standing far too close to be taken as anything other than territorial, but I wasn't about to chastise him for it, considering what we were about to deal with.

In the next moment, a furious shifter was in our space, fists clenched as his sides. "Nicole. What *the fuck* do you think you're doing?"

I bristled. "Excuse me?! Shouldn't I be asking you that?"

Cristian cleared his throat, his pupils dilated as he swayed. Was something wrong with him? "You're not allowed here, shifter." He opened and closed his eyes, his tone dazed as he tried to focus on Alexei.

"Are you okay?" I asked him.

"Is *he* okay?" Alexei roared. "You're fucking worried about this bloodsucker?!"

Cristian shook his head as though he were trying to settle his mind. "I think you're too powerful, Nicole. I've never actually gotten drunk from someone's blood before, but that's very much what this feels like."

Alexei shoved Cristian before I had a chance to reply. "Who the fuck do you think you are? Feeding from Nicole when she's—"

"When she's *what*, Alexei?" I challenged, noticing the growing crowd. Shirtless vampires had gathered around and were closing in on us, likely ready to defend their prince. "Go ahead and announce to the entire party what it is you *think* we are."

Alexei stammered and straightened his spine. "Nicole is still shifter property."

Cristian laughed mockingly. "Look around. You have plenty of shifters that are happy to donate their blood. It's not against the rules. You should probably get used to it, though. Once Nicole and I make a blood oa—"

Alexei was breathing hard, his chest rising and falling with every inhale. "Let's go, Nicole."

I gaped at him. "I'm not going anywhere with you."

He growled threateningly. "Woman. I'm barely hanging by a thread here."

"Well, so am I. It's taking a lot of restraint not to kick you in the balls right now, Alexei. How dare you show up here and act like a"—I lowered my voice to barely a whisper—"jealous *boyfriend* when you're engaged."

He looked around once more. "I'm simply acting in the best interest of the pack. We're still negotiating your allegiance—"

"My *ownership*, you mean," I hissed. "How many times do I have to tell you, Alexei? *No one* owns me."

Cristian stumbled again. "Shit. I just got hit with another wave."

I placed my hand on his arm to steady him. "Maybe you should—"

"Fuck this," Alexei spat, right before he crouched down and flipped me over his shoulder.

"What the hell?!" I pounded my fists on his back. "Put me down, you goddamned caveman!"

His forearm banded around my upper thighs as he marched out of the house.

"Nicole!" Bee shouted from behind us. "Hey! Put her down, asshole!"

I lifted my head just in time to watch Cristian fall forward as my best friend barely caught him from face-planting on the hardwood.

"Figure out what's wrong with him!" I called out to her. "I'll deal with this idiot."

Alexei's grip on me tightened. "You're pushing it, Nicole."

I was infuriated.

"*I'm* pushing it?!" Dammit, too much blood was rushing to my head to have this conversation. "Put me down, Alexei!"

A cool breeze tickled my legs as he carried me down the front steps of the frat. He finally let me down on the side of the house where we had a modicum of privacy. "What the fuck were you thinking letting a vampire feed from you like that?"

I looked around, wondering if any of Cristian's frat brothers would follow after us to rescue me. "What I do is none of your goddamn business."

"What are you looking around for? You think your little vampire prince is going to help you? Asshole couldn't even stand up straight, and his men don't give a shit about some donor. Now explain what in the hell you were thinking back there! You could have been hurt, Nicole."

I straightened my spine. "They'd care about me if I made a blood oath with their prince."

Alexei stalked closer, his hot, heaving breath washing

over me and making my residual arousal flare to life. I hated my body's reaction to him. Loathed it, actually.

I held my hand up. "Back off, Alexei."

"You think a blood oath will keep me from you, Nicole?"

"I think I'll do whatever the fuck it takes to get as far away from you and your goddamn father as possible."

He wrapped his arm around my back and pulled me flush against his body, our lips brushing against one another as he glared at me. "You can run as far as you'd like, sweetheart. You can hide. You can even let some prissy vampire prince try to get you off. But—" He paused to pull me even tighter against him, letting me feel the length of his hard cock against my stomach. "You won't *ever* escape me. I'm in your bones, baby. I'm carved so deep in your soul not even death could separate us. And you can deny it all you want, but I see the truth in your eyes. In the way your body naturally molded to mine just now. That awareness you're feeling? That sense of dread that you couldn't run from me if you tried? That's because you *know*, without a doubt, that no one else will ever measure up. You are *mine*, Nicole Fairweather. And I don't give a fuck if your mind hates that fact. It doesn't change reality. We're *fated*. But for the record, I have no problem claiming you over and over..." He paused to lower his hand, cupping my ass in a way that let his fingers slip under the short hem. "And over again until your brain gets on board with what we *both* know your body wants. This alliance you're seeking is pointless. *I will keep you safe from my father.*"

"Fuck you," I rasped, hating how breathy my tone was. "I don't need your so-called protection."

Voices in the distance shattered our moment, Bee's shouts being the loudest.

"I have to go," Alexei said with a curse. "But before I do... I changed my mind about letting someone else get you off. If I *ever* feel another man giving you pleasure like I did tonight, I swear on everything that I am, I will *kill* him, Nicole. *Brutally.* So, unless you want some prick's death on your conscience, I would think long and hard about who you turn to for supposed protection."

With those ominous words, Alexei left like a thief in the night, disappearing into the shadows.

"Nicole! Are you okay?" Bee panted as she ran up to me.

I watched the dark space where Alexei had vanished as my heart throbbed.

"Yeah," I croaked, my emotions bleeding through my voice. "I am."

At least physically.

But on the inside? Not so much.

TWELVE

Alexei

"But, *Alexei*, a couple's account on Wolfebytes could be so cute. I already got sponsors, look! A perfume company wants us to promote their mate pheromone line, and they'll pay us ten thousand dollars!"

Fuck. I'd rather stick my dick in a blender than listen to Mara whine and scheme.

"Absolutely not," I growled. It was obvious that she was leveraging our fake marriage to assert herself as the future luna in the pack.

"It could be fun. We could use the same photographer for our engagement photos to share on the page, and have a lifestyle shoot to really highlight our love story—"

"I said no!" I practically shook the walls with my roar.

My wolf was almost impossible to contain. Just being in the same room with this woman was enough to make me shift and tear the building apart with my teeth.

"I talked to your father," Mara said, unbothered by my outburst. "He thinks the publicity would be good for the pack. People want to know about our love story! And it's always good to have multiple streams of income. We need to start saving for our future pups, Alexei. You might have more money than God, but I want our babies to have *everything*."

It made me sick to my stomach to think of having a baby with her. Nothing mattered if both parents couldn't stand each other. My father wanted me to breed Mara to produce the next alpha heir, but she wasn't right. She was selfish and self-absorbed. While I had never given much thought to having children, I always envisioned myself with someone gentle and loving. Someone who fiercely defended our pups while still cuddling them tightly.

Someone like Nicole.

Mara couldn't pull herself away from her own reflection long enough to care.

"Drop it, Mara." I sneered. "You're not getting anywhere near my dick, so you might as well accept that fact right now."

She may have been wearing a flashy ring on her left hand, but I wasn't going to allow her to believe she'd ever have a chance to be my mate. My balls practically crawled back into my body at the thought of touching her.

Her green eyes narrowed. "What's that supposed to mean? We're *expected* to start producing heirs as soon as we get married, Alexei. Maybe even before, hmm? How do you suppose we accomplish that without me having access to your dick? Are you actually suggesting *artificial insemination*?!"

I wanted to plug my ears from the shrill tone of her voice, but I shrugged instead. "No. I'm saying you will not carry my heirs through *any* means of insemination. I don't want you to raise my pups, Mara. Is that clear enough for you?"

Her eyes brightened, which confused me. "Oh. Well, that's not a problem since I plan to hire a nanny immediately. I have no desire to actually *raise* our children. I've never really liked kids. Once they're old enough for boarding school, we can ship them off."

I pinched the bridge of my nose. I didn't know if she was being deliberately obtuse or if she was delusional. "How about we drop the subject and you tell me why you're here so you can get the fuck out as soon as possible? I don't appreciate the fact that you dropped by unannounced, especially after I told you I was busy. Didn't you have a nail appointment or something? I told Corbin to book one for you." *Specifically so she'd stay the hell away from me.*

Mara stomped her foot like a toddler. "You've been keeping me busy since the moment we got engaged. What is wrong with you, Alexei? Is this because of *her*?"

"Watch it," I warned.

"Or what?" she challenged. "You may think you're in charge here, Alexei, but I know things you don't that say otherwise. And if I were you, I'd start showing me a *helluva lot* more respect since I'm your *fiancée*."

Mara was a shit talker, but the confidence infusing her tone gave me pause. "What are you trying to say? Are you threatening me?"

She tilted her chin up. "What if I am?"

Taking three long strides, I pushed her against the bookcase in the lounge where we were having this awful conversation. "How many times do I have to tell you, you do *not* want to fuck with me."

Her glossy lips turned up in the corner. "Maybe I have someone more powerful on my side, so I'm not so afraid of you anymore. Ever think about that?"

I reared back. "Wh—"

"Alexei!" my father's voice boomed, interrupting us. In the next moment, he burst through the double doors to the lounge, with Corbin frantically trailing behind him.

I tried not to cower at the sound of his angry voice. A lifetime of abuse made it hard not to immediately want to duck and submit, especially after what I saw him do in his office. But I needed to be stronger for Nicole, so I sucked it up.

"Yes, Father?"

"Why the fuck are you making changes to Dr. Fairweather's meal plan? And who signed off on getting him a new bed and comforter?"

I tilted my chin up. "I did."

He clenched his fist at his side, the frustration flowing through him. I had no doubt he'd hit me for it later.

"Why?" The way he spoke through clenched teeth sent a shiver down my spine.

"Because the vampires have a lawyer documenting Dr. Fairweather's living conditions. If they suspect that you're mistreating him, it won't help our case."

"Fuck the vamps. The human is *mine.*"

My wolf growled in my chest, angry at the idea of this man claiming any part of my mate or her family. "We need to show the council that—"

"Fuck the council. We're shifters. I don't answer to witches, fae, or vampires. I run my pack. I control whoever I want to control. They have no claim over my scientist or his slut of a daughter."

Corbin moved to my side, while I wrestled with my wolf, who was getting more agitated lately. More driven to prove our worth and challenge my father. Hearing him talk about Nicole that way was making him rage.

"Your doctor can't function if he's malnourished or sleep deprived." By some act of God, I managed not to grit my response. "We want this cure as quickly as possible, especially if the vampires want a war with us." I had to appeal to his bloodthirsty nature if I wanted to get anything done.

His eyes thinned to slits as he assessed me. "I don't want the scientist to be *too* comfortable. Although, I'm glad you're taking the initiative, after your most recent failings. But I want that filthy human working himself to the bone."

"He's made great progress since his mental block's been lifted," Corbin piped in, saving me from responding. "Have you seen the latest reports?" My beta handed him a folder, and my father ripped it from his hands.

Mara leaned over his shoulder as he scanned the documents within, her proximity making my eyebrow raise.

"This is good," Dad murmured. "He's already figured out the missing protein."

Corbin nervously cleared his throat. "Discovered three hours after Alexei's order for better food. I know I work better on a full stomach." Corbin then patted his stomach and winked, trying to draw attention to himself while I focused on keeping my cool.

I cleared my throat. "He is also requesting a test subject. Someone born without their wolf counterpart. Professor Viden mentioned she had a suitable candidate, but you denied her request to bring him in. Why would you do that when it could hinder Dr. Fairweather's progress?"

My father waved his hand. "I've been conducting my own... *research* on the wolfless pack members, but I suppose I can spare one of them now that the missing protein has been discovered. Give the damn scientist whatever he needs."

"Your own research?" I asked, feeling nervous. "What kind of research?"

What was my father up to?

"It's none of your business," my father snapped. "Worry about getting David Fairweather his guinea pig. The sooner he figures out the problem, the better."

I swallowed and tried not to freak out. "Thank you, Alpha. Things seem to be moving along now that his mental block is gone."

He frowned. "I still think his whore daughter has something to do with the block removal. Something isn't right about her. The vampires *must* know something we don't. Why else would they bother staking a claim on her?"

His words made my gut churn. Was it possible Nicole shared what she knew about her mother with the Luca clan? I couldn't imagine her being so careless, but I had to admit my father had a point. Were they looking to exploit her as well? I knew Nicole didn't want to speak with me right now, but I needed answers, whether she liked it or not. She was terribly naïve when it came to supernatural politics. It didn't matter how much information she had downloaded in her brain. She even said so herself at one point. The data she had was based on fact, but reality left a lot of room for interpretation. And I didn't trust that any Luca would protect my mate unless it benefited them somehow. The question was, what did they want? Was it truly about having a regular source of blood? Or did they know she could potentially be more than human?

"I will look into it," I assured him.

My father studied me, nodding as he heard the conviction in my statement. I *would* look into it, but I sure as shit never said I'd share that information with him.

"Good." He pointed a stern finger at me. "But no more provisions without my approval. Understood?"

"Understood," I repeated.

"It's bad enough that bitch went against my orders and moved into the Kappa Zeta house. She's aligning herself with witches and vampires when I explicitly gave her orders. I need to remind her that her father is at *my* mercy."

"She's well aware," I snapped. "She seemed very upset at the lab."

"Good. I want her too scared to fucking think, and when this bullshit with the council is over, I'll break her nice and slow, and show her who's in charge. Fucking humans thinking they can challenge us."

I bit my tongue so hard blood pooled in my mouth. I didn't trust myself to speak without saying something that would result in dire consequences, so I simply nodded in acquiescence, which seemed to appease my father.

"Mara, would you like to accompany me to lunch with the editor for *Shifters Weekly*? They would like an exclusive on the future luna." I didn't think it was possible for my father to purr, but that's exactly what his gentle tone reminded me of. *What the hell?* He didn't even speak to my mother that kindly.

Mara gleamed. "Oh, I'd love to!"

He nodded toward the front door. "I'll meet you outside. I need to talk to Alexei about something."

"Of course, Alpha!" She pranced out the door, not even bothering to say goodbye to Corbin and me.

My father turned to me. "Why did one of my enforcers tell me you were at the vampire coven the other night?"

Fuck, I couldn't get that night out of my mind. I couldn't stop thinking about how Nicole felt so close and yet so fucking far. The way her eyes were heavy with fury and a hint of lust. Her soft skin against my palm...

"I expect a response when I ask you a direct question, son."

I jolted out of my impromptu daydream. "I was watching them. Trying to gain intel."

My father's eyes thinned to slits, his expression full of skepticism. "Did you learn anything?"

My heart started to race, a timeless fear that had been quite literally beaten into me at a young age. "Nicole hasn't taken the blood oath yet, but the vampires seem *very* interested in solidifying that alliance."

It took everything I had not to grit my teeth in frustration.

"Of course, they are," he spat. "I want to know what

they know about that nasty little human slut. Whoring herself out to a vampire like she's worth something. If they think she's the key to stealing my scientist, they'll have a war on their hands."

I saw his anger as an opportunity. "I could follow her! See what is happening."

He snapped his cruel gaze to me. "Absolutely not. You're too invested. Too soft. I don't want anyone to see you following that girl. I can find someone more suitable for the job."

Corbin raised his hand like a schoolchild. "I could follow her, sir. I don't even want to fuck her. I mean, gross. She's absolutely not my type."

My father rolled his eyes. "No. Both of you stay away from the Fairweather girl. I'll have one of my men tailing her. She needs a firm hand to keep her in line."

"Yes, Alpha," Corbin and I said at the same time.

My father checked his watch. "I'm leaving with Mara. Be good." For some reason, he had a mischievous smile when he said Mara's name, as if he had an ulterior motive.

I felt like I could finally breathe once he left.

"That was close." Corbin exhaled harshly. "I thought you said you weren't followed when you went to the Rho Eta house."

"I thought I dodged them." I sighed. "But I'm not surprised. My father has spies everywhere. We need to be more careful. We'll be under extra scrutiny now."

He plopped down on a chair. "Hey, did you think he

was acting weird around my sister? They seemed... famil-iar. Like really fucking close or something." He winced while cocking his head to the side. "Weirdly fucking close."

I waved my hand. "If he's keeping her busy, I don't care. I'm sure my father just likes the media attention. Her compulsion gifts are impressive, even if it pisses me off to admit it, and my father's not above outright bragging about that. She's the perfect little luna in his eyes."

"Too bad she's a psycho." Corbin shook his head. "In another world, I would have been really excited to finally call you my brother. But Mara..."

I knew he felt obligated to feel some sort of affection toward his sister, but it was difficult to care for such a bloodthirsty bitch.

"What did my father mean when he said he was conducting his own *research*? Do you think Mara is involved somehow?"

Corbin's shoulders slumped. "I don't know, but it didn't sound good. Your father is def up to some evil-villain-type shit. He's more angry and ambitious than ever before. I have a feeling something really bad is about to go down."

"Me too." I nodded in agreement.

"Any ideas on what he's planning?"

I combed a hand through my hair. "With all his talk about strengthening the pack... weeding out the weaker shifters... it almost sounds like he's building an army of some kind. I have no idea how he plans to accomplish that, but I do know we need to step up our game to protect Nicole."

"Your father is crazy, man."

"My father was right about one thing, though. We need to figure out what Nicole is," I whispered. "You don't think she told the vampires, do you?"

"I don't know what to think anymore. Cristian annoyed the fuck out of her; now she wants to make a blood oa—"

I growled, the sound cutting him off. "We have to figure out what she is and why there is so much secrecy about her family. None of it is adding up. Can you find some way to talk to her under the radar?"

Corbin looked around. "If I could, I would have done it already. I miss my little Nicky-Poo." He pouted, and a spike of jealousy hit me in the chest.

"Don't call her that."

He rolled his eyes. "Nicole and I were friends. I hate thinking she's mad at me. Makes my fucking skin itch." I watched as he scratched his neck. "The dude tailing me has relaxed some, but it's not like I can go anywhere unnoticed. And your father made it very clear he'd have eyes on Nicole at all times. My fan club calls me out every damn time I try to sneak away. I'd buy a mask if I thought it would work."

An idea struck me. "What if we could *make you* a mask?"

He frowned. "I was kidding, dude. It would look fucking weird if I strolled around campus wearing an actual mask unless it was Halloween."

"Not necessarily," I countered.

"What do you mean?"

"Juniper..." I began, suddenly feeling a little shitty for asking my best friend to do this. The purple-haired witch may have given him a change of heart spell to make their breakup easier on him, but he could still remember the feelings he had developed for her. Was it selfish of me to ask him to seek her out?

It wasn't for me, I reminded myself. It was for Nicole.

Corbin raked a hand through his dark blond hair. "What *about* Juniper?"

I cleared my throat as I decided to just go for it. "You should call her. Ask her to come over."

"Why? What would that accomplish?"

"She's powerful," I reminded him. "I'm sure she's capable of casting a masking spell, don't you think? Do you think she'd make us one so we can speak with Nicole? We need to figure out what she knows *and* warn her about my father sending more enforcers to watch her."

"Maybe." Corbin shrugged. "But maybe not. June seems to be firmly on *Team Nicole*. I don't know if she'd do *anything* that'd force Nicole to talk to us."

"That's why we need to insist that helping us do this would *benefit* Nicole." I exhaled, scrubbing a hand down my face. "We have to try, Corbin."

He pulled his cell out of his pocket and pressed a button before switching the call to speakerphone.

"Corbin?" Juniper's familiar raspy voice sounded through the line. "This is... unexpected."

"Don't worry, I'm not calling to try to convince you to take me back or anything." Corbin laughed nervously.

Juniper let out an audible sigh. "Corbin—"

"Yeah, yeah, I know," he cut her off. "We were never actually *together* for you to take me back. This is awkward. Can I please just get to the point? I'm calling about Nicole."

"What *about* Nicole?" Her tone was wary.

"Can you come over to the frat house?" he asked. "This would be better said in person."

"I don't know..." she hedged.

"Please, Junie," he begged. "I wouldn't ask if this weren't incredibly important."

I arched a brow at Corbin's nickname for Juniper. The tender way he spoke to her made me feel like an asshole for asking this of him. But we needed an ally on the inside, and Juniper was our only option—our only connection.

"Fine. But only because I'm curious about what you have to say and I'm worried about Nicole."

I couldn't help myself, the words poured out of me. "Is she okay?!" I leaned over the phone, as if I could somehow see my mate.

"She's fine," the witch replied. "She's just been through a lot, and it's obvious she's worried about her dad. Is it safe for me to go to your house? Alpha Jones isn't going to jump out of the bush and attack me or anything, is he?" Although there was a playful lift in her tone, I sensed a hint of seriousness in her question. Evidently, my father's aggressive nature and recent determination had not gone unnoticed by anyone.

Corbin answered for me. "He isn't here, but maybe you should enter through the *private* door." Corbin scratched the back of his neck again. There was a slight blush to his cheeks as he eyed me nervously.

"*What* private door?" I whispered.

Juniper giggled. "I'm not the only supe that likes to sneak into the shifter frat house after hours, Alexei. I spelled the south wall to have a hidden entrance for whenever Corbin and I would meet up for fun. Don't worry; I know how to be discreet when need be. I'll meet you both in Corbin's bedroom."

When she hung up the phone, I glared at my beta. "A secret entrance? Really?"

Corbin swallowed, his Adam's apple bobbing anxiously. "Hey, I'm not the only adventurous shifter here. Plenty of us like to have fun with the other supes, but since it's frowned upon, we have to get creative."

I clenched my jaw. "You don't think this is a security risk?"

"We take necessary precautions. It's all very high-tech. There's a secret password, and I get an alert on my phone anytime someone goes through it. Even though we're allowed to fuck whoever we want, there's a lot of shame in our community, dude. You know that. Sometimes it's easier to just bang in secret so people won't give you shit for it. You would be amazed who's hooking up with who right under your nose. Caleb has a rotation of three vampires he sees weekly."

I pinched the bridge of my nose. "We're going to talk about this later."

Corbin simply smiled. "Jonathan is sleeping with a fae dude who glows when he orgasms. It's actually pretty cool. You can see streams of light from under his door. Wesley is hooking up with a witch and—"

I held a hand up. "I don't want to know."

"But she's really cool. One time, she spelled his dick to be bigger and—"

"I still don't want to know, Corbin."

He continued anyway. "The spell was fucked. Dude had a fucking *tree trunk* for a dick. Juniper had to spell it back to normal, but then she made it too small and—"

"Please stop. I'm begging you."

"I'm just saying." Corbin exhaled. "I think more members of your pack would be open to interspecies relationships than you realize. Some are tired of hiding it."

That may have been true, but it didn't escape my notice that Corbin didn't mention a single hookup with a human. Shifters were permitted to have sex with anyone they liked—humans included—but it *was* frowned upon in male-female pairings, as there were no guarantees against accidental pregnancies. We had an unspoken rule that if you engaged in relations outside of your faction, you didn't flaunt it. Human-supe encounters rarely happened, even casually, because a supe would have to exercise extreme caution unless that human were a masochist and enjoyed a little pain while they played. It was inevitable the difference in physical power would become a problem if the supe lost control, and most supes didn't like the idea of restraining themselves during sex.

Although... I didn't hold back with Nicole, now that I thought about it. In fact, restraining myself hadn't even occurred to me at the time, which I should be reprimanding myself for. In theory, I could've hurt her. Was it possible our mate bond recognized her strength? That I instinctively knew she could take everything I had to offer that night?

"Fuck," I muttered.

"What's up, bruh?" Corbin asked.

I shook my head. "Nothing."

Now was not the time to think about that. I needed to focus on what mattered, which was how to convince Nicole's new sorority sister to assist us.

THIRTEEN

Alexei

JUNIPER WALKED through Corbin's bedroom door like she had been there a million times before. She strutted confidently to the loveseat against the wall and plopped down as if she didn't have a care at all. "I like what you've done with the place. New bedding?"

Corbin squirmed, and once again, I felt bad putting him in this position. "I wanted something different after we—um—ended our arrangement."

Juniper gave him a tender look, and I sensed that she genuinely felt bad for how things turned out. "Well, I like it. The comforter looks cozy."

There was no time for them to exchange pleasantries.

"We need your help," I said before sitting down beside Corbin.

"And why should I help you?" Juniper asked. A challenging stare emanated from her as she crossed her arms over her chest. "You broke my girl's heart. And you keep breaking it. I don't like how you're handling this at all."

Her words stung my heart, and my wolf clawed at my soul. I knew that I was hurting Nicole, but hearing it from Juniper made me feel like shit. "I'm trying to protect her."

She arched her brow. "Are you?"

Corbin looked between us, and after an awkward moment of silence, he spoke up. "I need to be able to check on Nicole without Alexei's father knowing."

Juniper shrugged. "She has plenty of people checking on her already."

Corbin shook his head. "I'm worried about her. Alpha Jones is assigning more enforcers to watch her. He thinks there's something up with Nicole."

"I'm capable of protecting my own, Corbin." Juniper pressed her lips together in defiance.

This was getting us nowhere.

My alpha wolf rose to the surface, demanding this woman help us protect my mate. Since Nicole and I completed half of our bond, it was getting harder and harder to control my inner animal, knowing she was in danger. My instincts were on hyperdrive, our bond urging me to race after Nicole and beg her forgiveness. I wanted to protect her. I wanted to take her away from here—away from my father.

Corbin dragged his hands down his face. "I care about her, Junie. She's my friend, and it makes me sick to think that she hates me. Never in a million years would I have done anything to humiliate her like that. I hate that fucking recording and the lies I had to tell my sister. You know me, Juniper. You *know* me. I'm not that guy. I'm loyal, and if one of my friends is in danger, I'll do everything I can to protect them."

Juniper nodded before turning to me. "And what about you? I don't see you groveling or coming up with a solution."

"I'm going to challenge my father," I whispered, the truth like a burden on my chest. Even though I had been thinking about it since I'd mated Nicole, it was the first time I admitted it out loud. In order to keep her safe, I had no other choice.

"You're going to challenge him?" Juniper's brows lifted in shock. "Like, *formally* challenge him for alpha rights?"

I nodded. "I'm going to *try*. His combat skills are better than mine, but I'm bigger and stronger—"

Corbin cut me off. "Pack Daddy's gotten lazy and hasn't kept up with his fitness regime. You've been working harder for years. Besides... it's a mental game, bro. You just need to get out of your head."

I knew Corbin was right, but it felt nearly impossible to escape the many memories of my father beating the shit out of me. The abuse I'd been subjected to over the years had built up in my mind. Logically, I knew my lack of confidence was a trauma response, but logic didn't erase the lifetime of mental damage my father had done. In the moments he was wailing on me, it was hard to view myself as powerful enough when he'd been showing me the opposite since I could walk. But like I told June, I had to try. Nicole needed me to find a way around this roadblock, and unfortunately, no magical solution existed for this particular problem.

"And you're more motivated," my beta continued. "You're fighting for *Nicole*, man. Your wolf won't allow anyone—or anything—to get in between you two."

Taking a deep breath, I let out a shaky sigh. "I'm asking for your help to buy some time, Juniper. I can't challenge my father until I'm ready. Physically *and* mentally. I'm only going to get one shot at this." I met her golden gaze. "In the meantime, I need to make sure Nicole has as much protection as possible. To do that, we need to talk to her, but with my father's extra surveillance, we need to tread *very* carefully."

Juniper rolled her eyes. "I still feel like there's something else you're not telling me."

I nodded. "There is... but it's not my secret to tell. We need to talk to Nicole before I can say anything else."

I had no idea who Nicole had confided in, if anyone. She obviously trusted Juniper enough to move into the sorority house, but that could've simply been a matter of it being the lesser of all evils. Juniper clearly didn't trust me to share what she knew, and I wasn't about to share Nicole's secret without her permission. We were at a standstill, and the only thing that could fix this was if I had time to speak with Nicole individually. It was damn near impossible to do that when she was angry with me, and every spare moment we had together, I was trying not to rip her fucking clothes off and show her how much she meant to me.

Fuck, I hated that my mate was in this situation. She shouldn't have to worry about any of this. I should be at her side, protecting her. Helping her solve the mystery of her mother's identity. Instead, I was relying on others to get messages to her like we were kids passing notes in class. I'd had her all to myself at the vamp house, and I fucked it up. I should have brought it up then, but neither one of us were in the right frame of mind to discuss anything rationally.

"What exactly are you asking of me, Alexei?" Juniper tilted her head, like she was trying to solve a puzzle.

"Can you give us a masking spell?" I asked. "So we can safely speak to Nicole? It needs to be in private, Juniper. I can't tell you why, but it's important. Price isn't an issue. I'll pay anything."

She took a moment before turning to Corbin. "I'll give *you* one. *If* Nicole approves." She then pointed her finger at me. "But not *you*. Nicole has already made it pretty clear she wants nothing to do with you."

My chest tightened. "You know that's not true. Our mate bond... it must be killing her to be away from me. I know she's upset, but if I just had the chance to explain..."

"That's the thing, Alexei," she interrupted. "You've had plenty of chances to explain. And you keep making it worse and worse. Besides..." June's full lips curved upward. "I know *you* don't trust Cristian, but Nicole *does*. And *that's* what matters to me."

My jaw clenched in irritation. "Fine. If I can't personally speak with her, Corbin is the next best thing. As my best friend and my beta, I trust him more than anyone else. And *way more* than that fucking *bloodsucker*."

Corbin shook his head in warning when I growled.

The purple-haired witch simply raised her eyebrows, looking unimpressed. "Did you just *growl* at me? I guess you don't want my help after all, do you?"

"C'mon, Junie," Corbin pleaded. "Don't be like that."

Juniper stood and started walking toward the door. "I'll talk to Nicole when I get back to the house. And if she gives me the green light, I'll gather the ingredients and we'll arrange a time to meet. But I meant it when I said I will only give Corbin a spell. That part is non-negotiable. Take it or leave it."

"I said *fine*," I gritted. "But in the meantime, do *not* let her make a blood oath with that asshole. Or do anything else with him for that matter."

She gave me another sassy grin. "Now, what kind of feminist would I be if I tried to tell one of my sisters who she can and cannot share her body with? Especially at the request of a man who is *engaged*?"

My nostrils flared as my fists clenched. "I am *not* engaged."

June shrugged. "That hideous rock on Mara's finger says otherwise."

With that, she walked out the door, leaving me to chew on her words.

"Dude," Corbin said. "You look like you're about to wolf out at any moment. Maybe we should go for a run?"

My animal counterpart really fucking liked that idea. He was clawing at my insides, dying to take over.

I stood, stashing my cell and keys in my nightstand. "Let's go."

I barely made it out the back door of the frat house before I was stripping out of my clothes and shifting. My wolf came quickly, rising to the surface with a vengeance. Fur sprouted along my arms, as my back arched and cracked. Soon, my senses switched into overdrive as I landed on all fours.

My consciousness fell to the background as my wolf pulled forward, his tumultuous emotions waging war in my mind. He was feeling agitated and possessive, drawn instinctively toward our mate with a sense of determination. There was a faint tug at my soul, the beginnings of the bond I was building with Nicole. Even though we hadn't completed the mating ceremony, there was an undeniable tether between us.

My wolf knew exactly where she was at that moment, and he started chasing after the faint connection we shared.

Corbin was hot on my heels, but he knew better than to stop an alpha in pursuit of his mate. I didn't care about the consequences at that moment. I didn't care if we were being followed. It seemed like my wolf was brimming with angry energy. I was filled with a sense of confidence in myself, the urge to challenge my father coursing through my veins. My mate was the greatest motivator, but I had to work on my skills as a fighter so I could assure my dominance.

Corbin was right. It was a mental game, and I had to get over the trauma my father put me through so I could be worthy of Nicole and keep her safe.

I sniffed the air, catching a whiff of my mate's sweet scent. I ran hard through the woods after it, tracing the perimeter of our campus wall hidden by the large towering trees. When I stopped at the Kappa Zeta house, my heart sank. Nicole was sitting on a patio, a sketchbook clutched in her hands as she patted her familiar on the head.

Macey snapped her attention to us, barking in warning.

I wondered if Nicole could still hear my mind at this distance. There was still so much between us; I wondered if I had ruined our mate bond past the point of repair.

"I'm going to make this right, Nicole. I promise."

Nicole's chin lifted, her eyes scanning the tree line, as if she heard my telepathic message. Corbin and I sunk deeper into the shadows. I wanted to run up to her, take her in my arms and reassure her that everything was going to be okay.

"Alexei?" She stood as her voice rang loud and clear in my head, taking a step forward.

Corbin nudged my shoulder, silently urging me to turn back.

Nicole's familiar growled, hackles raised as she stalked toward the tree line.

My beta nudged me again, snapping his jaws to prompt me to move. It wasn't in my nature to run from confrontation, but I knew I'd do more harm than good if I hurt my mate's companion, so I tucked tail and ran in the opposite direction. Macey quickly gave up her pursuit as Nicole called her back to her side. I howled in frustration, Corbin echoing the sound as we ran through the forest. The canopy was so thick, moonlight barely shone through the leaves. My paws kicked up dirt as I ran faster, adrenaline flooding my system.

My wolf was a ruthless creature. He had alpha power coursing through his veins but no experience to back it up. My father thought that by beating me into submission, he was making a stronger alpha. But instead, he just made me a coward. I wasn't confident in my abilities to challenge him, and even though I knew I bested him in bulk and power, there was still an uncertainty buried deep in my soul that was impossible to ignore.

But I was working on that. For Nicole. For *us*. Even with so much distance between us, she was making me a better person.

I howled once more, and every step I took away from my mate made my wolf more agitated. Anger was a powerful motivator, and at that moment I felt nothing but pure, unadulterated rage. I wanted to destroy my father for ruining such a precious mate bond. I wanted to challenge him for power, because I knew that he was an unworthy leader. My pack was suffering under his guidance. My mate was in danger as long as he was alpha.

I stopped running and turned to face my beta, feeling a sudden need to spar.

Corbin's wolf was panting from trying to keep up with me, bracing himself as he read my intentions.

I crouched low, snapping my teeth at him. Corbin wasn't the enemy, but he was the best sparring partner I had. I didn't have another alpha to practice with, so he took every hit.

Corbin stared at me for a moment, his wolf eyes taking in the way my hair stood on edge. A low growl simmered in my chest. I could see the wariness in his expression. Corbin was devoted to me as a friend and as my beta. We practiced because he knew how important this was, but it wasn't easy for him. I was stronger. Faster.

He wasn't really that much of a challenge.

Slowly, he nodded, letting me know that he was ready. And then, I charged.

Corbin was light on his paws as he jumped away from my advance. But it was only a matter of seconds before I was pinning him to the soil, fangs pressed against his throat. He whimpered in submission before shifting back into his human form. I did the same, rolling onto my back next to him. Dried leaves and brambles were digging into my skin uncomfortably as I caught my breath, but the pain was minimal compared to the ache in my chest.

"I fucking hate this."

"I know you do, dude," Corbin said. "But you need to think about the endgame. If you go running up to Nicky anytime you want or challenge your father before you're ready, there'll be consequences neither one of us wants. I hate to say it, man, but maybe you need to play into this thing with my sister for a while to throw him off the scent. If June will give me the masking spell, I can talk to Nicole. Find out exactly what she's learned and who she's shared that information with."

"And if Juniper won't give you the spell?"

I saw him shrugging in my peripheral. "Then maybe I have to sweet talk some other witch into doing it. And when I say *sweet talk*, I mean *eat out*."

"I'm not going to let you whore yourself out for a problem I caused," I snapped.

Corbin laughed. "Why not? It's not like I wouldn't enjoy myself. You know how much I love going to *Chow*

Town. As long as the lucky lady isn't sporting a seventies bush, that is. I have no idea who thought they should bring those things back, but it's so wrong. I tried it once, because the girl had the best rack I've ever seen, but I can guarantee it'll never happen again." He shivered dramatically. "I was picking pubes out of my teeth for two days. I can't even watch hairy-bush porn, no matter how hot the chick is. My gag reflex instantly kicks into overdrive."

I curled my lip in disgust. "I don't understand why you feel the need to tell me these things. That visual is almost as disturbing as the time you told me about your adventure with anal after meeting that girl at that jalapeño popper eating contest."

He sat up and arched his brow. "We're literally two dudes lying naked in the dirt right now. If I can't tell you about my sexual horror stories, then what are we even doing here, bro?" I grabbed a handful of dirt and tossed it at him, the gritty ground sticking to his sweaty skin. He shoved my shoulder with a laugh. "Is now a bad time to talk about your training?"

I scrubbed my hands down my face. "What about it?"

"You and I have been sparring since we were old enough to walk. But you're so strong now that I'm not much of a challenge. Don't get me wrong, I could totally go in for the sneak attack and kick your ass—"

"You wish!"

Corbin grinned. "Challenge accepted."

I let out a sigh. The playfulness fled my body once

more. "You're right, though. I need someone who actually knows what the fuck they're doing to train me—"

"I take offense to that," he deadpanned.

"You know what I mean. I need an alpha. Someone that's not deliberately trying to sabotage me. My father talks a big game about wanting me to take over, but everything he does is holding me back."

Corbin nodded. "I've been putting some feelers out for other alphas in the area. Maybe we could find someone willing to work with you."

I shook my head, immediately feeling apprehensive at that idea. "My father has too many trade deals with every alpha in the world. If I started working with one of them, he would immediately know about it. It's not like we're going to find some lone wolf capable of training me."

Corbin patted me on the back. "We'll find someone, okay? You have the strength and the motivation. And if we can lure your father into a false sense of security, then you'll also have the competitive edge. We just need to work on your skill and your confidence. I know you talk a big game, but your dad has pulled some psychological bullshit over you these last few years. The stronger you get, the more he tries to take you down."

I thought about that for a moment, knowing he was right.

"I can't let him win, Corbin," I whispered.

"And you won't," he assured me. "Like I said earlier, you're fighting for your mate. It's the strongest motivator there is behind protecting one of your pups. We just need to be smart, because one thing Pack Daddy is not, is a dumbass."

I sighed. "So, what now?"

"Now..." Corbin stood, his dick now at eye level, so I stood, too, to get the damn thing out of my face. "We run. There's no way we're gonna solve this tonight, so we might as well let our animals loose. But let's stick to this half of the forest, yeah? Do you think you can control your wolf well enough to do that?"

"Of course I can," I grumbled.

Maybe.

I guessed there was only one way to find out.

My wolf sprang from my skin, paws smacking against the earth with a loud thump. I took off at full speed with my beta right behind me, hoping I could live up to my promise.

FOURTEEN

Nicole

Juniper hovered over a basin of moon water, eyeing the concoction with her brow raised. "Corbin is going to regret asking me for help," she cackled, sounding like an evil villain as her laughter bounced off the walls.

"I'm making the right choice, aren't I?"

Juniper smiled sweetly. "If your gut is telling you to talk to Corbin, then I think this is a good idea. He seemed genuine when I spoke to him."

I scratched my arm, the nervous tic driving me crazy. I wanted to talk to Corbin, morbid curiosity fueling my decision more than anything else. But I also missed the mischievous beta wolf. Corbin and I had become friends in a short amount of time, and even though I struggled to trust him, I missed him. I wanted to know what was going on, and I was curious what he wanted to talk about. Knowledge was power in this game. I was working on building alliances, so perhaps having an inside look at what was going on behind the scenes would help me better defend myself—or even rescue my dad.

The fact that Alexei went to Juniper for help, and conceded defeat when she refused to give him a masking spell, solidified the decision for me. Plus, if Corbin was willing to swallow his pride and accept help from the girl who dumped him, then I could be open to listening to him.

"I can't wait until he looks in the mirror," Juniper said, snapping me out of my thoughts.

"Do I even want to know?"

Juniper added a vial of something that looked disgustingly similar to snot, but in the short time I'd known her, I'd learned not to ask what went into her potions. "I'm just making him work for it. What Corbin said on that recording was messed up, and I will always choose a Kappa sister over one of my hookups. But I do care about him. I just like messing with him, too."

I forced a smile. "He *is* fun to mess with."

She started stirring the potion counterclockwise, her eyes trained on me. "Is there something you want to tell me, Nicole?"

"Why do you ask?" I replied, feeling nervous.

She stopped stirring and tapped her spoon on the rim of her cauldron three times. "You know you can trust me, right? Whatever you tell me is safe."

I'd been struggling with telling anyone about my mother and her potential supernatural heritage. But since the visions Macey showed me created more questions than answers, I figured it wouldn't hurt to have Juniper on my side. She had already proven herself to be a trustworthy friend and a strong ally in this mess.

But I was still so fucked in the head. I felt unsure of everything, but I knew my reluctance to trust was holding me back. If I let Juniper—and maybe even Cristian—in fully, maybe I'd have a more solid plan to get out of this mess.

"Okay," I breathed. "I *do* have something to tell you. But I'm nervous because I'm not quite sure what it means."

Juniper nodded, as if she expected this. "Okay. Tell me. We can work through it together, and I swear I won't share anything you tell me in confidence."

I sighed before spilling the truth that had been haunting me. "Mace gave me a vision of my mother running with friends of hers who were shifters. Then, someone tried to capture her. The vision faded before I could get any real answers. But after talking with Hannah and Jade, who were my mom's best friends, I've learned that my mom wasn't human. Which means..."

If Juniper was surprised by this information, she didn't

show it. "*You're* not entirely human. But you don't know for sure? Jade and Hannah don't know any specifics?"

I picked at my jeans before responding. "That's the problem. They *do* know. But they can't say a word because they cast a secrecy spell with my mother to protect her secret at all costs. All I know is that whatever she was, was exceedingly rare and put her in great danger."

Juniper wrinkled her nose in disgust. "Secrecy spells are awful. And *very* difficult to get rid of if one of the original casters passes away."

"So I hear." I released a sigh. "I just want to know what I am. Jade says it's possible I could be in danger, too. There are so many questions I don't even know where to start. My father had this lock on his mind, and somehow, I was able to break it. How did I manage that? I have *no clue* what I did. Alexei told me that his father had a whole team of witches trying to figure it out, but they couldn't pull it off."

Juniper set the spoon down and crossed her arms over her chest, eyes scanning my body, as if she could identify my faction with a single look. "Well, you're definitely not a witch."

"How do you know?" I asked.

"You have power, but it's not witchy magic."

"I didn't realize there were different kinds. How many types of magic are out there? And how do you know my supposed magic isn't witchy magic?"

"Can you feel the potion I'm brewing right now?" Juniper lifted a delicate brow.

I cocked my head to the side, not sure what she was asking. "Feel?"

She nodded. "Whenever someone performs a spell, I'm drawn to it. I can *feel* the magical energy shift in the air. Every witch can. If you were a witch, you would be drawn to our spells like moths to a flame. I just performed a pretty big one when I made this potion, and you barely flinched. Like magic attracts like magic, and you, my friend, are *not* a witch. I'm sure of it. But there are countless other possibilities."

Of course, there were. God forbid this be simple.

Relying on the process of elimination was frustrating. I knew I wasn't a shifter because I couldn't transform into any animal, nor did I feel the presence of one in my soul. I definitely wasn't a vampire, because I had no desire to drink blood. Hannah had told me that even half-bred vampires needed it for sustenance.

"I don't feel like I identify with any supe I've met so far. Besides that one freak incident with my father, I don't feel like I'm harnessing *any* kind of power. What if that was just a coincidence? And why hasn't my mental encyclopedia kicked in? I have all this information about witches, shifters, vampires, and fae stored in my head, but nothing about any rare beings, other than the fact that they exist."

She thought about that for a moment before responding. "From what I understand, the rare beings are quite reclusive and not very... forthcoming. There's not a whole lot of information about them stored in our magical archives because they don't allow their abilities to be documented. Most of what we know is based on legend. As far as *your* powers go, that could simply be a matter of you not reaching magical maturity yet, which is kinda like the supernatural equivalent of puberty. Some supes don't come into their gifts until they reach a certain milestone. For example, a succubus's powers don't awaken until they lose their virginity." June sighed wistfully. "I met an entire clan of succubi once. Best orgy of my life."

I let out a bitter laugh. "Well, you saw my video with Alexei. I'm definitely not a succubus."

Her golden eyes widened. "Alexei was your first?!"

"No." I shook my head. "But it was the only time someone had video proof of me not being a virgin."

Her face fell. "Nic—"

I held a hand up to cut her off. "Please don't. I don't want to talk about it."

Juniper nodded, chewing on her fingernail with a look of deep contemplation in her expression. "Elementals are a very rare demon breed, but there is a community of them in Northern Canada. They come into their power after brutal exposure to the elements. When they turn eighteen, they put them through a series of tests to see what their affinity is. I had to watch the ceremony once, and it made me sick. They tied this girl's legs to weights and threw her into a lake."

I shivered. "Well, I definitely hope I'm not an elemental."

Juniper walked over to me and grabbed my arm, her kind eyes scanning my expression. "We'll figure this out. Redwood is full of supernatural creatures. Witches, shifters, vampires, and fae are the most common ones— but there are so many in this big ol' world. I'll help you, I promise."

My eyes filled with tears, but I managed to keep them from falling. "Thank you, Juniper. Please don't make me regret trusting you with this information. I don't know if I can handle another betrayal."

Macey wove around Juniper's legs, as if she were trying to assure me I could trust the witch.

June crouched down to Mace's eye level, scratching behind her furry ears as they seemed to be communicating telepathically. "I know, sweet girl," Juniper told my familiar. "I would be wary, too, but between the two of us, we'll find the answers one way or the other, right?"

Juniper was obviously speaking out loud for my benefit, which I appreciated. The cynical part of me knew she could be misleading me with her reply, but my familiar's next actions told me to have faith.

Mace's pink tongue slobbered all over June's golden

brown cheek, making her fall back in a fit of laughter. My beautiful wolf playfully bounced on top of the witch, coating her face in doggy saliva, but June took it in stride, planting a big kiss on her snout before getting to her feet.

"Man, she's full of energy today." June smiled down at Macey. "Tonight would be a great night to run under the moon, wouldn't it?"

Macey barked excitedly.

"I'll take that as a yes." I laughed. "God, I'd love to have your gift of communicating with animals. I'm so grateful for the visions Macey's shown me, but there's still so much information missing. It'd be much easier if I could just talk to her." I gasped when a thought came to me. "Wait a minute! Can you ask her what she knows about my mom? Can she tell you directly instead of feeding me cryptic visions?"

June tucked a purple curl behind her ear. "I've already tried that, babe. Unfortunately, Mace is as clueless as the rest of us. When she shares a vision with you, it's because a god has gifted her with that information. She has no control over what she shows you, or any information beyond that."

"God?" I frowned. "*What* god?"

She shrugged. "I don't know for sure—neither does Macey—but there are plenty of gods and goddesses that like to intervene. Maybe one of them took pity on you."

I knew supernatural beings worshiped gods and goddesses, but my brain download didn't give me any information beyond that. I honestly thought they were just imaginary celestial beings like in Greek mythology.

"So gods and goddesses are real?"

June nodded. "*Very* real."

I frowned in confusion. "Do they have tangible form? Or is it more of a *have faith and your prayers will be answered* type of thing?"

"To be honest, there's a lot of misinformation out there," she explained. "I suspect the gods do that on purpose, because information is power, and they don't want to give us lower beings any advantages over them. I think they took a page from the rare supes' book, or vice versa. But what I've been taught is that they exist on another plane... It's called Elysian Point. And they've been rumored to slum it on other realms while in disguise, but never with humans."

I mulled over her words for a moment. "Why would a god want to give me information, though?"

Juniper shrugged. "Why do gods do anything? If I had to guess, I'd say immortality gets pretty boring after you turn a thousand, give or take a few centuries."

"You don't think my mother was..." I didn't even finish my sentence, because I felt it was too absurd saying it out loud.

My witchy friend's brows raised. "Absolutely not. That would be... more rare than anything I've ever come across. Gods don't marry or mate mortals. I've heard of one having a fling with the fae, but even that is mostly myth. You would be like a flashing beacon with all that power."

I sighed, feeling hopeless that I would never figure out what I was. "I just wish I had answers. It's hard enough not knowing my mother, but now there's this whole secret side to her that I can't even process. She's always felt like a stranger to me, but now..."

Juniper chewed on her lip. People always got awkward when I talked about her, mostly because they didn't know what to say. "You know the parts of her that matter. You know her friends and that she loved your father."

"But this matters, too." My frustration grew the more I thought about it, and Macey nudged my thigh.

"Of course, it matters. But her entire identity wasn't wrapped up in this. Regardless of what supernatural being she was, you and your father were her priority. Her life with you all was what she wanted. She wouldn't have done the secrecy spell otherwise."

My eyes misted with emotion. "It's just so frustrating. I've always wished that I could talk to her—get to know her. But now I have more questions than ever before. Not only did I miss out on having a mom, but I missed out on knowing this whole different side of myself. Redwood has brought me nothing but headaches, but at least now I know about the supernatural world. I should've been a part of this community from the start. Maybe then Alexei—" Saying my mate's name out loud sent a lightning bolt of pain straight to my heart. I couldn't believe what I had been about to say.

Maybe then Alexei would have picked me...

Juniper looked at me with pity. "Alexei has to come to terms with everything on his own. There's nothing you could have done to make this relationship easier on the two of you. It's not your fault that you aren't a shifter. And it's not Alexei's fault for having to fight through decades of prejudice against humans. I'm not saying how he has handled things is okay, but you can't fault yourself for not being what society thinks you should be." She grabbed my hand and stroked my skin with her thumb. "At the end of the day, you are not a shifter. Alexei has to choose to love you regardless, not because you fit in his world, but because you make his world a better place."

I stared at her for a moment, soaking in her words. As much as I hated to admit it, I missed Alexei. I *loathed* the thought of him and Mara as a couple. Even if I wasn't ready to forgive him, that didn't mean I wanted him to be with her.

"Well, I think the mask potion is ready for the next step. Why don't you go hang out with Jade, Hannah, and Bee while I deliver this to him."

I was looking forward to whatever devious plans Juniper had for Corbin. I needed a bit of levity to survive the turmoil I'd been under. "Thanks, Juniper. For... well... everything."

She grinned. "That's what Kappa sisters do."

As I walked out of the potions room, I felt a bit lighter. I'd come to college looking for a sense of sisterhood and to feel closer to my mother. And even though it didn't happen in a way I'd expected, I still found that.

Now I just needed to learn more about my heritage, save my dad, and figure out what to do with the whole mating situation.

Easy, right?

FIFTEEN

Alexei

THE POTION HAD to sit under the moonlight for three nights after Juniper dropped it off. I spent the last few days pacing my bedroom floor and trying to avoid Mara whenever I wasn't in class. It was excruciating to wait so long, but I knew it would be worth it. My father had men hidden in every corner of this university, so I had to be safe. Today, Corbin would finally be able to talk to Nicole.

The most god-awful bloodcurdling scream I'd ever heard sounded from Corbin's bedroom.

"What the hell?" I muttered, narrowing my eyes as Juniper giggled.

"What did you do?!" Corbin cried from the other side of the door. "Juniper! Whhhhhhhyyyyyyy?!"

I pounded my fist on the wood. "What's wrong?"

"Don't!" my beta shouted as I jiggled the door handle.

Now the quirky witch was straight-up cackling.

I turned my attention to her. "What the hell did you put in that spell?"

Juniper arrived a few minutes ago to witness the big reveal. She told him it was best to undress before drinking it; otherwise, he'd ruin the clothes he was wearing. Corbin and I assumed that was because his new form would be a lot more muscular like mine since she recommended I lend him something to wear from my wardrobe.

Based on Corbin's reaction, I was pretty sure we were dumbasses in assuming that.

She waved me off. "Oh, just a little lesson in humility, that's all."

Fucking hell.

Corbin was a vain motherfucker, and if his witchy ex just gave him a bunch of warts or turned him into an ogre, he was not going to handle it well.

I slammed my fist on the door again. "Corbin, open the goddamn door and let me see what we're dealing with."

I could swear I heard him whimper. "Why, June? Do you hate me that much?"

She rolled her uniquely colored eyes. "Oh, don't be such a baby, Corbin. I'm sure it's not as bad as you're making it out to be."

I heard the telltale sign of the door unlocking a second

before he whipped it open. "Not that bad?! NOT THAT BAD?!"

I looked him over, and I couldn't figure out what the hell he was griping about. It wasn't like she turned him into something grotesque. June's potion gave Corbin thick wavy brown hair, deep green eyes, and a muscular build that had significantly more bulk than his usual swimmer's frame. He was conventionally attractive like an A-list movie star would be. I couldn't find a single thing wrong with him, and considering he was currently half naked, there was a lot to look at.

I frowned in confusion. "I'm not seeing the problem."

Corbin turned, showing me his back. "Do you see the problem now?"

My lips twitched as I took in the tiny sprite wings that fluttered rapidly from the middle of his back, tossing rainbow-colored glitter in their wake. It took me a few seconds to gain my composure before speaking.

"So you have itty bitty wings. You can easily cover them up. It's not *that* big of a deal."

"Oh, yeah?" Corbin challenged. "Well, what do you think about *this*?"

He dropped the bulky comforter he had wrapped around his lower half, exposing his naked ass. I'd seen many naked asses in my life—it was part of being a shifter—but I couldn't say I'd ever seen this. A lion's tail swung back and forth, sprouting out of his skin right above his butt crack.

"Hey!" I shouted when the damn thing swatted me.

Corbin groaned. "I can't control it. It's just there, doing whatever the hell it wants."

I side-eyed the laughing witch. "You couldn't resist, huh?"

"You haven't even seen the best part," she replied.

My brows rose. "Corbin? What is she talking about?"

My beta whimpered again as he started turning toward us. "*This.*"

My jaw dropped when I got my first glimpse of the gargantuan appendage hanging between his legs. I was absolutely speechless, and I couldn't stop staring if my life depended on it. Corbin's dick looked normal... ish. It was humanoid, albeit a bit red and angry looking, but this was no ordinary cock. This wasn't even a porn star jumbo cock. The poor guy's dick was literally the width of my forearm, and it hung just past his knees.

"What's the problem, Corbin?" Juniper asked. "You were always so proud of your massive cock. I thought I was doing you a favor by making it even bigger."

Corbin grunted as he lifted it. "*You gave me an elephant peen!* How could you *ever* think this would be okay?! How am I supposed to walk around with this thing? What am I supposed to wear? How do I take a piss without dunking it in the toilet?" He gasped. "Oh my God! What if I had to use one of those toilets with automatic flushers and it got sucked down the pipes mid-pee? Those damn things always flush during inopportune times!"

"Maybe you should stick to urinals?" I suggested, barking in laughter.

"Not funny, asshole." Corbin glared.

I coughed into my fist to disguise another laugh. "Sorry, dude."

He leveled that same scowl on his ex. "You need to fix this!"

June held her hands up. "No can do, bud. You're stuck like this for at least a week. Maybe two. And it's not *actually* an elephant penis. Don't be so dramatic."

"Dramatic!" Corbin threw his hands up. "How am I supposed to put pants on, June? How?!"

Juniper and I were both mesmerized by the sway of his cock caused by his flailing arms. It was like one of those metronomes hypnotists use, luring us into a trance as it swung back and forth. Back and forth. Baaaaaack and forth.

She shook out of her daze with a shrug. "I dunno. Maybe an ACE bandage would help? You could strap it to your thigh like a holster or something."

I cocked my head to the side, still staring at the gigantic dick. "You need one of those slings people use when they dislocate their shoulder."

"I need a fucking army to hold this thing up!" He squatted like his lower back was hurting, and his tail poked between his legs as if playing a weird game of peek-a-boo. It waved at me from around the massive dick, then tickled Corbin's taint. "Ahhh! The tail is violating me!"

Juniper waved her hands around and produced a bandage out of thin air. "Come on, Alexei. Go strap his dick to his thigh so it doesn't drag on the floor."

I snapped my attention to her. "I love Corbin like a brother, but there is *no way in hell* I'm touching that *thing*."

Corbin whined. "Please." His tail started picking his nose, and he swatted at it.

"Absolutely not," I replied, my tone leaving no room for argument.

Corbin sighed before snatching the ACE bandage from Juniper's outstretched hand, and he made quick work of wrapping it around his pants python. It was like a fucking third leg.

"You should probably avoid getting excited," I said solemnly. "I'm putting you on a porn ban, effective immediately."

He grunted. "You think, asshole?"

Juniper simply smiled while watching him. "Your balls are so tiny in comparison. I should have made them proportionate."

I nodded in agreement.

"Ooooorrrrrr... maybe you shouldn't have given me the world's largest dick!"

Juniper rolled her eyes when he struggled to fix the bandage at his knee. "You're constantly bragging about how well hung you are, Corbin. I just wanted to give you a little perspective. By the way, your new name is Skidmore. You're a quarter lion shifter, a quarter sprite, and half-unicorn shifter. You like dancing in gardens, eating snails, and every woman who isn't an equine shifter is terrified to have sex with you because you'll split her in half."

"Skidmore? What the fuck kind of name is that?" Corbin looked up at her as his bandage unraveled. "Juniper, I swear to God, I have never felt more murderous in my life!"

"You're not doing the best job embracing your new persona. Skidmore is a lover, not a fighter." Juniper was struggling to contain her laughter.

Not that I could blame her.

"No fucking shit, Junie," Corbin seethed. "*Skidmore* doesn't even have to lift weights. He just jacks this gigantic boulder off." He threw both hands down, presenting his angry penis in exasperation. His tail tickled the head of his cock, as if enticed by the idea of getting off. "Oh no you don't!" Corbin grabbed the tail and separated it from his dick.

The lion's tail started fighting Corbin, struggling to get out of his grip.

"This is possibly the greatest day of my life," I murmured while his dick swung around and Corbin fell to the ground wrestling his tail.

Juniper cackled for a good five minutes while Corbin tried to keep his tail away from his third leg. Every time he slammed onto the ground, he cried out in pain because his appendage was too big and kept getting crushed beneath him.

"Enough," I said after a while. Even though this was the most entertained I'd been in a while, we didn't have time to fuck around. I was thankful for Juniper's help, but Corbin was going to be completely useless as my beta for the next week or two.

With a flick of her wrist, Juniper magically hoisted Corbin up on his feet, wrapped his dick to his thigh, and settled his tail. "Grab those gray sweatpants and get dressed. Nicole is waiting, Skidmore."

"Fucking witches. I ate your pussy like it was my job, and this is how you repay me?" Corbin asked while angrily getting dressed. Much to Juniper's delight, the outline of his monster cock was very visible in the sweatpants.

She shrugged. "You hurt Nicole's feelings. Consider us even."

I winced and made a mental note to make sure the vengeful witch didn't tamper with anything of mine. I didn't want to wake up with a micropenis. "Thank you for helping us, Juniper. And for talking to Nicole."

Corbin struggled with his white tank top, his wings straining against the thin material but still easily covered. "Yeah," he huffed. "Thank you *so* much."

She blew him a kiss. "You're welcome, darling."

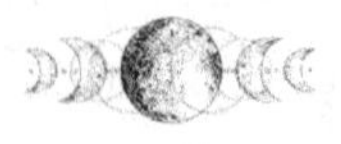

IT TOOK a lot of coaxing to get Corbin to go outside. He walked like he had a stick up his ass, and I wasn't sure if it was because of his dick sling or his intrusive tail. I could see the outline of his wings and their rainbow glitter through his shirt, and the moment we walked onto the front porch of our frat house, I noticed another interesting feature that wasn't visible until a beam of sunshine hit his skin.

"Oh, fuck."

"What?" Corbin whirled around to face me.

"Nothing."

Juniper slammed her hand over her mouth, trying to suppress another giggle.

He took another step, putting him in direct sunlight, and fuck, I needed a pair of sunglasses. I squinted at the sight of him.

My newly disguised beta let out another high-pitched wail. "Why, Juniper! WHY? I'm a fucking disco ball!"

Juniper had to brace her hands against her knees, she was laughing so hard. A dude on a bicycle crashed into a tree because Corbin's skin blinded him. "You couldn't stop at the massive dick? You had to make my skin fucking *glitter*, too?!"

I ran back up to the porch and grabbed one of the umbrellas sitting there. Somehow, I managed to open it up and hand it to him without laughing, probably because I was too busy trying not to get blinded by his sparkling skin.

Corbin flipped us off. "I hate you. I hate all of you."

"I don't know why you're complaining," Juniper choked out. "I added some good things to your mask, too. You're impossibly fast and strong..."

"And my skin is pale white and glitters in the sunlight," he deadpanned.

I pinched the bridge of my nose. "You really need to go."

Corbin growled. "I'm going, okay? I'll fucking be there with bells on."

Juniper let out another snort. "Sometimes you speak like—like you're from a different time. How old are you?"

"Fucking twenty-one. My grandmother used to use that phrase, alright?"

"How long have you been twenty-one?" Juniper giggled. "I'm having way too much fun with this."

"What? Like six months. You know that. You gave me that sexy little birthday present with the whipped cream and the handcuffs." Corbin frowned before pointing an accusatory finger at her. "Oh my God! Are you quoting that vampire movie?! *Did you make me glitter like a goddamn fictional vampire?!*"

"Team Edward 'til the day I die!" June fist-pumped the air.

Corbin's jaw dropped. "What? That's ridiculous! Everyone knows that Edward was a—"

"Enough!" I growled once more. "We're drawing a lot of attention to ourselves. The whole point of this mask was to get Corbin in there undiscovered. The two of you need to stop fucking around and go to the Kappa Zeta house." I could practically *feel* my father watching me. I knew he was having a meeting this morning, so there were fewer of his enforcers walking around, but we couldn't be too careful. Luckily, Juniper used a spell to scan the area this morning, and there was one sleeping enforcer a half mile away, but we couldn't be too careful.

Corbin was still seething, but like a good little beta, he straightened his spine and nodded. "Yes, Alpha."

"You're right. It was just a bit of fun," Juniper added.

"Fun is over. Go talk to Nicole. I want a full update tonight, Skidmore."

And with that, I spun around and went back inside the frat house.

I just wished I could go with them.

SIXTEEN

Nicole

MACEY WAS WHINING at the back door of my room, pawing at the glass for us to let her inside. Jade was trying on one of my newest creations, an upcycled Gucci dress with studs along the seams. "I love this, Nicole. I can't wait until you're a big time designer so I can buy all the things."

I smiled and got up to let Macey in. My familiar had been acting strange lately, but I figured it was my own nerves about everything making her act up. The moment I opened the door, she shoved me toward Jade with her bulky body.

"Whoa, whoa, whoa." I laughed. She was acting like one of those herding dogs. "What's going on, girl?"

Macey whined, nudging me with her snout.

"It seems like she's trying to tell you something," Hannah said.

I crouched down. "Is that it, girl? Are you trying to tell me something?"

Macey's claws scratched the wooden floor as she paced the small space in front of me.

I placed my hand on her head to soothe her, but the moment I did, I was violently pulled into one of her visions. A thick forest replaced my bedroom so quickly that it was disorienting.

"What is it, Nicole?" Jade asked.

"Touch her," I suggested. "See if it'll work like last time."

The moment Jade and Hannah laid their hands on my wolf, the two of them appeared before me in their ghostly forms, just like when Mace showed us the vision of my parents.

The three of us watched as my mother came into view, kneeling beside a large spruce tree. She rubbed her swollen belly as she glanced inside a rectangular box.

My heart warmed at seeing her pregnant with me. It was the only time we were together, and I didn't remember any of it. She looked so beautiful, albeit a bit worried and tired.

"What's in the box?" Hannah asked.

"I can't see," Jade replied. "But I feel like this is important."

"Me too," I agreed. "I don't think we'd be seeing this if it weren't."

I strained my eyes, but we weren't close enough to see inside the box. The god, or whatever being was responsible for these visions, must've known we were struggling, because in the next moment, we were standing right above my mom, close enough to touch her had we been corporeal. It was jarring being this close yet unable to touch her. That didn't stop me from trying though. I reached out, but my partially transparent hand slipped right through my mother's shoulder. I held back a sob at the unfairness of it all as I tried to focus on what the vision was trying to show us.

My mom's long brown hair fell in a curtain around her face as she stared down into the wooden box. I followed her gaze, finding a golden blowing horn adorned with some of the largest gemstones I had ever seen. There were designs etched into it, but my mom closed the box before I could get a better look. She secured the latch, then placed her hand against the dirt, murmuring something I couldn't make out. In the next moment, the ground opened up, creating a hole big enough to fit the large box.

Maybe I was an elemental after all. What other creature could control the earth like that?

"I know where this is!" Jade's apparition said.

"Me too," Hannah offered.

I waited for them to explain, but they were too excited as they looked around. "Where?"

Jade smiled longingly at one of the trees. "This is behind our old sorority house. We used to have picnics here all the time. Your mom especially loved this place."

I was about to open my mouth and ask another question, but my mother started mumbling words I didn't understand. They sounded Latin. *"Vita et lux. Non sine luce vita."*

"That's not a spell I've ever heard before." Jade shook her head in confusion. "Come to think of it, I've never seen your mom using magic before either. I knew she had power, but I didn't know she could wield it like this."

"Me neither," Hannah agreed.

A blinding light seemed to rip through the air, and what started as a thin peek into another world expanded and shifted until a circular portal opened up. I held my breath as a man with honey brown hair and golden skin walked through. He was bright. It was as if life and light lived within his veins. His icy blue eyes took in the surroundings, and he tugged at his linen shirt.

My mom smiled brightly when she saw him. "Cyrus. It's been a long time."

He looked at my mother with gentle fondness, his expression slipping into something that mimicked familiarity. My mother held her stomach as she stood up, and his eyes zeroed in on the obvious bump under her palm.

"Oh, Celena. You're pregnant." His face fell, and a grief I hadn't expected took hold of him. He reached for my mother's hand, and she placed her fingers in his palm with friendly affection.

"I'm going to be a mom," she choked out.

"How is this possible?"

"I fell in love." Her eyes were glistening with unshed tears. "You'd like him."

He shook his head. "I doubt it. Celena, you know what happens when—"

"I know. I'm trying to find a cure, but we keep hitting dead ends. I'm due any day now." As she looked down at her stomach, a sense of longing overwhelmed me. "I fear I've run out of time, so I need to take precautionary measures."

"You should have called me sooner." The man frowned.

My mother's shoulders jumped as she giggled half-heartedly. "So you could throw me over your shoulder and carry me back home? I wanted to spend my last few months with my husband."

"You would have been a wonderful mother," he whispered, touching her bump with reverence.

There was a sinking sensation in my gut as alarm bells were going off in my mind. It was as if both of them knew my mother would die.

"I need your help." She swatted at a glistening tear before looking up at him with adoration. "You've always been there for me. I need you to look after this for my daughter. You know how dangerous it would be if it fell into the wrong hands before she comes of age."

"I swear it." Cyrus nodded. "But you know what I need to bond our magic together."

"I do." My mother produced a silver dagger from seemingly out of nowhere.

She held her hand above the hole in the ground before pricking the tip of her finger with the blade. She handed the weapon to the mysterious man beside her, and he did the same. A golden glow came from deep within the earth as droplets of their blood landed on the wooden box.

"I will be notified the moment anyone tries to unearth the horn," Cyrus stated. "Only a soul linked to our magic will be able to open it. When the time is right, I'll invoke your daughter's familiar."

"Her familiar?"

Cyrus grinned. "It is my duty to spoil your offspring, Celena. Besides, she'll need protection and support. It'll also allow me to keep a watchful eye on her. You know how dangerous this world can be."

"She'll be safe," my mother swore. "I've ensured it."

He smiled. "A fierce mother through and through."

"I do feel better knowing you'll be there for her. And a familiar is such a beautiful gift. It eases the pain in my heart to know she'll have such a special bond," she mused. "May I make a request?"

"Of course. Anything for you."

"Make it a wolf."

Cyrus shook his head playfully. "As if I would select anything else. Your daughter's familiar will feel my call when the time is right. I'll make sure the summoning horn is safe until then."

My mother smiled. "Thank you."

He gathered her into his arms, whispering something into her ear as they embraced. As he pulled away, my mom pressed two fingers to her lips before holding them out toward Cyrus as he stepped into the portal and disappeared.

My mom knelt to the ground once more, placing her hand in the dirt. In the next moment, the hole she dug had been sealed over, hiding the presumably sacred box.

"We need to get that box," Jade said the moment the vision faded.

"Agreed," Hannah added. "I can't believe Celena could wield magic like that, and we never knew. Why do I get the feeling there was a lot more she didn't share with us?"

"To be fair, she didn't talk much about her—" Jade gasped as if her voice had been choked off. "Damn spell. Let me try this again. Lena told us *what* she was, which for obvious reasons we can't tell you, but she never really spoke about her past. About the intricacies of being a *being that shall not be named*. Only that it was imperative to her safety that others assumed she was human. That they assumed *you* were human."

It was so odd to have confirmation I wasn't entirely human, but seeing my mother do what she did in that vision left no room for doubt. Physically speaking, we looked almost identical. There was no question Celena Fairweather and I were genetically related.

"You're sure that tree is behind your old sorority house?" I asked.

"Positive." Hannah nodded. "Or... it was the last time I was there. I can't imagine the university would've chopped it down though. They're really big on preserving green space."

"Only one way to find out." Jade clapped her hands together. "Looks like we're taking a trip to Massachusetts."

I sighed, feeling torn. "I know this is important. *I know* Macey's vision had purpose. But traveling across the country right now... with my dad being in the situation he is... I don't know if this is the right time."

Jade nodded in understanding. "I get that, honey. I really do. But you heard what that Cyrus guy said. You need a soul link to Celena to access the box. That's *you*, babe."

I replayed the vision in my head.

"Actually, what he said was, 'Only a soul linked to our magic will be able to open it.' So, in theory, I don't have to be there to dig it up, right? Only to *open* it? Could you two go by yourselves? It'd be easier for you anyway since you're alumni, right? If anyone asks why you're there, you could play the whole *visiting my old stomping grounds* card."

"I suppose," Hannah agreed. "But he also said he'd be notified if anyone tried to touch it. I don't know who that guy was, but I know he's powerful. I highly doubt he's going to just let us walk away with something so important to your mom."

"What if you brought Mace?" I suggested, causing her ears to perk up. "According to that vision, he's the guy responsible for sending her to me. Don't you think he'd recognize my link to her? He could easily deduce that you two wouldn't harm me since familiars can recognize intent to harm."

Mace barked excitedly as if she agreed with me.

Jade's dark brows furrowed. "I don't know..."

"Please. I can't go that far away from my dad right now, Jade. I just *can't*. And to be honest, I'd much rather know you guys are safe from this place, too. I don't think we should bring that horn back here while all this stuff with Alpha Jones is going down. If you can get it, you can protect it until the dust settles here and I can come to you."

Jade shook her head. "Nicole, the whole reason we're here right now is to help you. Leaving you defeats that purpose."

"I know, and I appreciate it. But you'd be helping me

by doing this." I placed my hands in a prayer position. "Please, you guys?"

"I don't like the idea of leaving you alone," Hannah said.

"I'd still have Bee," I reminded them. "*And* her father if shit really hits the fan. She's talking to him right now to give him the scoop on everything. He's been like a second dad to me my whole life. You know that. And you know he's capable of protecting me if need be."

Bee had stepped away to call her father only minutes before Macey gave us that vision. He'd been texting her, asking for an update, so I knew he was invested in the situation. I was genuinely surprised he hadn't brought in the cavalry yet. Bee said he had to be careful as a powerful alpha not to appear like he was challenging someone. But there was nothing that man wouldn't do for his daughter and, by extension, *me*.

Hannah and Jade exchanged wary glances before Jade said, "Well, I guess we have some packing to do then." She pointed at me. "But I expect regular updates from you, young lady. And if I don't get them *at least* three times a day, we're coming right back here."

I held my hands up in surrender. "Deal."

They held their arms out for a hug, which I readily accepted. "I love you, guys."

"Love you too, honey," they said in unison.

I pulled away from their embrace, tickling Macey behind the ear. "You take care of them, girl."

Macey barked in reply, licking my hand.

I laughed. "I love you too, Mace."

I had a good feeling about this. The fewer people I loved in harm's way, the better. And if we could get some solid answers about my mom's heritage in the process, bonus.

CHAPTER

SEVENTEEN

Nicole

Bᴇᴇ and I were sitting in the pair of Adirondack chairs located on the small porch outside of my room. Juniper was walking toward us, with some strange guy at her side. The dude's skin sparkled in the sunlight, making me giggle. I peered at him in confusion. Wait a second... Was the masking spell done already? Could it be?

"Corbin?" I asked, somehow picking up on his aura. Whatever her spell did made it easy for me to *sense* him.

"Apparently, you're supposed to call me Skidmore now," he grumbled in confirmation.

"Huh?"

Wow. Juniper's spell was impressive. Corbin looked *completely* different. He was taller, more muscular, and his facial features looked nothing like the boy I knew. But why was he walking funny? And why was he freaking glittery? My eyes widened when they fell below his waist and saw a clear dick print through his sweatpants. But that couldn't be right, because that thing was *way* too big to be an actual dick.

"Ouch," Bee said as her eyes settled on the same spot. "Homeboy is packing some disturbingly large heat, huh?"

Corbin froze mid-step as he spotted my best friend. His eyes widened, and he inhaled deeply. There were a few seconds where he just stared at Bee, as if in awe of her.

"Please..." he murmured. "What is your name?" He took a step toward her and reached for her hand, but my bestie snapped her fingers away.

"I'm Bee. Nice to meet you. Um, do you need to sit down? You look *very* uncomfortable."

Corbin glanced down at his body, as if suddenly remembering how ridiculous he looked before cursing. "Motherfucker. *Of course* this is happening right now." He turned toward June. "I really, *really* don't like you."

Juniper rolled her eyes. "Seriously, Skidmore. You're gonna have to get over it. It's just a little—" Her eyes widened as she looked between Bee and Corbin—er... *Skidmore*—and her lips curved into a grin. "Oh, this is too good."

What was going on? Why were they acting so weird? "Anyone want to clue me in?"

Corbin ignored Juniper and took another step toward

Bee, his eyes swimming with affection. "You're the most beautiful woman I've ever seen in my life. My name is Corbin, and I don't normally have a tail—"

At the mention of said *tail*, something long and furry reached from behind his back to stroke Bee's cheek.

My best friend swatted it away. "Personal space, dude."

He growled and grabbed his new tail, holding it behind his back before speaking to her once more. "I'm sorry. It has a mind of its own. Shit. I'm fucking this up."

"Are you okay?" I asked Corbin, deciding to take a break from punishing him for being so cruel to me. Something was obviously going on.

"No," Corbin spat. "I'm trying to talk to Bee here, but this fucking magical mask is messing up my game." Bee chewed her lip, and Corbin eyed her mouth with hunger, a slight groan escaping his lips. He then grabbed his thigh and started mumbling. "Football. Algebra. Mrs. Gertrude's granny panties."

"What is wrong with him?" Bee stage-whispered to me.

"I have no clue."

She lifted her long hair up off her neck and put it up in a messy bun. Corbin stared at the way she arched her back, her chest jutting out as she fixed her hair.

"God, it's hot out here," she complained.

"So hot," he murmured, echoing her.

"Hey!" I stood up, slapping him on the shoulder, forcing him to stop ogling my best friend. "No drooling!"

"Impossible. She is literally perfect." Skidmore wore a very Corbin-esque cocksure smile. "So... can I take you out sometime?"

Bee scanned his appearance once more, her eyes lingering on the clear package outlined by his gray sweatpants, obvious apprehension in her face. "You're sweet, but..."

Corbin looked down at his dick, which now seemed even bigger.

Ew. Was he getting a hard-on?

"Oh, don't worry about that. I don't normally have this big of a dick. It's the magical mask's fault. My real dick is actually pretty small."

Bee's brows raised. "Small?"

Corbin quickly realized his mistake. "I mean not *small*. Average. I normally have an average dick. Maybe a little *more* than average. Even better, I know how to use it. I will totally rock your world with my perfectly normal-sized dick, baby."

"This is very uncomfortable." Bee gave me a *Is this guy for real?* look.

Meanwhile, Juniper was laughing so hard she couldn't breathe.

Corbin scrubbed his shimmery hands down his face. "Look. All I'm trying to say is that my real dick isn't scary. I mean, this thing is a *weapon of ass destruction*." He gestured to his massive appendage. "But my normal dick is very satisfying and not at all dangerous. A perfect size, I promise. You'll see when this damn mask wears off." Bee just stared at him with wide eyes as his tail broke free and poked him in the eye. "Ouch! Motherfucking tail!"

Bee stood up, and before I could stop her, she grabbed his tail. The extra limb immediately wrapped around her wrist. "So you're the guy that humiliated my best friend on that recording, huh? You're not what I expected."

Corbin looked like he wanted to crawl into a hole and die. "I love Nicole like a sister. In fact, she's significantly better than my *actual* sister. I never wanted to hurt her."

"But you did hurt me, Corbin," I said.

"Shh, I'm talking to Bee."

I glared.

Jeez. I thought he came here to apologize for being so shitty, but all he can seem to focus on is my—

No.

No.

NO.

Realization dawned on me at that moment, and even though I wanted to be excited because I actually did sort of still like Corbin, I was horrified by what this meant for my best friend's safety.

"You asshole!" I yelled before slapping Corbin on the shoulder. "You went and mate bonded my best friend?"

He turned to look at me. "It's not like I had a choice!

And way to just announce it all willy-nilly. I was working up to that!"

"Mate?" Bee asked. "Oh. Yeah, no, I don't do the whole shifter thing. My dad would have an absolute shit fit." Bee untangled herself from his tail and took a couple of steps back. "Plus, you know, the whole thing you've got going on there"—she made a swirly motion in the general direction of the oversized bulge beneath his pants—"is not my cup of tea. It's boyfriend dick or no dick for me."

"Boyfriend dick?" I questioned.

Bee's lips turned up in the corner. "Yeah, you know... not too big that you'd be too sore to go back for seconds, but at the same time, not too small that you have to wonder if he's even inside you yet. Boyfriend dick is like the Goldilocks of peen. Juuuuusssst right."

Juniper, Bee, and I started cracking up.

Corbin pointed at my best friend. "Yes! That's what I've got! I mean... normally. I'm one-hundo-percent a boyfriend dick kinda dude."

Bee looked skeptical. "Uh-huh. Sure you are. But even if that were true, you're still a shifter, so thanks, but no thanks. I may have been raised by a shifter, but that doesn't mean I have any interest in being in a relationship with one. I know how most of you guys feel about humans."

"But..." Corbin's face fell so much I actually felt bad for the guy. "We're mates. I'm sure of it."

Her brows climbed toward her hairline. "Since you're

acquainted with Nicole here, I'm assuming you know she's my bestie, yeah?"

Corbin nodded dumbly. "Yeah. Of course."

"Okay... and so it would be fair to assume she told me *all about* how poorly she's been treated since *your* bestie realized she was his mate, right?"

He blanched. "Um... maybe?"

Bee snickered and pointed dual finger guns at him. "So, if you're such a smart guy, why would you *ever* think I'd be interested in going through something like that? I may know all about your little shifter world, but I'm human, dude. That's not gonna change."

Now he was frowning. "But..."

Oh, man, I really needed to change the subject. It was getting all kinds of uncomfortable here. Plus, knowing my bestie, I knew she was mostly all bravado right now. I could tell by the way she was pinching her brows together and choosing her words carefully that she was concerned about Corbin's claim. But she was also too prideful to show her anxiety in front of some guy she just met. I was sure she'd be on the phone again with her father the moment Corbin left. She knew all about mate bonds. When she finally opened up about her knowledge of the shifter world, she talked about how much her father still missed his mate.

"What did you come here to say, Corbin?" I asked.

The love-struck beta kept staring at Bee, his eyes full of sadness. "Right. Um..."

Juniper finally stopped laughing and pulled herself together. "Corbin wanted to grovel," she said encouragingly. "Right? Give it your best shot, bud."

"Right. Grovel," Corbin echoed, his tone faraway.

"And he wanted to ask you a few questions," June added.

He frowned. "Yep. Just a few."

Poor Corbin seemed to be having an existential crisis, and we weren't going to get anywhere at this rate.

Bee turned to me, my best friend seamlessly reading my thoughts. "I'm going to go grab some coffee—"

"Don't go to the local coffee shop," Corbin interrupted. "Juniper's brother likes to spell drinks there."

Bee cleared her throat. "Okay then. I guess I'll go to the library—"

"Don't walk by the gardens on your way. There are deadly plants that'll eat you alive. And stay away from the Rho Eta Theta house. The vamps will try to suck your blood. Oh, and the shifters like to run in the woods. Actually, if you could just—"

Bee giggled. "I've already been to the vampire house. *Thirsty Thursday* was a *bloody good time.*"

Corbin's nostrils flared as he agonized over his apparent jealousy. "I can assure you I'm more fun than any *Thirsty Thursday.*"

"Sure, big boy. Whatever you say." Bee gave him a skeptical look and then turned to me. "Is anywhere safe on this campus?"

Corbin scratched the back of his neck nervously. "Can you just stand here for a minute longer? I'm having a bit of a panic attack thinking my mate is just going to be walking all around campus without protection. How the fuck does Alexei function without going homicidal?"

His question made my chest ache. That was the problem, wasn't it? Corbin had just met Bee, and he was actively pursuing her and trying to keep her safe. Alexei pushed me away right from the start and had done some pretty fucking cruel things to keep me at arm's length.

"Oh, Nicole," Corbin said, finally, *finally* tearing his gaze from Bee to look at me. "I didn't mean it like that. Alexei cares about you. So fucking much. It's killing him to be away from you right now. He's protecting you, too. In his own way."

I swallowed the thick ball of emotions in my throat and let out a huff. "I kind of wish he'd stop trying to *protect* me."

Corbin's face darkened. "No. You don't. Trust me. Alexei is the only person standing between you and Alpha Jones."

Bee reached for my hand, offering me silent solidarity. "Maybe we should go inside to continue this conversation?" She looked over her shoulder, into my new bedroom. "So we can have some more privacy? Wouldn't want to risk some of those shifters who like running in the woods overhearing us, now would we?"

"God, I love you, Bee." Juniper tapped her temple.

"Smart, independent, and a good friend. If you ever want to join a coven, I'd love to have you." She turned to Corbin. "C'mon, Skidmore, let's get inside."

I held the door for them until all four of us were safely inside before closing it and turning the lock.

Corbin looked around. "Where's Mace?"

"She's with my aunts, Jade and Hannah. They went on a little adventure."

"Adventure?" June questioned. "What *kind* of adventure?"

Bee and June took a seat next to me on the edge of my bed, while Corbin painstakingly lowered himself into the chair at my desk, wincing because his third leg was straining against his pants.

"A supernatural exploratory adventure," I replied.

Corbin looked at the two women beside me before locking his green gaze on me. "How much do they know? How freely can I talk here?"

"They know everything."

"And what exactly *is* everything?" Corbin asked. "I've been in the doghouse for a little while but would really like my best-friend status reinstated so I can know all the dirt. Please and thank you. Also, I love you, and my sister is a major *see-you-next-Tuesday*, if you catch my drift. Your hair looks great, by the way. Have I mentioned that? I'm trying really hard to get back in your good graces, Nicky. Please love me again; I'm adorable, and I'm carrying around a dick the size of Texas to prove how much. Like *literally*. Do you have any idea how heavy this mofo is?"

Bee stifled a giggle. She really was a sucker for funny guys. Corbin definitely wouldn't let her down in that respect.

I let out a sigh. "It's hard to be mad at you when you're so... festive. And if you were trying to throw Mara off by lying, I *guess* that's a valid reason to be a complete asshat. As long as you swear you didn't mean it."

"I would never talk about you that way. You're Alexei's mate." He paused to look at Bee. "I take the mate bond *very* seriously. Nothing—and I mean nothing—would get in the way of me and my mate."

"Down, dog. You've made your point," Juniper said, breaking up the intense moment with a laugh.

I knew in my heart Corbin was a good guy and that I could trust him. And as much as I hated to admit it, I knew Alexei would go out of his way to protect me, regardless of whether or not I agreed with his methods. I supposed it was in my best interest to fill Corbin in on everything so he could share that with Alexei. It saved me the trouble of doing so. I may have trusted Alexei with my safety, but I didn't trust him with my heart. He'd been negligent with it too many times, and with everything else going on, heartbreak was the last thing I needed to deal with. It was easier to just stay away from him as much as possible.

"Just so we're all on the same page. My mom's not human. We know that for sure after Macey showed us a vision of my mom hiding some magical thing in the forest behind her old sorority house that is apparently super-duper important. *So* important that she's got some weird guard to watch over it. Jade and Hannah went to retrieve it, but they needed a link to my mother to access it, so I sent Macey with them."

"Macey? Why Macey?"

"Because she's Nicole's familiar, and Nicole shares DNA with her mother; therefore, Mace is that link by extension. Keep up, Corbin." Juniper waved her hand for me to continue. "Go on, Nicole."

"I don't know what my mom was, but I have a good feeling she was in hiding because she was in danger."

Corbin turned pale. "So being on Alpha Jones's radar is a bad thing."

"I guess we can just add it to the list of reasons that bastard wants to kill me." I started ticking off my fingers. "I'm Alexei's fated mate. My father is searching for a cure that's very important to shifters and he thinks I'm standing in the way of that. My mother is some sort of rare supernatural—"

"Don't forget that you defied a direct order and moved here instead of the Beta Phi house." Juniper beamed. "I would like to take credit for that, by the way."

"That too," I replied. "Oh, and I've formed an alliance with the vamps and the witches."

"My bestie is an overachiever," Bee said playfully, though her expression slipped into a frown.

Corbin cleared his throat. "About that. Maybe a blood oath with Cristian isn't a great idea, Nicole. It's one thing to donate on occasion for some extra cash, but a blood oath can be... sexual. Emotional. It's essentially a committed relationship."

I felt my anger rise. I didn't owe Alexei anything. "Neither you or Alexei have the right to make that decision for me, Corbin. I learned early on that I had to protect *myself*. Alexei isn't some knight in shining armor out to save me. If working with the vampire prince is the best way to keep me safe, that's what I'm going to do."

"Alexei *is* keeping you safe," Corbin argued.

"Is he? Because he isn't here right now. He doesn't want to be with me. Mara is the one with a ring on her finger."

"He would be here if he could."

Juniper and Bee watched our back-and-forth with rapt attention. "But he isn't. I get that he's scared of his father. I'm scared, too."

"You don't have *any clue* what Alpha Jones is capable of, Nicole. You've only seen a small fraction of the shit he's done. Alexei is smart to stay away."

I stood up, my voice rising in frustration. "Then tell me! Tell me why Alexei is so fucking terrified of his father."

Corbin's expression darkened, a shadow of pain flickering across his features. "It's complicated. Really fucking complicated."

I sighed. "Well, try to uncomplicate it, Corbin."

He leaned forward, propping his elbows on his knees. "Alpha Jones has never been a good man. For a long time, he *was* a good alpha. You don't get to run the largest shifter pack in the country without being a natural leader. A powerful leader."

"Why do I get the feeling there's a *but* coming?" Bee asked.

Corbin swallowed. "*But*, lately, Alpha Jones has been… short-tempered. Much more so than usual. And he's been… lashing out against weaker members of the pack. Alexei's worried about their safety. His dad's been… Well, he was *always* a firm believer in keeping our bloodlines pure and growing our numbers as fast as possible. But lately… simply being a wolf shifter isn't enough. Alpha Jones doesn't just want the biggest pack. He wants the *strongest* pack. We suspect he has a more… nefarious motive for hiring your father."

I frowned. "Like what?"

He shrugged. "Keep in mind this is all conjecture, and really, we've put the pieces together so recently that we haven't had much time to consider other angles, but maybe… we think it's possible Alpha Jones wants to find the missing wolf gene because he's trying to *make* more wolf shifters. Like an army of test-tube soldiers or some shit. It's the only thing that makes sense."

"Well, that's terrifying," Juniper said.

I knew Alpha Jones was a psycho, but this was next level. An army of shifters? For what? "So what do we do?"

Corbin let out an exhale. "That's the fucking question."

Bee pulled her phone out of her pocket. "I'm calling my dad. He needs to know about... well... all of this."

I nodded. "Yeah. Good call."

At my words, Corbin turned even paler than the glittery vampire he reminded me of. Turning to Juniper, he pointed an index finger in her face. "You'd better find a way to get rid of this"—he then pointed at his junk—"before I meet my mate's father."

Bee stood up and pressed her phone to her ear. "Not mates."

The moment she walked out the door, Corbin cursed. "Like fucking hell we're not."

CHAPTER

EIGHTEEN

Corbin

I wasn't the fucking main character. I knew that. Alexei knew that. If Redwood University was some soap opera, I'd be the loveable best friend that died tragically in some yacht accident, and my evil twin would run off with my girl.

But today I felt like I had the starring role in my own romantic comedy. Bee was the reluctant love interest. Alexei was the brooding side character. Nicole was the sassy best friend.

And the antagonist? Well, that would be General August Minifred, Bee's father. Yeah, I knew the man's name. What kind of mate would I be if I hadn't done a full background check on Bee and the people she was close to?

I practically ordered it the moment I looked into her beautiful eyes and realized I'd be eating her pussy for life. I had to admit, the general's military career was impressive. And to be honest, he scared the shit out of me now that he was going to be my future father-in-law.

I had a tactical plan of attack that involved flowers, puffing out my chest, and hiding this motherfucking tail. I stole some of my sister's Spanx to contain my massive eclipse of the dick, and even though it felt like I'd put a tourniquet around the annoyingly large appendage, it ensured that I wouldn't poke the man in his jugular when his daughter inevitably gave me a hard-on.

My girl was beautiful. Like "I wanted to put a baby in her belly *yesterday*" kind of beautiful. It was infuriating to know she wasn't on board with the whole bonded-for-life thing, but I was confident in my abilities to woo her. Disco skin, tiny wings, tail, and elephant dick be damned.

"You're sweating," Alexei pointed out.

He was enjoying this a little *too* much. I loved the man, but his roadmap to success had pissed his mate right the fuck off, and there was no way in hell I'd make the same mistakes as him.

Step one, convince Bee to love me back. The second I got my body back, I was dropping my pants to show her I had a boyfriend dick. There was no way she wouldn't fall for me on the spot. Then, I'd take her on dates where I showered her with gifts, compliments, and attention. I had a personal goal of her adding #Corbinsgirl to her

Wolfebytes bio by the end of the week. Wait... I supposed I needed to send her an invitation to Wolfebytes first. Then our social media coupledom could commence.

Step two, tell my parents I was mated to a human *after* draining my trust fund so that we had a nice little nest egg. Sorry, Mom and Dad. Your boy was all grown up now and found himself a nice human to marry. Either get with the program or enjoy spiteful holiday cards every December with photos of my epic life with my epic mate doing epic things. I had a feeling they'd come around once I got Bee pregnant. My parents wouldn't be able to resist little versions of me running around and causing chaos.

Step three, step down as beta. Run away to a quiet little town where no one will give us shit. Live happily ever after. The. End.

Easy, right?

Well, maybe not *that* easy. My entire career trajectory was built around being Alexei's beta. I'd already fallen head over heels for Bee, but the thought of leaving Alexei high and dry was giving me hives. Then, there were my parents. Carl and Mary Sullivan—also known as Dad and Mom—were strict as shit sometimes, but I loved them. Even if they were responsible for bringing Satan's spawn, aka Mara, into the world. The fact that my mom made the best chocolate chip cookies in the world softened that particular blow a little. I'd be crushed if she didn't give me her secret recipe to pass along to my kids one day.

So step four, help Alexei take over as alpha so that he

could change the shifter prejudice bullshit from the top of the hierarchy. If he publicly claimed Nicole and got Alpha Jones out of the way, then I could possibly-maybe-sort-of stay here with Bee.

"*Of course* I'm sweating. My mate is on her way here with her father." I was whining, but I didn't care if that sounded emasculating. This whole situation was fucked. "What if she gets into a car accident on the way? What if she's attacked? What if a guy with a normal-sized dick sweeps her off her feet and they run away together to Switzerland?"

Alexei snorted. "First of all, you hired an armored car."

"A necessity." I nodded.

"Secondly," he continued, "her father is a shifter and a general in the military. I'm sure she's *very* safe."

I pouted. "*I* want to be the one to keep her safe."

"And if she finds a guy with a normal dick, well, then I guess you could whip yours out and scare him off."

My best friend was an asshole.

"How do you function? I mean that seriously. I feel like my wolf is going to crawl out of my ever-loving skin." I scratched my arm for emphasis.

"I'm *barely* functioning," Alexei murmured.

He'd been such a broody asshole since he'd mated Nicole, and now I understood why. But we were completely different people. He liked to stew in his angsty corner and listen to poignant ballads that explained his feelings because he was too emotionally stunted to express himself like a normal evolved man. But me? I liked lists. And plans. And goals.

So... somewhere before step one, I needed to convince General Minifred that I was a fucking catch.

"You get to see Nicole today, though. That's a bonus."

I was trying to make my best friend smile. It took some careful planning and a secret back door that *wasn't* a euphemism for anal, but I'd found a way to get Nicole and Bee into Alpha Nu undetected. Juniper had some sexy witches distracting the enforcer watching us, and if that didn't work, she was going to make him fall asleep. Alexei couldn't come and go as he pleased without being followed like *Skidmore* could, but at least he'd get an hour or two with Nicole. I was kind of hoping they'd sneak off and fuck so he would stop being such a grumpy asshole.

If I were being honest, I wished we would have come up with this little rendezvous idea *earlier*—as in before I took this masking spell. That damn brilliant witch could have easily helped us sneak around the enforcers *without* turning my dick into a train wreck, but she couldn't resist giving me that damn lesson in humility. Total bullshit, if you asked me. There was nothing wrong with confidence, and I had that shit in spades. When I wasn't lugging around the monster in my pants, anyway. Fact of the matter was, I had to be smarter if I was going to protect my mate.

"And she's going to look at me like I'm the scum of the earth," Alexei deadpanned.

"Beggars can't be choosers, dude." I shifted in my seat. The damn Spanx was giving me a massive case of crotch rot. Why the hell did women wear shit that made them sweat so much? "It probably doesn't help that I'm doing such a spectacular job highlighting all the ways you're fucking this up. Sorry not sorry I'm so amazing at this mate bond thing, bruh."

If the dirty look he gave me was any indication, Alexei did *not* appreciate the reminder. "Speaking of... don't you think it's a little odd?"

I tilted my head to the side in question. "Don't I think *what* is a little odd?"

"That we both mated humans," he explained. "Fated mates have become such a rarity among shifters, yet both you and I have found our mates, and they're both human, which has never occurred before."

"That we know of," I pointed out. "Also... *your* mate probably isn't all that human, remember?"

He nodded in agreement. "Not entirely. But she *is* half, and we know that the other half *isn't* shifter. When has there *ever* been a record of a fated interfactional pair?"

"Never."

"Exactly," Alexei agreed. "So, why them? Why us? Why now?"

Those were all good questions. Fated pairings had become so rare throughout our lifetime that most shifters in our generation brushed off the possibility of finding one. Sure, we could all talk a good game, and some held on to the romantic notion of it, but for the most part, the word *mate* had become synonymous with spouse. Alexei's parents were proof that you didn't need to be fated to effectively lead a pack. Not that Alpha Jones was currently excelling at that, but he had in the past.

"Maybe we should research mate bonds more," I suggested. "Figure out what causes them and how they operate. This could also be another step in our evolution. More and more shifters are being born without wolves. Maybe fate has other ideas for us."

My solemn response was far too serious for my liking, but I genuinely believed it. Things were changing and you could either piss or get off the pot, and there was no way in hell I'd let a beautiful woman like Bee slip through my fingers just because the world decided we weren't meant for one another. Fuck anyone who stood in my way.

"I'll just add it to the list of shit I should have been doing the moment I found out Nicole was my mate," Alexei replied bitterly.

Damn, he was really rocking this whole martyr thing. I had half a mind to slap him across the face and knock some sense into him.

"We should make a ten-step plan—"

"You know I hate your plans."

I ignored him. "Step one, have sex with your mate. Both of you are too grumpy, and I think a couple dozen orgasms would loosen you up and clear your head."

A look of longing crossed his expression. The guy was

totally imagining himself eating my bestie out, and before Bee, I would have teased him for it, but I had my own mate now, and the amount of cold showers I'd had to take in the last twenty-four hours was downright shameful.

"Like she would ever even look at me. As long as Mara has a rock on her hand, Nicole is going to hate me. But I'm not ready to challenge my father yet."

"Step two, tell my sister to go fuck herself."

He gave me a wry look. "I just said I'm *not* ready to challenge my father. Don't you think going directly against his orders to propose to Mara would be considered a challenge?"

I shrugged. "Maybe. But a man can hope. She's really killin' your vibe."

Alexei frowned. "I can't shake the feeling she's involved in something really fucking bad, but I can't put my finger on it."

"Mara's always been a conniving bitch," I reminded him. "When is she *not* scheming?"

"This isn't her usual MO, though. She has this... confidence that wasn't there before."

I laughed. "Dude. My sister is the most conceited girl I've ever met. I don't think it's possible for her to *be* more confident."

"I'm not talking about her appearance," he countered. "She's acting like she has something on me. Like she's holding onto evidence that could destroy me, and she's just waiting for the right moment."

I cursed when I thought of something. "We know Mara set up that camera in Nicole's old dorm room, right? How long do you think it was there? And how often did you and Nicole speak openly in that room where she may have overheard something she shouldn't have?"

His brown eyes widened. "Fuck. I need to find out when that camera was planted."

"Yeah, you do." I nodded. "Knowing my sis—"

"Knock knock," a feminine voice called.

My heart fell right out of my ass. Like full on, it felt like I just took a massive dump and my heart was somewhere bleeding out on Alexei's floor.

"They're here!" I hissed before looking around the room.

I'd already made sure everything was cleaned up and had forced Alexei to put on a suitable outfit, but I still wanted to double-check.

Alexei sat up on his bed. Even though he didn't appear as nervous on the outside as I was, I still saw the way his eyes widened. Dude was freaking out about seeing Nicole and, as usual, I'd have to be the beta hero and smooth shit over.

Good thing I was a professional at my job.

"Come in!"

The door swung open and Juniper walked through first, her eyes scanning my appearance for a brief moment before she let out a short giggle. I seriously was going to get payback one of these days. The next person to walk through the door was my beautiful mate. Bee seemed to take great care with her outfit today. She wore tight black jeans and a button-down silk shirt. I was already mentally cataloging my closet so we could match. Yeah, I was man enough to be twinsies with my mate. Our Wolfebytes feed would be so epic.

And then Nicole walked in. She also put a little extra effort into her appearance, and I knew Alexei was probably trying not to pop a boner. *I hear that, brother.* Nicky wore a teal lace tank top and a cream cardigan over it. Her jeans were also tight, and whatever, she looked good. I didn't really care 'cause she was best friend territory, but I had to notice these things so I could compliment her better. Getting Nicole to love me again was step one-point-five. There was no way Bee would ever give me a chance without her bestie's approval.

Lastly, the general walked in.

Oh. Em. Gee.

Dude was a fucking *alpha.* I'm talking *the alphiest alpha there ever was.* The second my future father-in-law walked through the door, my wolf wanted me to crawl on the floor and submit. Even Alexei groaned at the ridiculous amount of power wafting off the man, and that was saying something. How did I not uncover this during my research on him? I felt so unprepared.

"Which one of you is the asshole that mated my baby girl?"

General Minifred had golden brown skin, fierce dark

eyes, and a buzz cut. His shoulders were broad, and I knew he could beat my ass with his pinky finger.

Alexei smirked and shook his head. Yeah, thanks a lot, jerk.

I slowly stood up, my tail straining against my Spanx like it was ready to cause some chaos. "Me, sir. I'm Corbin Sullivan. Future beta and business finance major. I have a perfect credit score, seventeen streams of income, and a list of references for you." I pulled out my leather portfolio and handed it to him. I truly hoped he appreciated the gold embossing on my resume. There was something to be said about fine stationery. People just didn't appreciate craftsmanship anymore.

His brows rose as I held it out for him to take, but he didn't grab it, so I just stood there like an idiot holding a heavy-as-fuck leather portfolio out. "Um, I included bios of both my parents. Health records proving I'm STD free—"

At that, General Minifred growled.

Okay, maybe mentioning my clean bill of health was too much. I was rambling. Fuck.

"He's great in bed," Juniper added. "A selfless lover."

I wasn't sure if she thought she was helping—witches were pretty open about their sex lives. She sent her twin brother a photo of my dick, for fuck's sake. But that was exactly the sort of commentary I'd been hoping to avoid.

Bee looked between us. "The two of you?"

"Not anymore," I quickly replied.

General Minifred looked at his daughter, then snatched my portfolio out of my hand. "I'm already not impressed."

I whined a bit, making his glare intensify. I'd never really cared that I was a beta before; it was still a high honor, but now I was worried he wouldn't think I was strong enough to take care of his daughter.

"Corbin is a phenomenal beta," Alexei said. "He runs everything in this place, and I trust him with my life."

General Minifred looked at Nicole. "Is this the idiot who broke your heart, Nicole?"

Whew. Shout out to Alexei for taking some of the heat off me. I was not above throwing him under the bus to make myself look better in this situation. I was a damn good beta and an even better friend, but this was my mate we're talking about. She's my number one.

"That's him, sir." I resisted the urge to point like a toddler telling his mother who pushed him on the playground.

Alexei arched his brow. Yep. He knew what I was doing.

The general gave my best friend a good once over. "Well, don't you look like a sorry excuse of a man."

I read on a blog that insults in the military were, like, a general's love language, so maybe this meant we'd all be hugging it out soon.

One could hope, right?

Alexei went all alpha and growled challengingly, though.

Not good, my man. Not good.

"Stop growling, maggot. I could take you with my eyes closed. How the hell do you think you're going to go up against your father in the current state you're in? You've got your alpha wolf locked down so tight I thought I was walking into a room full of she-wolves."

I smiled awkwardly. "Uh, good one, sir."

He turned to me. "Shut up. I don't care who the hell you are, but you are *not* dating or mating my baby girl. I don't trust you. I don't *like* you. And I have half a mind to make you run until you puke just for thinking it's okay to even look at my daughter."

I resisted the urge to whimper, because that clearly wouldn't go over too well with my future father-in-law. "Sir... I have nothing but the greatest respect for your daughter. And I take our bond *very* seriously."

Bee rolled her pretty brown eyes. "Dude. You seriously need to chill with this whole fated mates crap. I told you that's a *you* problem, not a *me* problem."

This time I *did* whimper.

Dammit.

I could definitely see why Alexei hated it so much whenever Nicole called him dude. I was usually a big fan of the word, but when these women wielded it toward their mates, it was pure flippancy. Leave it to me and my brother-from-another-mother to bond ourselves to smartasses.

Was this karma in action, or what?

General Minifred barked in laughter, pulling my mate into a side hug. "That's my girl!"

Alexei let out a cocky laugh, making everyone turn to him. I knew it was in his alpha nature to whip his dick out and tell people his was the biggest, but his little act wasn't fooling me. Probably because right now, *I* had the biggest one at the moment.

"You can try," he said with a chuckle.

"What's that supposed to mean?" Bee placed her hands on her hips in such an adorably sassy way that I suddenly became very worried about the structural integrity of my Spanx.

"*It means*, you can't fight fate. Nicole was just as drawn to me as I was to her. Doesn't matter how far you go or how much you fight it, you'll both end up together."

Nicole chewed on her tongue for about three seconds, which was apparently enough time for her to come up with a response that would rip Alexei a new asshole. "Actually, there are quite a few things that could make mates not want to be together. Betrayal. Humiliation. *Getting engaged to the devil.* I might have wanted you before, but when I look at you now, I feel nothing."

Well, smack my ass and call me Sally.

I didn't think the vibe in this joint could get any more awkward, but here we were. The moment Nicky's verbal punch hit its target, it felt like all the air got sucked out of the room. Her tone was laced with so much venom, so much conviction, I almost believed her.

Almost being the key word.

Because the one thing she couldn't hide was the pain in her eyes. The way her gaze sought Alexei out the moment she walked into the room.

Alexei ground his teeth together so harshly my own molars ached. "Keep lying to yourself, Nicole. It doesn't change the facts."

Nicky scoffed as she folded her arms over her chest but said nothing.

Bee and I exchanged a look that spoke volumes. I knew at that moment, she would be the perfect partner-in-crime to get these two fools back together. She wanted Nicole to be happy just as much as I did. And Bee could deny fate all she wanted, but I was confident in my ability to woo her to see what we had was real, too. Maybe if Alexei and Nicky could get past their shit, Bee would accept our bond. Then, it'd be a pussy-eating free-for-all, twenty-four seven.

Damn, I could hardly wait.

"Would you like to lose those eyes of yours, boy?" the general snapped, drawing my attention back to him. "Because if you keep looking at my daughter like you're imagining defiling her ten ways from Sunday, you're about to."

Crap. Evidently, I needed to add *don't get murdered by your mate's daddy* to my checklist.

Nicky's cell phone started ringing, drawing all of our attention to her. She looked at the screen, then up at General Minifred. "It's Jade."

My future father-in-law nodded.

Nicole answered the video call and smiled, but her surrogate aunt on the other line didn't even give her a chance to say hello.

"I've been digging holes for two days!" she screeched. "My blisters have blisters. My nails are cracked, and I have dirt in places where dirt shouldn't be!"

Nicky's brows shot up. "Heyyy, Jade."

"I just ordered a freaking metal detector, for God's sake! And I swear your familiar is laughing at me."

I could see the screen from my vantage point. Jade moved the camera to show off a very happy and very muddy looking Mace.

"I take it no luck finding the horn?" Nicky asked tentatively.

Jade huffed. "If I hadn't seen the vision myself, I'd say there *is* no horn. Do you want to know where Hannah is right now?"

Nicky cleared her throat. "*Do* I want to know?"

"She's meeting with the dean. Because apparently, two alumni digging dozens of holes on campus property in the middle of the night is *suspicious* and *concerning*. Stupid campus security caught us."

General Minifred cleared his throat and held out his hand for Nicky's phone. "Jade? Sounds like you're having a hard time. How can I help?"

"Can you dig?" she deadpanned.

General Minifred laughed. "I've got my hands full here. Want me to get clearance for your digging so the university will get off your back?"

"I want someone to rub my feet and hand-feed me grapes after all the manual labor I've been doing," she spat.

Nicky was holding her hand over her mouth, trying not to laugh.

"I'll book you a massage," General Minifred offered.

I didn't think it was possible for him to be kind, but apparently he knew how to be gentle when he wasn't talking to his daughter's mate.

Jade huffed. "And I guess some clearance would be nice. Make me sound super important and officially official. The girls at the sorority house keep looking at me like I'm crazy."

The general grinned. "Will do. Be safe and keep us updated."

Jade nodded. "Yes, yes. You keep Nicole away from her asshole mate."

Alexei grunted. "Nice to hear from you too, Jade."

"Oops," the mischievous woman chirped. "Talk to you later, I have holes to dig."

The moment the call ended, I spoke. "Is anyone

hungry? I had bread flown in from France and some champagne—"

"We're leaving," General Minifred said. "Wait for my instruction."

And with that, the love of my life walked out the door.

Alexei slumped in his seat, but I wouldn't let one bad meeting ruin my mood.

"I think that went well," I lied with a bold smile on my face.

I mean... well *enough*, right? It was the thought that counted.

CHAPTER
NINETEEN

Alexei

I WAS SITTING in my finance class, having trouble concentrating because I couldn't stop thinking about everything that had been going on. Failing really wasn't an option, but at the same time, grades were very low on my list of priorities right now. My mate didn't trust me. My father was up to something sinister, more so than usual. My best friend was walking around with a goddamned horse dick, pointing out what a shitty mate I was by showing Bee and Nicole how it should've been done from the start.

I just wanted to drag Nicole by the neck into my bed and fuck her until she couldn't see straight. But I didn't have time for that, and she didn't have an ounce of affection for me right now. I was getting so desperate for her that I was taking more cold showers than what was even remotely acceptable. I needed to get my shit together so I could work on winning her back.

"Mr. Koenig, would you mind answering the question on the board?"

I growled in frustration. Professor Asshole was one of Dad's informants, so I had to be on my best behavior; otherwise, I'd end up with another punch to the skull for being a disappointment.

I looked at the equation and knew I didn't have a fucking chance. I didn't review the chapter last night, and I already had to work twice as hard as everyone else because math wasn't my forte.

I grabbed the back of my neck in frustration. "I'm not sure, Professor Adamson."

Soft murmurs flowed through the room, no doubt out of shock or pleasure that I was dropping the ball.

The professor frowned. "See me after class, Mr. Koenig."

I could swear the entire class was thinking *ooh, you're in trouble now*. Fucking hell, this was my senior year of college. I shouldn't feel like I was about to be served with detention.

Fuck this. *I* was the future alpha. Maybe I needed to stop acting like a terrified little pup and start taking charge.

"Can't. Alpha business," I grumbled.

A human next to me blurted out, "The coffee shop is off Main Street."

At least the containment spell was still working, I supposed.

Professor Asshole stiffened, as if he wasn't used to being defied. "I *said* you'll see me after class. If you can't be bothered to learn the material, then there will be consequences—"

"Stanley. Can I call you Stan?" Rage and defiance were burning through me. I was exhausted and fucking tired of everyone pushing me around. Every minute of my day was scheduled by my father. My major and classes were hand selected by him, too.

"You most certainly *cannot.*"

"Stan, I'm *not* going to see you after class, and let me tell you why. You're *lucky* to be teaching here after you had that little slumber party with a coed three years ago and my father swept it under the rug."

A few giggles erupted as Professor Asshole turned beet red. It felt good to exercise a little power. Wasn't this what my father wanted? A ruthless alpha that took shit from nobody?

"Your father—"

I cut him off again. This guy wasn't my real problem. I knew he was just a sorry fucker in my path while I was having a complete breakdown, but I still aimed my rage at him. "I don't want to talk about my father. *I'm* your future alpha. And *I* am saying I have important business to attend to."

He seemed to finally get it. After a lingering moment, he relented. "Of course, Mr. Koenig. If you need more time to study the material, I'll send over some notes from my presentation."

I nodded once. "Good."

After a pregnant pause, the professor turned away and continued his lesson, going out of his way to avoid eye contact with me. I supposed getting your ass handed to you in public was something a man only wanted to endure once. I should feel bad about being such a self-righteous prick, but I didn't. Not when I knew this man was my father's lackey, doing his bidding like a bitch in heat, taking any scrap of attention my father would give him.

In fact, I was so pissed off that I decided class wasn't really interesting anymore. I stood up and all eyes fell on me. Stan's dry-erase marker froze on the whiteboard. I grabbed my shit and fixed my face into a furious scowl. I had a feeling my father would beat my ass for this later, but I wanted—no, *needed*—to fucking do something for myself.

My irrational anger drove me out of class, out of the business building, and somehow my feet dragged me to the one person who was able to calm me.

Nicole.

I sensed someone watching me, but I couldn't find it within me to care. Maybe my father would finally challenge me. Maybe I'd finally get the chance to beat his ass and take charge of my own fucking life.

I knew she was in Intro to Fashion Design right now with that fucker Cristian, which was driving me insane.

My phone pinged in my pocket just as I got to the door of her class.

> Alpha: Why did you storm out of class
> and insult Professor Adamson?

I groaned at the text. Of course Stan would cry to his alpha like a little bitch. I couldn't do anything here without it getting back to him. That was the problem, wasn't it? I couldn't be my own man. I couldn't make my own decisions.

I couldn't be with Nicole.

Not until I successfully challenged him, anyway.

I quickly typed a response, feeling bold behind the safety of my cell phone even though I knew he'd punish me for it, fabricating a lie on the spot.

> Alexei: I needed to check on the vampire.
> Heard whispers he's planning something.
> Also, Adamson is a spineless idiot who
> disrespected my role in the pack.

My father took a moment to respond.

> Alpha: Report back to me ASAP what the
> vampire prince is up to.

I let out a sigh of relief and pocketed my cell. If there was one thing my father hated more than me, it was anyone questioning our leadership. All the more reason why I was only going to get one chance to usurp him as alpha. I'd recently realized my father would never willingly step down from the role, despite the fact that I'd been training for it since birth. He didn't give a shit about tradition if he didn't think I'd be as ruthless as he was. I was capable, no doubt, but that wasn't the kind of leader I wanted to be. Especially not after learning about my father's suspected aspirations.

I needed to see Nicole *now*.

My wolf damn near exploded out of my skin when I spotted Cristian-fucking-Luca through the window, leaning into my mate, looking far too comfortable in such close proximity. Nicole laughed at something he said, making my proverbial hackles rise even further. I didn't know if she could sense my presence or if it was merely a coincidence, but in the next moment, she glanced up, looking directly at me through the glass. Her blue eyes flashed in warning, as if she could tell I was on the verge of losing my shit. When she gave a minute shake of her head, I knew without a doubt that was exactly what she saw in my expression.

I took a few deep breaths, gazing into her crystalline irises, allowing myself a moment to simply be. Her full lips curved into a sad smile as if she pitied me. I didn't want her damn pity, but I would take anything that wasn't the disgust she usually showed me these days.

In a brief moment of insanity, I raised my hand and curled my finger, beckoning her toward me. Her eyes widened for a fraction before narrowing in anger.

I swear to the fucking gods, my cock turned to stone. I quickly looked around and didn't see anyone in the hallway. This was my chance to get her alone on *my* terms.

Giving her a challenging look, I reached for the door handle, prepared to drag her out of there.

My wolf was on a warpath. Mates weren't meant to be away from one another, and after more than two weeks, I'd hit a breaking point.

She quietly excused herself, and Cristian looked my way. He must have seen the fury in my expression, because he moved to follow her, but Nicole touched his shoulder and shook her head.

The only reason he was still breathing was because he listened to her.

I felt feral.

Desperate.

Needy and angry.

I just wanted the taste of her on my tongue, her pleasure on my skin.

My wolf's instincts were in the driver's seat, and I was a willing passenger.

The moment Nicole stepped out into the hall, she grabbed my wrist and pulled me away from the door.

"What the fuck is wrong with you? Why are you here? What if someone sees?"

A low growl made my chest vibrate, my wolf urging me forward.

Claim her... claim her... claim her.

"*Mine.*" My proclamation made me sound like a brute, but I was more beast than man right now.

I took her by the hand, practically dragging her behind me as I searched for an empty room.

"Alexei!" she whisper-shouted. "What are you doing?"

I spotted a darkened room one door down and increased my pace. I tugged on the handle, grateful it wasn't locked, because I wasn't above breaking the damn thing down right now.

I pulled Nicole into the empty classroom and locked the door behind us. As was typical in the arts building, there were long tables instead of desks, which worked perfectly for what I had in mind.

"Alexei!" she repeated, jerking her hand out of my grip. "What the hell do you think you're doing?"

I crowded her against the wall, tucking my face into her neck. Nicole shivered as I took a deep breath, inhaling her sweet lilac scent.

"Alexei, what... are you doing?" This time when she asked, her tone was needy, not nearly as angry as it was a few moments ago. It was proof that she felt this magnetic pull between us. That her body knew where it belonged— in my arms. She scoffed when I said as much, but it morphed into a low moan when I pressed my lips against the nape of her neck once more.

"I'm so sick of being without you," I murmured as goose bumps scattered across her skin. "Please, Nicole. Just for a few moments, can you please stop fighting and give in to what we both want?"

She shook her head but gasped when my tongue snaked out, tasting the salt on her skin. "Stop." Her words said one thing, but the breathy tone she used said another.

"You want me to stop, baby?" I grabbed her hip and shoved my fingers up the hem of her tight little shirt so I could touch the soft skin there.

"You're engaged." Nicole braced her palms against my chest, though she didn't push me.

"The only person that owns me is *you*, Nicole. You know it. I know it. And Mara-fucking-Sullivan *definitely* knows it. I couldn't have made it any clearer to her that our engagement is a farce that I *never* intend to see through."

"I hate you," she croaked as I pressed tighter against her body.

My cock was eager to prove her wrong.

"No, you don't," I insisted. "You may wish you did sometimes, but you don't."

"You make me so mad! Why did you pull me out of class?"

I didn't want to talk about stupid classes. I wanted Nicole to give in, even if it was just temporary. I'd take whatever scraps I could get at this point. And maybe if I let her coat my chin with her pleasure, she'd forget that she loathed me altogether.

It was a long shot, but I was willing to put in the work.

"Because I want you. And deny it all you want, but you want me, too. But if it makes you feel better, rage. Scream." My mouth formed into a smirk as I dipped my finger behind the waistband of her skirt. "Be loud, baby. Don't hold back. Drag those sharp nails down my spine and bite my lip until it bleeds. I'll take your hate. I'll make it feel good for both of us."

I think we were both surprised when she started pawing at my belt buckle. "This doesn't change a damn thing, Alexei. It doesn't mean I forgive you. It sure as hell doesn't mean I trust you. I just really need to get off right now. I'm so sick of feeling numb."

My cock was trying to punch through the zipper of my jeans as she popped the top button. "Whatever you say, baby."

Her eyes narrowed into slits. "Don't call me that. Matter of fact, if you could stop talking entirely, that'd be great."

I raised my brows in challenge. "Make me."

She slammed her lips to mine, shutting me up the only way she knew how, and *fuck*, I was a goner. She tasted so sweet. Nicole was too damn good for me, but the way she swept her tongue across mine and sunk her teeth into my bottom lip made me want to do everything in my power to be good enough for her.

She broke the kiss with a gasp and shoved my pants over my hips, freeing my dick.

"I know I'm going to regret this," she said before jumping up to wrap her lush thighs around my hips, aligning her perfect pussy with me. I could feel how soaked she was through the thin barrier between us, and it made me groan in satisfaction.

She wanted me. She wanted *this*, no matter how much she claimed otherwise.

She sucked on my neck with an angry sort of passion, pulling my pulse through her teeth and biting down just enough to make it hurt. I cupped her ass and held her against the wall, grinding into her as I kneaded her flesh.

"Christ." I jerked away as her teeth clamped down even harder, drawing blood. There was no mistaking the copper scent in the air, nor the dark shine on her lips as she pulled away.

Jesus, why did I find that so hot?

"Fuck you, Alexei." She reached between us to slide her underwear to the side, pressing her wet heat against the head of my cock in invitation. "Consider it payback for all the times you've hurt me."

My wolf howled, the beast inside of me wanting to come out and play with the one raging inside of our mate.

"Let it out, Nicole. Show me how pissed off you are. Make me feel what you feel." I thrust inside of her with so much force her back climbed up the wall. "I'm an alpha to my core, baby. I can handle it."

"God," she whimpered. "Why do you have to feel so good?"

I pulled out almost entirely before pushing inside again. "Because this is meant to be, Nicole. Nothing will ever be better than this."

"Shut up," she groaned. "You're ruining it."

"You want to know why I pulled you out of class, Nicole? Because I wanted you. Because the idea of spending even one more second without your body clenched around mine was unacceptable."

Nicole's back arched, putting her round breasts on display beneath her tight shirt. "I said shut. Up!"

I banded my arm beneath her ass to free up one hand. I used that hand to push up her top, yanking the lace cups of her bra down until they acted more like a shelf for her perfect tits. "Fuck, you feel so good. You're choking my cock with that sweet pussy of yours."

"Goddammit, Alexei!" she moaned when I bent my knees, switching up the angle. "Seriously. Shut the fuck up, or I'm ending this right now."

Fine. If she didn't want me to talk, I would be perfectly happy using my mouth for other things. I sealed my lips around one dusky pink nipple, swirling my tongue, applying just the right amount of suction to make her toes curl. Nicole's shoes dug into my ass as I began to move in earnest, her nails clawing the back of my neck. "Tell me you hate me while I'm thrusting inside of you. I want to hear your breathy voice when you lie."

"I..." *Thrust.* "Hate..." *Thrust.* "You..." *Thrust.* "So fucking much." *Thrust.*

"Liar." I slammed my mouth against hers before she had a chance to protest. She yelped as I pulled back with a bite, returning the favor. "One of these days, Nicole. I'll be your peace. I'll make it right and we'll get our happily ever after. But right now? I'm going to fuck you to pieces."

"Then do it already!"

I would've laughed at the command, but there was nothing funny about the wanton look on her face. I pressed my mouth against my mate's, giving her what we both wanted as I fucked her hard and dirty. This was passion in its rawest form. Wild. Free. Pure motherfucking carnal desire.

I gripped her breast with one hand, rubbing the stiff peak between my thumb and forefinger.

"Oh, just like that!" she keened.

I stilled inside of her and smirked. "Let's get one thing straight, Nicole. *I'm* running the show right now." I pinched her lips together when she opened her mouth to reply. "Don't worry, though. You'll be too busy coming all over my cock to be mad about it for too long."

I began moving again to punctuate my statement.

Her head fell back as she whimpered, "Please... Alexei. Just... I need *more.*"

I dropped the hand that was on her chest down to her

clit. Nicole's entire body went taut as I circled my thumb over the sensitive bud. She was so fucking wet it was audible as I slammed in and out of her body.

"So demanding," I murmured, loving how heavily lidded her eyes had become.

I tucked my face into her neck, licking, nibbling, and sucking as I brought her to the edge of oblivion. Nicole was squirming so much I had to hitch her legs higher, holding on to her thighs with both hands again as I drove into her.

"So damn close," she whispered.

"I know, baby," I promised. "Just hold on."

She fisted my short hair with both hands, pulling hard enough to leave no question whether or not she intended to hurt me. Lucky for her, I'd seemed to develop a little taste for pain with my pleasure.

I could feel her impending release as she tightened her grip, her shapely thighs tensing around my hips. Her breaths grew ragged, her moans grew louder, as she tilted her body to chase me with every retreat. I quickened my pace, to the point where neither one of us was capable of forming words any longer. I ground into her with deep, merciless jabs that bordered on cruel, but Nicole was clearly loving every second of it. She took everything I had to give, and returned the favor. My mate screamed through one orgasm after another, pulling my hair, clawing my back, biting my lip. We would both be sporting bruises after this, but I didn't care. I thought our first night together was the most erotic experience of my life, but this topped it by a mile. Would it always be like this with her? Would each time be better than the last?

I couldn't wait to find out.

I was getting close, so I began toying with her clit again, determined to make her come one more time before I did. Within seconds, Nicole was a slippery, whimpering mess, screaming my name. I released a muffled groan into her neck as she clenched around me, choking my dick until I couldn't hold back any longer. I plowed into her with as much force as I could manage until I was falling with her into that pleasurable void where nothing else mattered. This feeling, being deep inside my mate, claiming her, *marking her*, was the only thing that held relevance.

Fuck.

As the aftershocks waned, I pulled out of her, wincing as the evidence of my oversight leaked down her thighs. Nicole shivered as I trailed my finger through the sticky substance, dragging it over her swollen flesh. I looked at her in question.

She nodded. "I'm on the shot. I got my last one right before I moved here, so we're good."

Part of me was relieved, but the more primal part loved the thought of her belly swelling with my child. I knew it was for the best right now though. Impregnating my mate was the last thing I should be thinking about with all these unknowns in our lives right now.

Nicole's palm pressed against my chest, prompting me to step back. "I meant what I said before, Alexei. This doesn't change anything."

She awkwardly righted her clothing as I growled. "The fuck it doesn't. The body doesn't lie, Nicole. What just happened here proves we're in this together. Whatever else happens, with my dad, your dad, what we learn about your mom, doesn't matter. We're on the same goddamned team! What's so bad about seeking comfort in each other?"

She lifted her chin stubbornly. "*What's so bad* is that I'm your dirty little secret, Alexei, and I refuse to be that girl! Do you have any idea how pissed I am at myself right now for giving in?" When she headed for the door, I thought about stepping in her way, but the icy glare she flashed made me reconsider. "Take care of the Mara situation. Stand up to your father. You do that, then maybe we can talk about whether we *have* a future. Until then..." She waved her finger back and forth between us. "This won't happen again."

I punched a fist-sized hole in the drywall as she left the room, leaving me in the dark with my fucking dick still hanging out coated in her cum.

"Dammit!"

I knew she was right, but that didn't mean I fucking liked it.

Nicole was mine. And I intended to prove it or die trying.

Nicole

GENERAL MINIFRED WAS a determined sort of man. I learned how resourceful he could be long ago. When Bee signed up for ballet lessons, he converted their basement into a studio, complete with a floor-to-ceiling mirror and a bar along the wall. He hired one of the best dance instructors in the area to give her private lessons. She didn't stick with it for long, but he was all in. Every whim she ever had, he supported.

When she took an interest in photography, he converted the forgotten ballet studio into a dark room and bought her one of the best cameras money could buy. Once he committed to something—especially when it was in the best interest of his daughter—he truly committed.

He wasn't afraid or ashamed to use whatever resources he had available to take care of her, and since meeting his daughter's fated mate, he seemed motivated by a new sort of objective:

Keeping his daughter away from Corbin.

I trudged through the leafy woods beside my best friend with Alexei and Corbin following about twenty feet behind us. They miraculously were giving us space because Bee threatened to never speak to Corbin again if they didn't give us some breathing room. General Minifred had been hard at work the last week on something—but we didn't know what. Part of me wondered if he was drawing us out here so that he could kill the boy hopelessly in love with his daughter.

We had to be secretive. After Alexei's and my moment in the classroom, Corbin—or *Skidmore*—said that Alpha Jones was watching Alexei more closely. I also saw my reluctant mate sporting a black eye on campus, but I didn't know where he got it. I didn't *want* him to get hurt, and even though I was still navigating my own pain and regrets, I worried about him getting in trouble by coming here.

"So you don't have any clue what your father is planning?" I whispered to my best friend. She shook her head, then looked longingly over her shoulder at Corbin. The spell Juniper gave him had not worn off, but he had somehow found a way to contain his tail and oversized appendage.

Bee seemed distracted. "I have no clue. Hey, do you think I should talk to Corbin? He's been sending me gifts practically every hour. Your bedroom is full of flowers."

I knew without a shadow of a doubt that Corbin would pursue Bee relentlessly. He was a romantic at heart, and when he put his mind to something, there was nothing that could get in his way. Corbin sent flowers, poems, designer purses, photography props—you name it. The last gift was a commissioned painting of the two of them cuddling in a forest.

Even though Bee was strictly against any sort of shifter mate bond, I could sense that she was flattered, at the very least.

"I think you should do whatever feels right," I replied, even though there was a bitterness to my words.

It stung to see Corbin jump with both feet into a relationship he knew would be looked down upon by his community. It kind of made me jealous, and I hated that I felt that way.

Bee nudged me. "I'm here to focus on *you*, not find a new boyfriend. It feels... wrong."

I laced my fingers through hers and gave her a gentle squeeze. "Corbin can be a pain in the ass, and he really hurt my feelings..."

"Why do I feel like there's a *but* coming?"

I sighed. "*But* he was one of my first friends I had here. Don't get me wrong, we had a very rocky start, but he quickly became someone I enjoyed spending time with. If you feel like you want to get to know him, don't hold back on my account."

At my back, I heard Corbin hiss an excited "Yes!"

Damn shifter hearing.

Bee blushed. "I'm not even sure what I want right now. My dad has drilled it into me that the shifter community isn't safe—especially for humans. I see how much pain you're in, and I—"

I let go of her hand to wrap my arms around my middle, feeling sad for a moment.

"It's a mess," I agreed. "At least your mate isn't rejecting you, lying to you, and getting engaged to a girl that made your life a living hell. Corbin's intentions seem genuine. I think if you're even a little curious, you should give him a chance to be your friend. The mate bond is unbelievably intimidating and not something I ever envisioned for my life. And I don't think you should tie yourself to someone because you feel like you have to. But there's no harm in getting to know Corbin."

The guys stopped walking, and a quick glance told me that they were watching our backs with devoted scrutiny. I wanted to know what Alexei was thinking. I also hated myself for still feeling so attached. Our hookup in the classroom a week ago had been admittedly hot, but it left me feeling even more hollow than before. I loathed the fact that I gave in so easily to the man who had hurt me. Not to mention, it felt wrong to be with him when there was so much up in the air. Alpha Jones was a dangerous man, my father was still imprisoned, and Jade and Hannah were out looking for some magical gift my mother set aside for me.

Movement in the woods ahead drew our attention. General Minifred poked his head through the thick brush of leaves and gestured for us to follow after him.

"Something tells me my father doesn't want me to talk to Corbin," Bee whispered.

I let out a choked laugh. "You think? I'm surprised the boy is still alive and not buried in a ditch somewhere."

Bee giggled. "Come on, my dad deserves more credit than that. He's a war general. He wouldn't just throw a body in a ditch like some average criminal. He'd probably use a wood chipper or dissolve the body in lime."

"True," I agreed.

Once again, Corbin spoke up at our backs to Alexei. "Are you sure it's safe for us to be following them deep into the woods where no one can hear us scream?"

"Why would *I* be screaming?" Alexei asked. "You're the idiot who mated with his daughter."

"Uh... did you miss Nicky's harsh recap on what a shitty mate you are?"

"Definitely didn't miss that part," my *shitty mate* huffed. "But I really don't think Bee's dad brought us here to off us."

"Then why was he being so cryptic as to *why* he wanted to meet?" Corbin questioned. "Dude, I don't wanna die with a damn lion's tail and a donkey dick."

My best friend giggled while I bit my tongue so I didn't do the same.

"Oh, for shit's sake!" General Minifred griped. "You do realize I can hear everything your dumb ass is saying right now, don't you? If I have to listen to you bitch about your raging case of elephantiasis one more time, I swear, I *will* make you scream!"

"Crap," Corbin muttered. "Save me, Alexei."

"Boy, you'd better stop moping and get your ass over here before I drag you by your tail," General Minifred shouted.

Corbin did a little jump, then sprinted through the woods, breaking through the thick brush in a hurry. Alexei sighed and quickly walked after him. I wasn't sure if it was because he was worried about General Minifred kicking his best friend's ass or if he wanted to make sure Corbin didn't do anything stupid.

"Drop down and give me twenty," General Minifred yelled as Bee and I made it over to him. Corbin dropped to the ground and let out a little scream when his pelvis hit the dirt a little too hard. He started doing push-ups while Alexei growled. "You too, boy."

I held back a laugh as Alexei did as the general-turned-drill-sergeant asked. I wasn't sure if General Minifred intended for Bee and me to start drooling at the sight of our mates doing push-ups, but that's what happened. Alexei's corded muscles flexed as he dipped down to the ground and back up.

Corbin's arms shook. "For the record, I'm great at push-ups when my body isn't—"

"Twenty more, boy."

I took a moment to look around, surprised by the cleared trees and workout equipment. It looked like the general brought us to one of those extreme warrior races crazy people always liked to participate in. There was one obstacle after another, starting with low-strung barbwire over a patch of mud. After that, was a rope climb over a giant wooden wall. The four of us walked around, taking in each part of the course, our confusion getting thicker by the second.

Corbin tentatively raised his hand. "Um… General Daddy… er, I mean, *sir*… what *is* this?"

A deep rumble sounded from the general's chest as he glared at the poor beta before turning his attention to Alexei. "Do you still plan to challenge your father?"

Alexei swallowed. "Yes, sir. But I need to make sure I'm ready first."

General Minifred spread his arms, gesturing to our surroundings. "Well, this is going to help you get ready."

Alexei's dark hair fell onto his forehead as he shook his head. "I don't understand."

"Are you an idiot? I'm training you. Welcome to hell."

Bee nudged me. "We should get your friend to help us conjure a couple lawn chairs, a margarita machine, and some snacks."

I rolled my eyes. I wasn't sure what sounded better—

watching the general scream at Alexei and make him run until he puked or watching my shirtless, estranged mate workout for hours. Definitely the first option. I wasn't about to lust after Alexei again. Last time I was weak, we fucked in a classroom, and even if some part of me felt like it was the hottest sex of my life, I would *not* be repeating that mistake again as long as Mara had a ring on her hand.

Alexei crossed his arms over his chest. "Why are you doing this?"

General Minifred scowled. "Are you questioning me?"

"I just want to know what you're playing at. I know you want to protect your daughter and Nicole, but you seem invested in me becoming alpha. I just want to make sure we can trust you."

I gasped, but Bee's dad didn't back down. "I work with a specific sector of the military. We keep an eye on things. I've been following your father's ambitions for a while with the help of an informant."

Bee's mouth popped open in shock, making me realize she didn't know this.

"Dad, you've known what was going on here?"

He nodded. "I wasn't exactly prepared to make a move yet. There's been quite a bit of red tape, but you moved up my timeline when you called to tell me you were visiting Nicole. But now, it's in everyone's best interest that Alexei is prepared to challenge his father. As soon as possible."

We all sat there stewing over his words, more questions forming in my mind as I processed everything.

"Wow," Bee said.

"Are you going to help me get my father back?" I asked, my tone small.

I'd been growing more and more anxious. Corbin fed me updates about my father when he could, but it wasn't enough.

"I think the best way to get him back is by making Alexei the alpha. My unit is prepared to go against Alpha Jones if need be, but I don't want to start a war. Not unless we're forced to."

I nodded, not feeling encouraged. A lot was riding on Alexei. Could he truly do this? Save my father *and* keep me safe?

"I guess we should get started. I need to find a nice shady spot to watch," Bee said, lightening the mood.

"You'll be participating," General Minifred said to us.

"I'm sorry... what?" Bee asked, her eyes wide with horror.

I, also, felt a little taken aback. My idea of a good workout was jogging through campus, not military boot camp.

"You want to prove to me you're good enough for my daughter, Corbin? You're going to rescue her."

"Rescue?" Bee and Corbin asked at the same time. It was kind of cute how they both squeaked that word out.

"Nothing more motivating than a mate." General Minifred cleared his throat before continuing. "You'll crawl through hell for your mate. Do anything to help them. I'm going to use that motivation to turn the two of you into worthy shifters."

"What do you mean *rescue*?" I asked.

General Minifred nodded to the intense course at his back. "I hope you aren't afraid of heights, girls."

I followed his gaze up to the highest point of the course and dropped my mouth open. A rock wall the height of a towering building led up to a platform with some chairs.

"Please tell me there's an elevator to the top," Bee said.

Juniper walked out of the trees, looking like a fairy princess in a green tracksuit. "I can magic you up there."

"What's *she* doing here?" Corbin asked, his face turning pale.

Ever since it came out that he and Juniper used to hook up, he'd been doing everything in his power to keep June and Bee apart.

The coy witch ignored Corbin and winked at the general. "Hello, August. The perimeter spell is complete. Your hair was very potent. Have you ever considered monetizing your pubes? You'd make a killing selling a few strands to a witch."

I gaped at my friend. Since when were she and Bee's father on a first-name basis? I had *never* heard anyone address him so casually before. Although, I supposed if anyone had the lady balls to try pulling that off, it'd be June.

Wait, a second... did she say *pubes*?

"No." General Minifred laughed. "But I'm glad it worked for our purposes."

"Did she say *pubes*?!" Bee hissed, echoing my thoughts.

Juniper seemed unfazed. "Anyone who's anyone knows that hair taken from more *intimate* places holds greater power."

My best friend gagged. "Please tell me you didn't collect the specimen yourself. And while you're at it, please tell me I'm having some really weird dream right now and we're not *actually* having a conversation about my father's intimate *anything*?"

Her dad flashed an admonishing look at the purple-haired witch. "Sorry, honey, Juniper here was supposed to keep that part to herself."

"I don't see what the big deal is." June shrugged. "We all have 'em. Well... not *all* of us, I suppose. I'm a Brazilian kind of girl myself. Right, Corbin?" She winked at him.

"Oh God," Corbin whimpered. "Junie, we talked about this."

The general glared at him.

Meanwhile, Bee laughed. "Please. Do you think I care?"

Corbin's head snapped to her as his mouth gaped. "You *should* care!"

"Why?" Bee challenged.

Corbin looked nervously between his mate and her father. "Bee... maybe we should have this conversation another time. Like, when your pops doesn't look like he's about to alleviate my head from my shoulders?"

"Like that's ever going to happen." The general scoffed before turning back to Juniper. "You're sure the spell is working? Nobody will be able to see or hear us?"

"I'm positive," Juniper replied. "I even sprinkled in a little extra diversion. Anyone who tries coming out this way will suddenly have an emergent need to find a toilet before they shit themselves."

General Minifred nodded. "Nice touch."

Juniper curtsied. "Thank you."

"Let's get started, shall we? If you manage to make it through the first four sections of the obstacle course, I'll be impressed." General Minifred gleamed, and I knew he was absolutely looking forward to running them ragged.

"Can we possibly have a rundown of said obstacle course? Also, do you have insurance on a thing like this? Has it been tested for health and safety standards?" Corbin rambled.

"A rundown? It's not that hard to figure out." General Minifred glared at him. "You make it from one side to the next. Period. And I can assure you, it's *a hell of a lot safer* than the things I'm imagining doing to you with my bare hands."

Corbin frowned. "I'm totally returning the *World's Best Father-in-Law* shirt I got you."

Bee's dad pinched the bridge of his nose as she swallowed a giggle. "Juniper. Please get the ladies to their station and light the fire."

"Fire?!" Corbin shrieked. "Do you really think it's wise to start a fire in the middle of a forest?"

Alexei, who had been notably quiet during all of this simply nodded once as he smacked Corbin's side. "Thank you, sir. I'll work hard." He shot a glare at his beta. "Corbin will as well. I know you didn't have to train us, but you are. Protecting Nicole, Bee, and Dr. Fairweather is of great importance to us. We understand what's at stake, and we won't let you down."

The general actually looked impressed for a second. "You can thank me *after* you pass. *If* you pass." He grabbed the whistle from around his neck and blew. Every one of us winced at the shrill sound. "*Now move!*"

Alexei and Corbin practically dove into the mud pit, army crawling under the barbwire. I winced as the jagged metal caught on the backs of their shirts, but they didn't slow their pace one bit. Then again, if General Minifred told *me* to move, I would probably run as far away from him as fast as possible, too.

TWENTY-ONE

Alpha Jones

"Oh, Alpha!" the bitch beneath me moaned. "You're so big I feel like you're about to rip me in half!"

I appreciated the compliment but needed her to shut the fuck up if I had any hope of coming. Mara Sullivan had a tight little cunt that choked my cock, and her tits were large and perky, but her voice grated on my nerves. My fingers flexed around the back of her neck as I rutted into her from behind. I really wanted to wrap my hand around the front of her throat and squeeze—always an effective way to silence someone—but I managed to restrain myself, making a note to gag her next time.

I was focused on the prize.

I was going to put a fucking baby in this bitch.

As irritating as the blonde little whore could be, Mara was one of the most powerful influencers shifters had seen in over a hundred years. And she was young and fit. There was no way a pup formed between the two of us wouldn't be worthy of being my successor. I could start over, ensuring his utter devotion. He'd be someone who knew what it took to lead.

My current heir certainly didn't fit that description.

My wife, Anya, was a decent companion for the first few years of our marriage, but she couldn't give me any more pups, no matter how often I filled her with my seed, which was infuriating. If I had known she wouldn't have been able to fulfill her breeding duties, I would've never pursued her. Well, okay, that wasn't entirely true. I saw her potential the first time I spotted her. It was at the annual alphas' banquet where each alpha in North America and their family donned their finest formal attire and got together. It was mostly a bunch of posturing, but the main purpose behind the event was to forge business connections with one another, to strengthen our race.

Anya and I were only sixteen when I first noticed her, but even then, I could see her effect on others. People naturally gravitated toward her, vying for an ounce of her attention. Not only was she drop-dead gorgeous, but she had this natural charm that made others want to bask in the warmth it provided. When I'd learned she was already mated to another future alpha—the sole reason she was even attending the event—I knew others would instantly respect her as *my* luna, provided I could eliminate the problem of her current attachment.

I wasn't one of those fools who romanticized the idea of finding their fated mate one day. I'd always been inclined to say *fuck the fates*. They didn't get to choose my destiny. I very much believed it was an issue of mind over matter, but I understood the power the idea of being fated held over the general population. To any respectable alpha, marriage was a business transaction, nothing more. You couldn't properly focus on your pack if you were worrying about pathetic feelings like love. But it was obvious my future bride and her mate were disgustingly enamored with one another, so I had my work cut out for me.

Good thing I was the most driven shifter I knew.

I put a plan in place. I knew it would take some time, but I also knew it would be worth it once my supposed competition was eradicated. It wasn't easy making murder look like an accident, but if you wanted something badly enough, you made it happen, no matter the conse-quences. It was the true test of a worthy leader. Many couldn't stomach the violence that was occasionally required to be an effective alpha. But I didn't suffer any conflict where my conscience was concerned. So, I bided my time, watching Anya from afar until I could set things in motion. Then, after allowing her a brief time period to grieve, I finally introduced myself to her and gave her the full courting experience any bitch would salivate over from a man like me. Anya didn't stand a chance of resisting my advances.

Sadly, the honeymoon period didn't last long. Once our family doctor confirmed she couldn't produce any more heirs, my interest plummeted and my frustrations rose. I was man enough to admit she did make a great luna. Maybe even *too* great. My pack adored her, which made divorce an unfavorable choice politically. Left with no other options, I began seeking comfort in she-wolves who were eager to please. I'd needed an outlet for my anger at the unfairness of it all, and those bitches didn't mind being slapped around a little. They *wanted* me to treat them like the whores they were, something I was smart enough to know my wife would *never* tolerate. Even though Anya was physically stunning all these years later, she was nothing more to me than a political advantage. A collection of holes to drive my cock into when I was sick of my playthings.

But now that the one heir she'd provided me had proven his worthlessness beyond a shadow of a doubt, it was time to implement Plan B.

"Yes! Yes! Yes!" Mara screamed.

I increased my pace, thrusting so hard the leather couch she was bent over was pushing across the floor. I jerked a few more times, filling her up with my godlike seed, and then slowly pulled out so I could take my index finger and shove what was seeping out of her back inside.

"Mmm, yeah, Daddy. Fill me up with your hot cum."

"Hold it in, Mara." I watched as her swollen pink pussy clenched at my command.

This filthy slut loved that shit, thought it was hot as fuck when I did it. But this wasn't a matter of her pleasure. I didn't give a shit whether she got off. But I wasn't about to waste a single drop of semen and continue meeting like this longer than what was absolutely necessary. Mara was a decent fuck, but every time we did this, we increased our chances of getting caught. And that was something I couldn't ever allow to happen. The consequences were too detrimental to my cause.

I fastened my pants as she pulled her little dress over her head. Mara never bothered with any undergarments when she came to see me, because there was no point. She was here to serve her pussy up on a silver platter, and she was expected to make that as easy as possible. Trashy lingerie, no matter how appealing it could be, had no place here. It only got in the way.

"Have you managed to bed my son yet?"

Mara's eyes shifted to the side. "Not yet. But I promise it'll happen soon!"

"What the fuck is taking so long?" I charged, caging her against the wall. "You have *one job*, Mara, and that's seducing my son! How are you supposed to play it off as his pup when you get knocked up if you haven't actually succeeded in fucking him?!"

Her eyes watered. "I promise I won't fail you again, Alpha! I'll make you proud!"

I slammed my fist into the wall right beside her head. "You'd better, you little cunt."

"I will!" she cried. "I won't let you down."

She'd better not screw this up for me.

We had a plan. Mara would seduce my son, while using a condom, of course, so his seed wouldn't compete with mine, and when I successfully impregnated her, she would name Alexei as the father and claim the condom failed. Once a new male heir was produced, I could rid this world of my useless firstborn once and for all. Should anyone question it, any standard DNA test would prove a blood relation, so Alexei couldn't deny his supposed paternity.

It was easy. A brilliant solution to my little problem. My son had been a disappointment for far too long, and it was time to rectify that.

"I think it's that nasty human's fault," Mara spat, eyeing me cautiously. "Alexei would be eating out of my hand by now if it weren't for her."

"Nicole?" I asked.

Mara took my one-word reply and ran with it. "He's always looking at her with these pathetic lovesick eyes. I overheard him talking to Corbin about her a couple of times, too. They never say enough for me to fully know what's going on, but something isn't right, Alpha. Alexei is practically obsessed with that slut. She can't be *that* good in bed, can she? Why is he so hung up on her?"

"I'm looking into it," I snapped. "You know that already."

Sure, I'd noticed my son's infatuation with the wacky scientist's daughter. He tried to hide it, but I wasn't ignorant. I didn't particularly care if Alexei wanted to fuck a human, but I *did* care if his intentions with one went beyond satisfying a physical need. I wouldn't allow him to embarrass me like that, regardless of whether his days were numbered. That was why I had Mara plant that hidden camera in Nicole's dorm room. I needed to know how deeply he was involved with this girl so I could prevent it from getting any worse. I didn't think my childish plaything would explode with jealousy and share the video with the pack, making a laughingstock of my family. But I took great pleasure in punishing her with a raw, relentless ass-fuck. I was confident she wouldn't dare defy me again.

Sadly, I didn't think of planting a camera until two days before the stubborn bitch moved into the witches' sorority house, so we didn't get anything more than a recording of my son sticking his prick into a human. Mara had another surveillance system set up in the room that was reserved for Nicole at Beta Phi, but seeing as she defied a direct order and was now living at Kappa Zeta, that wouldn't help either. While I could admit seeing Nicole Fairweather in all her naked porn-star glory had made me hard, I personally found humans to be too fragile for my tastes.

They had such brittle bones that broke during a good fucking. The cracking sound really got me going, but the mess afterward was such an inconvenience. Plus, I tended to bruise and bite my partners while fucking. A fellow shifter would understand the brutality when animal instincts took over, but puny little humans didn't. They always wanted explanations for things like that—and were quick to cry abuse—which was asinine in my opinion.

The most confounding part in all of this was that I had no doubt Alexei's callousness while Mara was playing the video for the entire sorority was staged for *my* benefit. His entire demeanor shifted the moment he saw me walk into the house. I did, however, believe my son's claim that he spouted all that mate bullshit to get the key to Nicole's chastity belt. Who *hadn't* told a little white lie in the name of getting laid? I certainly couldn't fault Alexei for doing something every man in history had done at some point in their lives. Besides, everyone knew a shifter couldn't ever be fated to a human. But what I didn't know was *why* he was so desperate to bag this particular human and why it seemed like he was *protecting* her. It made no damn sense that some average little nobody had my son and his beta wrapped around her finger. The vampire prince, too. Nicole Fairweather reeked of human in every way, but something wasn't adding up.

I didn't like it when things didn't compute. I wondered if Nicole's troublesome witch friend brewed a love potion. That would certainly explain things—at least partially—

although my gut was telling me something bigger was at play. Something far outside the realm of perceived normalcy. I still suspected she did, in fact, somehow remove the mental block from her father's brain, whether she was aware of doing so. And I knew without a doubt, a human wasn't capable of that without some kind of magical assistance. I *would* find the truth, because knowledge was power, but I had bigger issues on my plate at the moment. The world needed a strong leader to rally us into a new age. And since Alexei would be dead soon anyway, his crush was of little consequence in the grand scheme of things.

"If she was out of the picture, then maybe I could—"

"You'd let a human stand in your way, Mara? I thought you were more ruthless than that. Perhaps you *shouldn't* be the one to bear my heir after all."

Mara blanched. "No. Of course not. I just think getting rid of Nicole would make it easier."

"Not until Dr. Fairweather has a breakthrough. There's nothing more pathetic than a grieving human. It's obvious his offspring is the center of his world. My threats would be useless if he felt he had nothing to live for, and I need him to stay motivated to find the cure so I can fulfill my promises to the pack." Among other things. "Nicole stays. *For now*. I don't care if you have to drug my son and mount him in his sleep. You *will* fuck him. You *will* make sure there isn't a doubt in anyone's mind whose baby you're carrying once you're knocked up. Because if you don't, I won't hesitate to kill you and find a replacement. Understand?"

"Yes, Alpha. *Of course*, Alpha." She bowed her head, her trembling fingers making me confident she took my threats seriously.

"You're lucky you're young and breedable, Mara. Lesser men wouldn't put up with your failures. Be sure to remember that. You're the mother to a future alpha. Act like it."

Tears formed in her eyes, and her mouth popped open, giving me an excellent idea. "I take this responsibility *very* seriously."

"Prove it."

I took one step closer, looking down my nose at her. The sound of seams ripping apart echoed throughout the room as I pulled her dress over her head, tossing the flimsy garment aside. Mara's surgically enhanced tits bounced as I shoved her to her knees and pulled my cock out. I threaded my erection through her lips, straight back to her throat until her nose was buried in my meticulously groomed patch of hair, and she was gagging around my girth. I held her there for a moment while she struggled to breathe, before pulling out.

Saliva poured out of Mara's mouth as she gasped dramatically for air. I gave her just enough time to take one breath in before repeating the motion over and over until I felt my balls tingling in warning. Right before I blew my load, I yanked her upright, bent her over the arm of the couch again, and shoved myself inside her cunt. I grunted as I came, pushing her face into the cushion so hard she was clawing the leather with her fingernails, once again struggling to breathe. I preferred her like this so she couldn't talk.

Mara slowly stood after I was done. Her lithe body was absolute perfection, her blonde hair was wild, her cheeks were flushed, and her collagen-filled lips looked so abused it nearly made me hard again. No one could ever claim this she-wolf was hard on the eyes, that was for sure.

"Do you have anything to say to me?" I demanded.

She gave me a sultry smile. "Thank you for allowing me the honor of pleasuring you, Alpha."

I raised a brow. "*And?*"

She lowered her head in submission. "I'll fuck Alexei by the end of the week. There won't be a doubt in anyone's mind."

"Good. Now fix your fucking face and get the hell out of here before I get back. You're a goddamn mess."

She fell to her knees, black mascara streaking down her cheeks as I stormed out of the penthouse. I wasn't worried about leaving Mara alone in the condo. It served as my own little personal fuckpad—I didn't keep anything personal or business related there. Besides, I was confident she wouldn't risk my wrath by sticking her nose where it didn't belong.

Nobody fucked with me and got away with it.

TWENTY-TWO

Nicole

FROM MY VANTAGE point on the platform, I could see Alexei's abs flexing as he reached for the slippery ledge and curled his body up. Salty sweat dripped down his tanned skin, and the groan that vibrated in his chest made me squeeze my thighs together.

"Corbin fell off the rope swing again." Bee sighed before taking a sip of her water bottle filled with vodka. "But, damn, he sure does look great doing it."

She'd turned today's training session into a little drinking game and had a slight buzz going. Corbin was determined, so she hadn't had *too* many opportunities to take a drink. He scowled every time she raised that bottle to her lips. But then again, the spell Juniper had placed over him finally wore off in the middle of their third obstacle, so overall, his spirits seemed to have been lifted. I supposed no longer having to deal with a giant peen and a tail to boot would do that to a guy. Especially when my best friend made it *quite clear* she enjoyed looking at the original Corbin even better than the magical mask he wore.

Alexei assessed the next obstacle where a freakishly large ax swung over a balance beam like a pendulum. Juniper had spelled it so that the timing of its sway was constantly changing. Alexei couldn't trust it not to speed up once he jumped onto the beam, but not completing the obstacle wasn't an option either. I had to hold back a scream last time because the ax nicked his shoulder.

He jumped onto the beam and ran the instant he had an opportunity, his feet quick and his posture steady as he made it across—just barely. I'd been holding my breath every time he'd complete a level. I wasn't sure how this course was going to make Alexei a better fighter, but General Minifred was a smart man who knew what he was doing.

Alexei's eyes locked on mine as he approached the large tower. For the last three days they'd been training here, he always managed to get to this point. But climbing was the hardest part, and it was a challenge neither he nor Corbin had mastered yet. Juniper spelled the rock wall to have changing points. It was constantly a guessing game whether you'd lose your grip or footing.

Alexei seemed more determined than ever to get to the top of the tower as he put his foot on the first step and grabbed hold of a ledge. Last night, I dreamt he made it to the top, swept me in his arms, and crashed his lips to mine. But I awoke in a seriously foul mood, knowing in reality, that was a pipe dream.

"Whoa." Juniper whistled from her seat beside me on the raised platform. "Your aura just went from hot-and-heavy to doom-and-gloom in two seconds flat."

I tongued my cheek, not wanting to reply with shifter ears in such close proximity. "I'm fine."

June snorted. "Right. And I'm the queen of the fae."

My best friend laughed from her place on my other side. "You would make an *excellent* queen."

Juniper's golden eyes twinkled as she smiled. "Why, thank you."

My smile spread across my face, as did a feeling of lightness that hadn't been there a minute ago. I had to admit, when Corbin staked his claim on Bee, I was worried about the whole Juniper situation. I didn't want to have to give up one of the few allies I had on this campus, but if being near a woman my best friend's mate banged repeatedly would've been uncomfortable for her, I would've made it happen. In retrospect, I shouldn't have been concerned. These two were actually a lot alike—it was probably why I felt so in sync with Juniper from day one—and Bee wasn't someone who'd hold anyone's sexual exploits against them. It sure was fun watching Corbin struggle with it, though.

As a loud curse echoed throughout the area, our attention was drawn back to the shifter currently splatting on the ground.

"Ouch," the three of us said in unison.

Alexei had fallen again, about halfway up the tower.

"Fuck!" he roared. "My phone was ringing, and it caught me off guard."

He looked back up at me and practically pouted.

"Focus, Alexei!" General Minifred barked. "Start over."

Alexei groaned while pulling his cell phone out of his pocket to check it. "It's my father."

Bee's father smirked. "He can wait. Start setting the precedent now that you won't be an obedient little pup every time he summons you."

In the distance, Corbin pulled his own cell out of his pocket. "Shit. Alexei we have to go."

General Minifred frowned as Juniper snapped her fingers. I squeezed my eyes shut as she sucked us through what felt like a magical straw and teleported us to the general down below.

"What's going on?" Alexei frowned.

"Your father summoned every shifter on campus *and* in Ridgeview," Corbin replied. "He's demanding the entire pack's attendance. This can't be good, bro."

I chewed on my lip with worry. "Has he done something like this before?"

Alexei's dark brows pinched together as he shook his head. "Not like this."

Bee's father stood taller, all traces of his previous annoyance gone. "Any idea what it could be?"

Alexei exhaled. "Only one way to find out. He says to meet him at the quad on campus."

General Minifred arched a brow. "Interesting choice of location. I'm coming with you." He turned toward his daughter. "You three go back to the sorority house and *do not* leave until I tell you it's safe to do so."

"I agree," Alexei added.

"What?" I said. "No way!"

"I'm with her." Bee jerked her thumb in my direction. "Dad, you know how stubborn Nic and I can be by now. There's no sense in fighting it. I *am* your daughter, after all."

The general smiled proudly.

"I'm going, too." June swung her arm around my shoulder. "Don't worry; I'll make sure no one sees us."

The three imposing men considered that for a moment before nodding their acquiescence in freaky synchronicity.

"Damn, that was way easier than I thought it would be," Juniper murmured.

"Now that I think about it, I'd rather have you close if anything happens," Alexei said, his eyes locked on mine.

"Fact," Corbin agreed.

The corner of General Minifred's lip quirked, which

was basically a giant proclamation of approval, even if he didn't say so. "Let's go."

Juniper took a deep breath. "Daddy Minifred, I'm going to need some more pubes with all this magic I'm using."

She snapped her fingers, and once again, I was sucked through air. Nausea rolled up my throat as I felt like a weightless entity hurtling through space. My head hurt as everything around me seemed to expand. My knees buckled, forcing me to fall toward the hard ground. I groaned in pain as I landed on all fours.

Bee stumbled a little, but she managed to remain standing. "Whoa. That'll sober a girl up real quick."

We were between two buildings on campus, hidden in a shadowed corner close to the quad. Strong arms wrapped around my middle and yanked me up until I was standing. Alexei held me for a moment while staring at me.

"How did you not fall when you landed?" I pouted while looking up at him.

Witch travel was not my favorite.

He forced a smile, though I saw the worry in his expression. "Practice."

I could hear his father's voice echoing in the distance. "Line up!"

"You have to go," I whispered, hating myself a little for worrying about him.

We still weren't together. Nothing about our situation had been resolved.

"Be safe, Nicole," he whispered.

"I will."

"And if anything happens, I want you to run. Don't stop until you're safe. I'll make sure your father gets out, okay? Just worry about yourself."

I chewed on the inside of my cheek, mentally rejecting that idea. If anything bad happened, I refused to leave my loved ones behind.

With our backs plastered to the brick building, Bee, General Minifred, and I all watched as Alexei and Corbin made their way toward the quad.

June closed her eyes in concentration, holding her index finger in the air. "And, we're officially invisible." She pointed toward a bench about twenty feet away. "There's the end of our cloak. As long as you stay within the boundary lines, no one will be able to see or hear us." She pointed in the opposite direction. "That bush is the other end of it."

I squinted my eyes as the air seemed to shimmer a bit around the shrub, which was located about halfway down the building. "Am I seeing things, or does that bush have a rainbow-colored halo around it?"

Juniper's eyes widened. "You can see that?"

"Uh... yeah. Is that bad?"

"See *what*?" Bee stretched her neck, glancing at the bush. "I don't see anything."

"I wouldn't say *bad*," June answered me. "Just... *interesting*. You shouldn't be able to see *anything*. My cloaking spells are top notch. Seamless to the naked eye to anyone other than the spell caster."

General Minifred looked that way briefly before turning back and studying me carefully. "That *is* interesting."

We didn't have time to ruminate any further, because Alpha Jones's commanding tone stole our attention.

"Ladies and gentlemen, welcome."

The four of us moved toward the corner so we could see what was going on, being careful to stay well behind the bench.

"I don't like this one bit," the general grumbled.

I didn't either. There was a large crowd gathered in a semicircle, hundreds, maybe even a thousand. In the center of the quad stood Alexei's father, along with at least fifty badly beaten men and crying women, who had been forced to their knees with their hands bound behind their backs.

A couple of humans were staring in a daze and mumbling, "The coffee shop is on Main Street," over and over again.

Juniper snapped her fingers, and they shook their heads in confusion before scattering.

"What did you do?" I asked.

"Every human in the vicinity suddenly thinks they have a big test they need to study for at the library. Mrs.

Norris, the librarian, is a friend of my mother's and will keep them safe until we figure out what's going on." Juniper pulled her cell out of her back pocket and began texting someone, presumably the librarian.

"We are gathered here today to witness something *spectacular*," Alpha Jones said.

The crowd was growing, other supes joining in, likely wondering what was going on. I spotted Cristian and a few of his frat brothers in the mix, taking in the scene with obvious concern. He pulled his cell out of his pocket, and it appeared as if he was typing something on the screen.

A moment later, my own phone vibrated. I pulled it out to see a message from him as Alpha Jones continued to greet everyone and hype up the crowd.

Cristian: Where are you?

I quickly typed a response.

Nicole: At the quad. Juniper is keeping me hidden.

Cristian scowled.

Cristian: Get out of here right now. Alpha Jones is up to something.

I rolled my eyes. No shit, Sherlock.

Nicole: I'm safe.

"Under my leadership, shifters have become the most powerful supernatural faction in the world. We're stronger, faster, and have more money than any other organization." Alpha Jones's booming voice was filled with pride, but I saw his ego for what it was: incredibly dangerous.

Chatter instantly coursed through the crowd.

Alpha Jones held his hand up. "Silence!"

And just like that, you could hear a pin drop.

"As I was saying... we have grown leaps and bounds since my reign as your alpha began. And what I have planned next will only ensure that continues."

No one dared to utter a word, but I could see the questions in their eyes.

"What is he doing?" I asked. "Why are those people lined up like that? It looks like a firing squad."

General Minifred stiffened. "This is worse than my source led me to believe."

"As alpha," Alexei's father continued, "sometimes, I must make difficult decisions. I must take action in the best interest of the pack. *Nothing* is more important to me than my pack. And while at times, I've been accused of being a bit harsh, I can assure you I am *not* a heartless man." He puffed his chest out, pausing in front of the bound shifters. "That's why a team of my most trusted men are currently transporting their children to a new facility where they will remain until they become of age. I have designed a comprehensive training program that will afford these children the opportunity to grow into more powerful shifters. They will *not* fail this pack as spectacularly as their parents have."

A collective gasp rang through the air.

"What the actual fuck?" Bee jerked her chin toward the psychopathic shifter addressing the audience. "Did he just announce the fact that he *kidnapped* a bunch of kids and shipped them off to some kind of internment camp?"

The general growled deep within his chest.

"This is so bad," I whispered, choking back a sob.

Those poor kids probably had no idea what was going on.

Alpha Jones looked down on the line of shifters he deemed unworthy with a scowl. "You have disgraced your pack and disappointed your alpha."

One of the women had a gash on her head and blood dripping down her face. She let out a whimper as she bowed lower, her nails digging into the concrete.

Alexei stormed up to his father, a determined look on his face, fists clenched at his side. "What is going on here?" There wasn't a hint of submissiveness in his tone, which filled me with a sense of pride.

Alpha Jones spun to face his son, disgust evident in the crawl of his thin lips. "Where have you been?"

Alexei straightened his spine. "It doesn't matter. I'm here now, aren't I? What are you doing with all these people here?"

I wasn't expecting Alexei to be so defiant. Usually, he cowered whenever his father was near.

"I'm showing everyone what happens when you are weak," Alpha Jones said with a gleeful smile. The glacial man turned to face the bound shifters again. "My son—my future heir—is here to help me show all of you what it means to be a good leader. We have to make difficult decisions for the best of our pack. You were brought here today because you are holding us back. You are not worthy to be a part of the Ridgeview pack."

The woman with blood running down her face started sobbing uncontrollably. Her hot tears littered the concrete, and with a shaky voice, she spoke. "My baby. What have you done with my baby?"

Alpha Jones walked up to her, and she stared at his Italian leather shoes as he spoke. "Your son will have a better life because he's no longer held back by you. I'm going to build him up in my image and mold an army. You are lucky to have such a considerate alpha. I'm giving your son the opportunity to rise above his breeding and become a better shifter."

She continued to sob as we all watched in horror. "Please don't hurt him. Do anything to me, just don't hurt my son."

Alexei took a step forward. "Father? What is this? What are you planning to do with them?"

Alpha Jones's smile was cold and calculating. "The better question is, what are *you* going to do, my son?"

Alexei frowned. "What does that mean?"

His father walked down the line of captives as he spoke. "It *means*, are you going to take your *final* opportunity to prove your worth, or are you not man enough? Not *alpha* enough?"

"What *needs* to be done?" Alexei repeated, gesturing to the line of shifters. "You've taken their children. You've beaten them into submission. What more do you want?"

Alpha Jones reached the end of the line, next to a scrawny middle-aged man. The guy was black and blue, his right eye swollen shut from forceful blows, but he lifted his chin proudly as the alpha fisted his hair. This was obviously a man who felt he had nothing left to lose.

"This," Alexei's father replied, bracing his other hand on the man's jawbone and twisting.

A sickening crack rang through the air right before the man's lifeless body fell to the ground.

Alexei lunged for his father's victim, but it was too late. His face fell in defeat as he knelt to the ground, placing a finger on the dead man's pulse point.

Corbin looked poised to assist Alexei at any moment. He briefly glanced our way, pleading with us to leave before we had to witness any more brutality.

Fuck that noise. I wasn't going anywhere.

People were openly crying and displaying signs of shock. But not a single one was doing anything to stop Alpha Jones from doing the same to the next person in line.

"Dad!" Bee cried. "You need to stop this!"

General Minifred shook his head solemnly. "I can't, baby." He gestured to the two dozen or so giant wolves that were now corralling the crowd, snarling in warning. "If I went out there without backup, I would be just as dead as that man." He pulled his phone out of his pocket, facing it toward the quad to record what was happening. "But I *can* get as much incriminating evidence as possible."

"What about Alexei?" I asked, panic evident in my tone.

"This is his battle, Nicole," the general said. "He was born to be an alpha. Maybe this is his chance to prove it."

"But he's not ready," I argued. "He *just* started training."

As Bee and June huddled near me, perhaps out of comfort, they looked at me with a sense of solidarity. They knew as well as I did that this wasn't going to end well.

"It doesn't appear as if he has much of a choice, sweetheart." The general sighed.

"We can't just do nothing!" I insisted.

Before Bee's dad could say another word, Alexei's voice boomed through the crowd, drawing my attention back to him.

"Father, *stop*. This is unacceptable." Alexei jerked his head toward the wolves. "Call off your muscle."

Alpha Jones belted out a sinister laugh. "I knew you'd pussy out." He made some kind of weird hand gesture right before all hell broke loose. "Oh, well. I suppose I have to take matters into my own hands."

The wolves attacked the bound people en masse, blood spraying as their powerful jaws tore limbs from their bodies. People screamed as they ran away, while some exploded out of their clothes, the bloodlust bringing out their inner animals, before jumping into the fray. Alexei lunged for his father amidst the chaos, but the alpha was faster on the offense, landing a solid uppercut followed by a series of kidney jabs.

Juniper locked her arms around me as I screamed. Blurs of bodies passed through my vision as Alpha Jones beat the shit out of his son. His fist landed on Alexei's eye, surely breaking the socket, and then he kicked his shin, the bone snapping on impact.

"No!" I screamed as Alexei reached for his father's neck.

"If you fight back, I'll *kill you*," Alpha Jones warned. "If you want a formal challenge, then I accept."

Alexei froze.

The crowd froze.

Dead bodies littered the ground, guts and blood painting the pavement in gore.

Alpha Jones kicked him again, the crunch of bones making me sob harder. "Alexei!"

"Go ahead, boy, *challenge me*. Give me permission to end your pathetic existence once and for all."

"Is this it?" Bee asked, her own eyes swimming with tears. "Is this Alexei's one shot?"

"If Alexei fights back, then he's formally initiating a challenge," General Minifred confirmed before tucking his daughter under his arm.

I swallowed as Alexei seemed poised to fight back. "He's never been able to fight back. He's just had to sit there and let his father beat him or risk..."

The weight of our situation seemed to land right on my chest. I could barely breathe. The thought of Alexei growing up with such a monster without the means to fight back was abhorrent to me.

"Hit me!!" Alpha Jones roared.

What kind of monster wanted a reason to kill their own child?

Alexei coughed up blood. "No."

I wanted nothing more than to run out to Alexei and help him out of there, but I knew it would be a suicide mission should I try.

Alpha Jones kicked Alexei in the face, and I pressed my palm to my mouth, muffling the scream rising up my throat.

Alpha Jones was going to kill Alexei.

And there was nothing I could do to stop it.

TWENTY-THREE

Alexei

BLOOD POURED FROM MY WOUNDS. The sound of my bones snapping was ringing in my ear. I could only see out of one eye, but my father's murderous expression stood out amongst the gore.

"Hit me!" he screamed again. "You know you want to challenge me." He grabbed me by the neck and tossed me with a grunt. My body slid across the concrete, and I landed in a puddle of someone else's blood. "You could end this suffering, boy. All you have to do is hit me back and I'll end it."

I grabbed my middle and groaned. I knew he couldn't kill me. Pack law stated you could only kill an alpha that challenged you. He wanted an excuse to end my life, but I wasn't going to give it to him.

"No," I grunted once more, about two seconds from passing out.

Damn, I was seriously fucked up. I probably needed a doctor.

"So spineless," my father spat.

I rolled over and writhed in agony. I had been this asshole's punching bag my entire life, and I was sick of it, but I knew I didn't stand a chance against my father *and* his enforcers. I was man enough to recognize my limits, so I had to endure the worst beating of my life, knowing my mate was watching the entire time.

He leaned over and pressed against my broken eye socket with his thumb, my entire body tensing from the pain. A cry escaped my lips, the sound mixing with his malicious laughter. I breathed as deeply as my broken ribs would allow, latching on to that elusive, quiet space in my head that allowed me to disassociate from my body. As my father continued to taunt me, I devised a new plan in my mind.

I was done with this. Done playing by his rules. Done letting him control my life and beating me into submission. I was done letting him keep me from my mate. It felt unnatural and downright cowardly to walk away from my pack, but if I wanted to save them eventually, I had to survive this *now*. This was literally the only way I could get out from under my father's rule without formally challenging him and claiming the throne after his death.

"I..." I sputtered and coughed before sucking in a deep breath. "I renounce my claim."

My father shot up, his mouth hanging open.

"What?!"

I dug my fingers into the gravel, my nails bending as I pulled myself onto my stomach and forced myself up on my hands. I looked weak, sitting before him on all fours, but I refused to lie down on the ground as I told him this. I'd been waiting my entire life to stand up to him, and I would damn sure do it with dignity.

His lips pressed into a tight line as I stood up. My insides hurt so bad, the agony pierced through my strength, but still I stood.

"I, Alexei Koenig, renounce my claim as the future alpha of the Ridgeview pack."

A surprised gasp traveled through the crowd.

"What is the meaning of this? I tell you to challenge me and you *quit*?! You're no better than the worthless shifters dead at my feet right now. What kind of man just gives up?"

"I don't want to follow in your legacy," I gritted. "I want *nothing* to do with you. If that means being a lone wolf, so be it."

My father clenched his fist. I knew I was embarrassing him, but I didn't care. I refused to continue giving him the upper hand.

"You're even stupider than I thought. The only thing keeping you alive was your position as my future alpha. If you're not in line to lead a pack, your life is utterly dispensable."

I had a feeling he'd say that. "I'd rather die free than live as your son. And I won't let you hide behind a challenge. If you want to kill me, then be a man and *do it*. You have no one. No heir. No respect. Your people may *fear* you, but fear doesn't create loyalty—only resentment. A good leader doesn't kill their weakest members. They *protect* them."

A vein bulged in my father's neck as he stared me down. "I'm going to enjoy watching you take your last breath."

I braced myself, praying like hell Juniper would take the cue and teleport me out of this mess. Just as my father took a step toward me, a blur of movement crossed my vision.

Twenty vampires formed a tight circle around me, with their teeth bared and fists clenched at their sides. To my shock, Cristian led the charge, placing him about a foot away from my father.

"Alexei Koenig is under vampire protection. You might want a war, Jones, but if you attack one of ours, I can assure you that you won't be prepared for the vampire king's wrath."

My father looked around in shock. "What is the meaning of this? Alexei would *never* work with a vampire."

"His mate made a blood oath to me, which means *her father and her mate* are under my protection. I take that responsibility *very* seriously. *As does the council.*" Cristian gestured toward the vampire at his side. "And for insurance purposes, my second-in-command, Phillipe, has been recording this entire conversation for their review. So, if I were you, I would be mindful of *every word* that comes out of your mouth."

Alpha Jones flinched, and rightfully so. While my father may have been the top dog of the shifter world, even he couldn't blatantly defy the council without some serious consequences.

"Alexei doesn't have a mate. Unless you're suggesting he mated that pathetic *human*?"

My blood boiled at my father's tone. Nicole wasn't a pathetic human. She was *mine*. I didn't want him to know about our mate bond yet. It put an even bigger target on her back than before, but I didn't have many options right now. If the vampires wanted to help out, then I wasn't too prideful to accept it. Considering the alternative, at least this gave me a chance of repairing things with my mate. Proving to her once and for all that I wasn't ashamed of her. That I would fight my father tooth and nail to save her.

I looked around the quad, taking in the massive wolves picking through their kills. The shocked expressions of those still in their human forms, who waited with bated breath for my answer. I didn't dare glance Nicole's way, though I could feel her gaze burning into me. Even if Juniper was protecting everyone with a cloaking spell, it wasn't worth the risk. Being invisible didn't mean someone couldn't touch you if they were in close proximity. My father was strong enough to resist a compulsion spell if he had reason to investigate an area. If I did anything to tip off the infuriated alpha right now, he'd go after Nicole in a heartbeat.

I spat a wad of blood onto the ground near my father's feet, doing my best to ignore my battered body. I had multiple broken bones. Countless contusions. Possibly some internal bleeding. Yet, somehow, I managed to lift my chin and level my father with a matching glare.

"You heard the vampire. Nicole is my mate. My *fated* mate." Gasps and murmurs echoed through the crowd. "And since she is under the vampire's protection, that means *I* am, too."

My father was so enraged his face was turning purple. "Impossible!"

"I'll admit..." I took a moment to breathe through the pain in my ribs. "I thought so, too, at first. And I did things I'll regret for the rest of my life while I was fighting fate. But it's true. Nicole Fairweather *is* my mate, and that means I will do *anything* to ensure her safety."

"You're a disgrace to this pack," he growled. "You're a disgrace to shifters everywhere!"

"He's lying!" Mara shouted while pushing through the crowd. Her strappy tank top was falling off one shoulder as she made her way to us. "They're not mates. *We're engaged.* All of this is just one massive misunderstanding. Alexei, tell your father you're joking. Tell him you don't mean it."

I saw the fear in her eyes, but it wasn't for me or for my safety. The future she had planned for herself as luna was publicly going down in flames, and this was her last-ditch effort to prevent that.

She smiled nervously at the crowd before continuing. "R-right, Alpha Jones? We had everything planned."

"Shut up," he barked at her.

It shouldn't have made me laugh, but the way she cowered made me smile. "Mara Sullivan, I wouldn't marry you if you were the last woman on earth." She gasped. "You're a vile, cruel cunt. And I'd rather saw my dick off than spend another moment in your presence."

Some of the crowd laughed. Most of them stared in horror.

"Shut up!" Alpha Jones screamed. "You will *not* defy me this way!"

My split lip curved up in the corner. "I'm not a part of this pack anymore, remember? I denounce you, Alpha Jones. I denounce the Ridgeview pack. I have *zero* interest in marrying that bitch you tried saddling me with *or* leading anyone who blindly follows you after what you've done here." I gestured to the mutilated bodies littering the ground. "But I promise you this. One day, I *will* seek retribution. And that day will be your *last.*"

His nostrils flared and his chest heaved. "And your beta? Does he support your foolish aspirations?"

Corbin stepped forward, toward the center of the macabre circle. "I do *not*, Alpha. As far as I'm concerned, Alexei is dead to me. I support your cause of making this pack as strong as possible, in whatever manner is necessary."

Cristian raised his brows beside me, not knowing Corbin and I had already planned for this.

I hoped my expression displayed shock at my best friend's supposed betrayal. I knew it was smart for him to stay behind and feed us intel. I just worried about his safety. But Corbin was the best beta I'd ever known, and he insisted on doing this, should the need ever arise. That day may have come sooner than we expected, but he fell into the role without any hesitation.

My father flashed a sinister smile. "Well, at least someone has some sense around here."

The vampires closed in tighter, as if they could sense the crowd's tentative hold on their inner beasts. If I didn't get out of here, there would undoubtedly be even more bloodshed today. And considering my weakened state, I wasn't sure it wouldn't be mine.

"Let's go," I said to Cristian.

My father raised a hand as his men started toward me. "Let him go. We have more important things to take care of than *a worthless mutt*." His jaw tightened as his eyes roamed around the crowd. "Make no mistake. If any of you are seen associating with Alexei or his supposed mate, you *will* be marked as my enemy. And you've seen today how I take care of useless members of this pack."

As I walked through the river of blood and away from my father, it felt like a weight had been lifted off my shoulders.

I was finally free. Finally rid of him.

And soon, the rest of my pack would be free, too.

I COLLAPSED the moment I was out of the quad. It was humiliating, but my body had completely given up. After all the adrenaline had faded, I was nothing more than a bleeding, broken mess. To my utter humiliation, flashes of memory made me realize that at some point, Cristian picked me up and cradled me against his chest, carrying me across campus like I was a helpless animal.

I had a feeling he would hold that over my head for a long time.

When I woke up, Nicole was hovering over me, dabbing my brow with a wet washcloth. Her crystal blue eyes peered into mine as I coughed.

"Everything is going to be okay," she whispered. "I promise."

The compassion in her gaze confused me for a

moment. I never thought we would be like this again. Closer. Together.

"Where are we?" I asked.

"We're at the vampire house. Cristian set you up in his room, but we can't stay here for long. He had a doctor look over you, and he said it's going to take a while for you to heal." She reached up and grazed the tip of her index finger over one of my bruises. I winced, causing her to snap her hand back.

"No," I rasped. "Don't stop." I wrapped my hand around her wrist and pulled her palm to my cheek, breathing in her calming lilac scent and soaking in the feel of her skin on mine.

Her eyes were bloodshot, as if she'd been crying. "You could've died, Alexei."

"It'll take a lot more than that to get rid of me." If Nicole's crestfallen expression was any indication, she didn't appreciate my poorly timed joke.

"Not funny." She scowled.

"You didn't actually go through with it, did you?"

I could've sworn our mate bond would've forced me to feel her bonding with anyone else, but maybe I'd been so inside my head with everything else going on, I missed it somehow.

"Go through with *what*?" she asked.

I groaned as I shifted a little on the mattress. "The blood oath. Cristian said..."

"No." Nicole's dark hair swished as she shook her head. "Not yet, anyway."

"Not *ever*," I promised.

My mate's musical laughter flowed through the room. "You're unbelievable, you know that?"

I narrowed my good eye. "Why do you say that?"

"Oh, I don't know." She waved her hand breezily. "Maybe the fact that you were just beaten within an inch of your life, and—"

"I think that's a bit of an exaggeration," I grumbled.

There was no missing her extreme eye roll, even with my limited vision. "*As I was saying*, you were just beaten *within an inch of your life*, and yet you still have the energy to be your jealous-possessive caveman self. Is this part of the accelerated healing thing, or are you just *that much* of a cocky ass?"

"Maybe a little of both," I admitted. "So why did Cristian do it, then? Why did he defend me like that?"

"Because I'm not an asshole," Cristian supplied. I hadn't even noticed him leaning against the doorframe, looking ridiculously well-coiffed in his button-down shirt and a cocky smirk. "Your father wants to rule the supernatural world, and we want to work together. Plus, I kind of like Nicole, and even though I'd gladly comfort her if you died, something tells me she'd prefer to keep you alive."

Nicole smiled at him before turning back to me.

"How bad is it out there?" I asked.

Nicole frowned. "Really bad. All humans and non-shifters are being asked to leave campus."

I sat up with a wince. "What?"

"We're being kicked out, Alexei. All of us."

I looked at Nicole. "What about your father?"

Her eyes misted with emotion. "Still locked up. I'm terrified to leave him here, but your father has enforcers everywhere. I don't know what to do. We've been given twenty-four hours to vacate."

"No. He can't—" I frowned, trying again. "Where is everyone going to go on such short notice?"

"The witches can head to New York to regroup at their coven's headquarters," Cristian answered. "My Rho Eta brothers and I will probably head to my clan's compound in Canada. You and Nicole can come with us if you'd like."

"I'm not leaving Corbin or Dr. Fairweather here."

Nicole flinched. "Did you forget the part where Corbin abandoned us? Bee's been bawling ever since. I can't get her to leave the little closet she sequestered in the basement."

"Do you honestly think Corbin would do that? He stayed behind to spy on my father. Fucking put himself in harm's way so he could feed us intel. We can't leave. None of us can. It would give my father the advantage."

Juniper entered the room, her eyes stormy. "So what do you plan to do, Alpha Alexei? If we stay, we'll have to fight. *Immediately.*"

I looked around the room at the future leaders of the

supernatural world and at my mate. "We stay. How many people can you hide in the training center?"

"Training center?" Cristian asked.

"Juniper and General Minifred set up a remote training facility for me. It's about six square acres, three miles from here. Close enough for us to stay in the game, but secluded enough for us to keep safe." I turned my attention back to Juniper. "So? Will your magic conceal all of us? Can we go there?"

She released a puff of air. "I don't know. I'll need a lot of pubes to maintain the protection spells. We need to figure out the logistics of it all to sustain that many people. We'd need food. Tents. Plumbing. It's a *huge* undertaking, but..." Her eyes widened. "Hold up. We moved the Kappa Zeta house here. Maybe I wouldn't have to start from scratch. We'd just have to—"

"Are you suggesting we move *your sorority house* to this training facility?" Cristian asked.

June nodded. "I think I am. But it'll require some major power."

"How many witches will that take?" I asked her.

"All of them. Maybe my mother, too. I can send word to her. I'm not sure we can make room for *all* of Greek Row, but the KZ house is big enough for us, you guys, and the vamps. It's already spelled with wards, and my house-elf can handle the food, though she might have a problem with the vampire diet."

Cristian scratched the back of his neck. "I have

enough blood stores for a month if we're conservative. We'll need security. My vamps can handle the perimeter."

I nodded in agreement. "We can set up shifts. Invite some fae to join, too. They're selfish creatures, so I'm not sure they'll be eager to work with us, but there might be a few who are interested."

Cristian shook his head. "We might not have enough soldiers, though."

General Minifred entered the room. He cleared his throat, drawing our attention. I wasn't surprised to see him, but the woman with the concerned expression on her face behind him made my heart stall.

"Mom?"

"Oh, Alexei," she sobbed before running over to the bed. Nicole moved out of the way so she could grab my hand. "What has he done to you?" My mother's hair was tied up in a tight bun, and her clothes were wrinkled. The tears streaming down her cheeks landed on my arm.

"What are you doing here?" I asked her. "Did he hurt you?"

Now that I thought about it, she was noticeably absent at the quad. I was thankful but also thoroughly confused.

My mother gingerly sat on the edge of the mattress. She smoothed some hair away from my forehead like she used to do when I was a pup. "Honey, I never thought he'd go this far. If I had known you were at risk like this, I would've warned you."

I winced as one of my broken fingers fused back together, sweat dripping from my brow.

"Mom, what are you talking about?"

She frowned, her espresso eyes slicing to the general. "August and I have been working together for quite some time. I wanted to tell you—I swear—but I couldn't risk exposure. I've no doubt your father would've killed me, just like he killed my mate."

"What?!" Nicole, Juniper, and I asked in unison, our shock and outrage evident in our tone.

My mother shook her head dismissively. "That part doesn't matter right now. What *does* matter is giving you a chance to heal properly and taking your psychotic father down once and for all."

I didn't let her brush it off that quickly. "Mom, what happened?"

She peered at me, her eyes swimming with tears. "It's a long story. Let's just say your father isn't afraid to remove anything in the way of getting what he wants. I found out some time ago. He let it slip one night while he was drunk. I was... devastated. And when August... er... *General Minifred* reached out to me shortly thereafter... Well, I suppose it's serendipitous that our paths crossed this way. We're very lucky to have him."

I felt the heavy weight of my mother's grief. Now that I had my own mate, the reality of her losing hers felt more tangible. To know my father was the one who killed him made me sick to my stomach.

"He'll pay for this," I promised her.

She gave me a sad smile. "I know he will, honey."

"Anya," General Minifred interrupted. "We need to get you to the safe house."

Safe house? *What* safe house?

My mom reached over to hug me, being mindful of my many injuries. "I love you, Alexei. And I'm *so proud* of the man you've become. No matter what, don't forget that."

I frowned as she pulled away, grunting at the pain that shot across my jaw from the motion. "Why does it sound like you're saying goodbye?"

She stood, joining the general in the doorway, tears filling her eyes. "I'm sorry I didn't protect you, Alexei. I'll never forgive myself for that. But I hope you know I never wanted this for you." She sighed. "It's safer if I'm away. I know he has that young Sullivan girl to keep him occupied, but I'm worried he'll do something rash."

I shook my head in confusion. "Wait, what?"

Nicole sat up. "Are you talking about Mara?"

Anya nodded. "They've been sleeping together for a while now. I thought it was strange that he wanted you to marry the girl he was screwing every night, but I can't begin to make sense of your father's mind."

The idea of my father hooking up with Mara filled me with dread. Mara's confidence boost made complete sense now. Whatever my father had planned, she was in on it. I had no doubt.

My mother spared a quick glance at my mate, and then

she met my eyes again. "I know you two didn't get off to the best start... and I'm sorry for my role in that."

"Mom, don't—"

She held her hand up. "I *did* have a role in you pushing Nicole away. But I can assure you, it was with her safety in mind. But after speaking with Nicole and August while you were asleep, I know you'll figure out how to overcome this." She looked Nicole's way again. "I'd be proud to welcome you into our family."

Nicole seemed like she didn't know how to respond. She appeared part flattered but also part wary. Not that I could blame her for the latter. "Um... thank you."

The general and my mother exchanged a few quiet words in the hall before I heard her descending the staircase.

"I need to contact my men to ensure everything is set up for your mother's arrival," he said upon his return.

"You're moving her to a safe house?" I asked. "*What* safe house? Why? Is she in danger for working with you?"

"The less you know, the better. I'm sending her away from here for a little while. Her husband is too unpredictable, and I don't want your mother caught in the crosshairs." General Minifred had a moment of shyness as he looked down at his feet.

A surge of protectiveness washed over me. "You seem close to my mom. Why is that?"

He scratched the back of his neck while everyone watched us speak back and forth like a tennis match.

"We've corresponded a lot these last few months. I'm sorry for not being as forthcoming. I wanted to protect her."

Nicole peered at the general. "Are you blushing, General?"

"That's ridiculous." He snapped his gaze to her. "I don't *blush*."

What the actual fuck? If I didn't know better, I'd swear the general had a goddamn *crush* on my mother.

I narrowed my eyes. "So, you've been making plans for a while now. How often, *exactly*, did you and my mother talk?" It was pretty ironic, considering he was ripping me a new asshole the moment he arrived.

"Watch your tone, boy." The general returned my glare.

Bee entered the room, her brow arched. "You're withholding all kinds of important information, aren't you, Dad?" She crossed her arms over her chest, leaning against the wall. Nicole's best friend had red-rimmed eyes and a haunted expression. "I mean... I know secrets are a big part of your job and all, but don't you think this is something Alexei should've known before now? He could've helped protect his mom."

He shook his head. "Omitting Anya's involvement was absolutely necessary until now. It's a delicate situation with many moving parts. You just have to trust me."

Bee shrugged. "So what now? My supposed mate is working with Alpha Jones, and—"

I grunted while shifting on the mattress. "He's *spying*. Corbin would never betray me like that. We had it all planned in advance, just in case my father lost his shit and it became necessary."

Her lip quivered, and Nicole crossed the room to comfort her best friend. "That's not any better, because that means he's in danger. He's with your deranged father right now. I don't... I don't know how I feel about this mate business, but I definitely don't want him to get killed before I have the chance to figure things out."

Nicole rubbed her back before wrapping her up in a hug. "We'll get him out of there, Bee. I promise."

Juniper spoke up. "And what about Mara? She's fucking the alpha! That makes zero sense."

It made me nauseated, imagining them together, but really, I thought it made perfect sense. They were both ambitious to unhealthy levels and power crazed. They were an ideal match.

"We need to know what Mara knows," Nicole whispered.

I nodded, mentally adding that to the list of shit I needed to do.

"We *will* get answers," General Minifred promised. "But right now, Alexei needs to heal and we need to move every loyal supernatural in the vicinity to the training camp. Bee, I'm assuming I can't convince you to go to the safe house with Anya?" The man looked desperate for a moment, and I saw the worry in his expression.

Bee rolled her eyes. "As much as I'd like to grill my future stepmother—holy shit, does that make Alexei my brother? I could totally be your sister-in-law, Nicole!"

General Minifred pinched the bridge of his nose. "Anya and I are just friends."

"Sure you are, Dad. That lovesick look in your eyes when you just said her name says otherwise. *As if* you could hide something like that from me. Don't insult me by trying to deny it again."

What the fuck was she talking about?

"Honey—" the general started.

Bee waved her hand, cutting him off. "Either way, I'm not going. Nicole is here. *Corbin* is here."

He frowned. "I don't like it, but I suppose I can respect your decision."

Juniper started digging in her purse. "That settles it, then. We're all staying near Redwood and moving to the training camp. Everyone, drop your pants. I'm going to need enough pubes to knit a sweater with."

I choked out a laugh while Bee stared at the witch in horror.

Juniper found some clippers and a ziplock bag before looking around the room. She snapped the scissors before pointing the bladed-side at me. "Well. Come on, then, Alpha Alexei. You enjoy dick-measuring contests. Let's see how you fare."

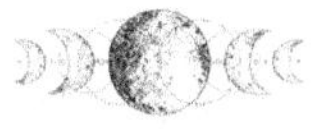

"Would you sit still?" my mate groused, running an antiseptic-coated cotton ball over my split brow that was taking its damn time to heal. It'd been two days since we relocated the witches' sorority house to the same woods where the general set up my training course. My injuries were slowly but surely repairing themselves thanks to my supernatural genes, but several lacerations were stubbornly refusing to get with the program. Nicole had told me on more than one occasion that this particular gash would probably heal faster if I wasn't such a *broody, frowny ass* all the time.

"It stings," I complained.

Nicole's stunning blue eyes rolled back. "Quit being such a baby. You had several cracked ribs, sprains, and ungodly bruising, yet you can't handle a little sting from antibacterial wash? Are you being serious right now?"

"*It stings,*" I repeated, standing firm on this. I didn't care what the damn label said. This brand of wound wash was *not* pain-free. Come to think of it, did any of them support that claim? "Maybe it would hurt less if you put on a sexy nurse costume?"

She gave me a look. "I'm sure." She pressed the antiseptic to my cut with a smile, and I let out a hiss of pain. "Oops."

I looked at my mate, who had been so caring and concerned since my father publicly beat the shit out of me. I hadn't expected her to ever talk to me again, let alone be so determined to take care of me. "Can I ask you something?"

She pulled the cotton ball back and tossed it on the tray beside her. "Sure."

"Is this real?" I asked, my throat bobbing with emotion.

She furrowed her brow. "Is your head hurting? Are you seeing things?"

I shook my head and reached for her hands. "No. I mean this... us... is it real? Are we... real?"

She seemed to understand my line of questioning, because a small, pitiful smile crossed her soft face. "Alexei, we've had our fair share of trials..."

"I've fucked up more times than I can count," I blurted out. "If I could go back, I would do so many things differently. You deserved better, Nicole."

She squeezed my hand. "I understand why you did some of the things you did now, though. Watching you just lie there while your father kicked you over and over again, never losing sight of pack politics. I could tell you wanted to fight back, but I also could clearly see your mind working, knowing you *couldn't* do so without dire consequences. I knew your father was dangerous, of course. My dad is still locked up in his lab. But I don't think I quite made the connection between us and your role in the pack. I didn't realize how much it governed everything you did until that moment. Our mate bond has put you in an impossible situation. I know that now. And while I may not agree with the harshness of your methods at times, nor your insistence to make decisions on my behalf, I get it."

"Not impossible," I promised. "We belong together. I know that now, Nicole. Maybe I've known it all along. But I'm done fighting it. If it takes the rest of my life, I *will* make it up to you."

"I believe you, Alexei." She sighed. "And I'm sick of fighting it, too."

"You are?" I asked. "What are you saying, Nicole?"

Nicole nodded. "I know we haven't known each other long, but I also know that no matter how hard I try to infuse logic into our situation, the way I feel inside *isn't* logical. It's... instinctual."

"And what are your instincts telling you?"

"That you're it for me." A beautiful smile stretched across her face. "And we have the rest of our lives to iron out the details. So... I'm in this for the long haul if you are."

Holy shit.

Who knew getting beaten by my father would've been one of the best things that had ever happened to me?

Nicole laughed as I pulled her into me and smacked a hard kiss on her mouth. I was so fucking ecstatic the pain barely registered. "You're really mine?"

She nodded once. "I'm really yours, Alexei."

TWENTY-FOUR

Nicole

My FIST SHOOK as I knocked on the door to Alexei's room. The vampires and witches were currently roaming the grounds and setting up more protections. Word got out that Alpha Jones had sent a team of enforcers to search the woods, so everyone was on high alert. Thankfully, these woods were huge and Juniper's coven was incredibly powerful. Her mother and sister had wanted to help once they heard about what Alpha Jones did in the quad. Between the three of them, they assured me the odds of anyone penetrating their cloaking spell were slim to none.

"Come in," Alexei said.

It had been six days since he'd gotten into a fight with his father and nearly died right before my eyes. I'd spent almost every waking moment at his side, nursing him back to health. I was surprised by how long it took him to get better, but Alexei assured me his shifter healing would kick in now that the bones had fully reset.

"Wow," I said when I opened the door. "You look *much* better today."

He stood at his bedroom window, staring out at the people below. His muscular back was on full display and nearly healed; only a few bruises remained. He didn't hunch over in pain, and there was a bit of color to his skin now.

He turned to look at me, his expression shifting from stoic concern to amusement. "I *feel* much better today. Was about to go talk to Cristian about the patrol schedule and see if I can grab a shift. It makes my skin crawl just sitting up here."

I walked over to him and wrapped my arms around his waist. "You were healing. It's okay that you've been resting."

He wrapped me up in a hug, cradling me to his bare chest as he stroked my back. "I've been training to be alpha for so long it feels unnatural to be severed from my pack. I know they're hurting right now, and every second I'm not training, someone else has to suffer."

"You'll be back to your pack soon. General Minifred said you'll be ready to challenge your father in no time."

"Speaking of the general..." Alexei rested his chin on the top of my head. "Has he heard from the council yet?"

After the evidence the general and Cristian collected during Alpha Jones's impromptu culling, the supernatural council demanded an emergency meeting, but they hadn't set a date yet. As of our last update, they were still in the process of gathering the council members and interviewing witnesses. According to Bee's dad, Alpha Jones had a team of high-profile attorneys ready to defend him when the moment arrived. Alexei was fairly certain his father would invoke his *constitutional rights*, whatever that meant. Our one saving grace was the fact that Alpha Jones's presence was required at this hearing, so he was currently on the other side of the country doing some prep of his own. Granted, that didn't stop his many minions from acting on his behalf here in Northern California, but I felt slightly better he was three thousand miles away.

"No." I shook my head lightly, careful not to disrupt Alexei's chin perch. "But he said it should be anytime now. Have you heard from Corbin?"

"About twenty minutes ago," he replied. "They're en route now."

Corbin's double-agent status had proven to be quite useful. He'd been keeping his ear to the ground, trying to locate the facility where Alpha Jones had sent those poor kids. The moment he got wind of its possible coordinates, he contacted the general so they could arrange a recon mission. I hated that Corbin was putting himself in danger like this, but I couldn't deny how much of an impact he could make. With Alexei's mother now underground, she could no longer feed the general information like she had been doing.

"Why does your father have to be such an evil bastard? I can't stand the fact that you're in this position. I know you miss your pack, Alexei." I looked up at him, melting at the sight of his warm gaze fixed on mine.

"I do," he agreed. "Well, the ones who aren't in my father's pocket, anyway. But *you're* my number one priority, Nicole. I want to rescue your father and build a safe space for us to exist. I'm more motivated than ever before."

I lifted up on my tiptoes to kiss him, and the moment my lips touched his, a frenzy of need made us deepen the connection. His sweeping tongue swept over mine as he dug his fingers into my back, pressing us as close as possible while he nipped at my lip.

"Alexei," I gasped as he walked backward toward the queen-size bed. He sat down and pulled me to stand between his thighs. I broke the kiss to speak to him. "Are you sure you're feeling better?"

He pawed at my clothes in answer, practically tearing the cotton T-shirt from my body. "Positive."

He moaned when his fingers traced my cleavage, and I reached behind my back with frantic fingers to unclasp my bra. The moment my breasts were free, his hot breath swirled around my nipple before he leaned forward and wrapped his soft lips around one of the pebbled peaks. Tossing my head back, I stared at the ceiling as his hands gripped my ass. The tight miniskirt I wore bunched at his touch, revealing the stark red panties I wore.

"I love this color on you." He brushed his knuckles over my mound.

My legs jerked, and I leaned forward as he slid his hand between my thighs and cupped me.

"I can tell," I panted, needing his lips on mine with a fiery desperation.

Alexei fell backward onto the mattress as I captured his mouth, taking me with him. I could feel his hardness between my thighs as I straddled him, the need inside of me ratcheting higher and higher every time he pressed into me.

"Fuck, Nicole," he groaned into my neck. "I need you."

"So take me." I gasped as he sucked on my pulse point.

I popped the button on his jeans, slid the zipper down, and reached into Alexei's boxers to grab his thick length. He bit his lip as I swiped the bead of pre-cum, spreading it over the tip before tracing the sensitive ridge with my thumb.

Alexei's fingers curled around my panties before a distinct tearing sound rang through the air. Before I could bitch about him ruining another pair of my underwear, he flipped our positions so my back lay on the mattress. In the next moment, I was crying out, clawing the sheets as his lips descended, licking and sucking my hot flesh, swirling his tongue around the sensitive bud until I was screaming his name. He gave me virtually no time to recover before his tongue went back to work, making stars explode behind my eyelids within what felt like seconds. I honestly didn't know whether I just had one insanely long orgasm or two. Whichever it was, it was freaking mind-blowing.

"Another," he growled.

"Oh my God," I panted. "I don't know if I can. That was *intense*."

Alexei lifted his head and gave me a wicked smile. "Oh, baby. Haven't you learned by now not to challenge my inner alpha? If I tell you to come all over my face, you're going to *come all over my face*. Got it?"

I shivered from his commanding tone and the filthy images his words conjured. I barely managed an unintelligible grunt before he resumed feasting on me like I was his own personal oasis in the middle of the scorching desert.

Goddamn, this man knew how to eat pussy.

Not that I was complaining.

After Alexei made me come two more times, he sat back on his knees, pulling my thighs around his hips. With one smooth thrust, he had buried himself inside of me to the hilt. My heels dug into his powerful glutes as he thrust in and out, making my body sing his praises. His hands gripped my hips with bruising force as he worked us both into a sweat. Slowing his pace, he slid one hand up my torso to knead my breast, while the other lightly grazed my swollen clit.

My mouth fell open. "Alexei... I can't take another. It's too much."

He slowly slammed into me, making my back bow off the mattress. "Yes, you *can*. Trust me, Nicole. I know what this fucking beautiful body of yours needs better than anyone. *Trust. Me.*"

I nodded, feeling the truth behind that statement. At that moment, I realized I *did* trust Alexei wholeheartedly. I wasn't sure when my mind had decided to let down its guard, but somewhere along the way, any doubt I'd ever had about him—about us—had been erased.

"Kiss me," I begged.

Alexei quickly complied, making love to my mouth just as thoroughly as he was making love to my body. I wasn't sure how much time had passed, or how many more orgasms I had, before he was spilling his release inside of me with a long, drawn-out groan.

"I love you, Nicole," he whispered into my ear as he held me tightly. "I'm so fucking sorry for everything I've put you through. I'm going to work my ass off for the rest of our lives to prove that to you."

I ran my fingers through his short, dark strands, placing a chaste kiss on his cheek. "I love you, too, Alexei. And I forgive you."

He pulled back just enough to look me in the eye. "Yeah?"

The sheer hope reflecting back at me made me smile. It was such an odd look for this man, but it was a damn good look. I vowed to do whatever I could to nurture that optimism until it blossomed into infallible faith that everything would be okay. No matter what we faced in the road ahead, I knew we were stronger together.

I nodded, my eyes swimming with happy tears. "Without a doubt."

TWENTY-FIVE

Alexei

IT WAS A BIG RISK, kidnapping Mara. But she had answers, and I wanted revenge.

She sure as shit wouldn't come if I called her, but thankfully, Luca had insider information. Much to my surprise, Mara and one of Cristian's frat brothers had a steady hookup toward the end of last school year. The way Cristian tells it, this guy was a bit obsessed with Corbin's sister, so much so that he had taken to documenting her whereabouts. Yes, I knew that was simply a fancy word for stalking, but in his defense, it turned out the guy's fixation with Mara didn't develop naturally. Evidently, Mara had been compelling him to bang her, and she was a little too good at it. He even dumped his longtime girlfriend so he could follow her everywhere she went. Needless to say, we now had a vampire on our side who was more than willing to sell out the conniving woman.

It rankled me, having to depend on Luca, even though we were kind of on the same team now. I still didn't trust him not to make a move on my mate.

"You sure about this?" I grumbled from the front seat of his ostentatious Aston Martin.

I mean, I had a fucking fat bank account, too, but he liked the entire world to know about his. Everything about the asshole was flashy.

"Positive. Damien said she goes on jogs through this park when she's stressed." He nodded at a towering redwood and grinned. "Brings back memories. The one time Mara and I hooked up was right there against that tree."

I rolled my eyes. "I'm not sure how you stomached it. She has the—"

"Whiniest voice in existence?" he finished for me. "Yeah. I know. Great tits, though. Too bad her rack doesn't make up for the weird, nasally noises she makes when she comes. I'll never forget it. I almost lost my erection, and that's *never* happened before. Did you have the same problem when you fucked her?"

"I barely talked to her, let alone touched her." I threw him a murderous glare. "I wouldn't know what Mara sounds like when she comes, and I plan on keeping it that way."

Cristian shrugged. "Guess that's good for Nicole. By the way, man, sorry about the whole blood oath thing. You can't blame me for trying. I get that she's mated to you and all, but I had to shoot my shot."

Seriously, this vampire had a death wish. If I wasn't working with him to keep Nicole safe, then I'd snap his neck. "As long as you don't ever touch her, look at her, breathe on her, or even *think* about her again, we're good."

He arched a brow at me. "You know, blood oaths can be... friendly. I mean, I wouldn't have to fuck her or anything. We could—"

"Absolutely not."

He held his hands up in mock surrender. "Just hear me out. You need this alliance. The supernatural factions need to unite so we can take down your father. If you become alpha and we establish a strong partnership, think of all the good it'll do."

I clenched my fist and twisted in my seat. "I think the only *good* you're thinking of involves getting off."

"No," he replied, his tone stern. "Consent is important to me, and unlike you territorial shifters, I respect boundaries. A blood oath only requires one feeding a year at minimum, and she can donate the clinical way, with a needle and a nurse. It could be—"

"No."

Cristian huffed in annoyance. "You have to start thinking like an alpha—an alpha that's going to *war*. Right now, my father is ready to stand at your side, but we need some skin in the game. He's honoring the blood oath because Nicole is *considering* it. But he won't wait forever, and my father won't risk lives needlessly. Nicole is powerful. *Really fucking powerful.* Do you know I haven't had to feed since I drank from her?"

I snapped my attention to him, my heart starting to race. "Powerful? How so?"

Cristian lowered his voice, even though there was no one around to hear us. "I know she isn't human, Alexei. In fact, I think she could be the most powerful person I've ever met, which puts her at risk. You're going to need people you can trust to defend her, because there are plenty of people who will want to *hunt her* if they ever discover how formidable her blood is. She's strong, but that wouldn't matter if she were severely outnumbered."

I growled. "Was that a fucking *threat?*"

"Fuck you. Of course not." The guy actually looked appalled. "I'm not the bad guy, Alexei. The sooner you figure that out, the better."

I had to choose my words carefully. Even if Cristian knew something was different with Nicole, I couldn't confirm his suspicions. "Assuming I'm playing along with your theories, what do you think she is?"

He shrugged. "Something fucking earth shattering. I was drunk off my ass after feeding from her. I feel... stronger because of it."

Shit.

This was really bad.

"Look," I began. "I'll talk to Nicole and discuss her options. I agree that she needs protection, but I want her to make that decision. I also think you and I could come to an agreement without using my mate as a blood bag. My family has lots of resources at our disposal. If and when I become alpha, I'll have plenty of leverage to keep your father happy, okay?"

He shrugged. "You have to *become* alpha, first."

Yeah. That was the fucking problem.

"Oh!" he exclaimed while pointing out the windshield. "There she is. Told you she'd be jogging this trail."

I followed his gaze and smiled menacingly as I saw Mara jogging in our direction "Shall we?"

"Let's catch ourselves a wolf," Cristian replied, his fangs dropping down.

"I will *kill* all of you," Mara said as Cristian set her down on a wooden chair.

She'd somehow chewed through the gag we put on her, and I longed for silence once more. She was a feisty little thing, and even though I hated her, I couldn't help but smile when she busted Cristian's back window trying to escape.

"Did you call the others?" Cristian licked his lips.

Mara had a nasty gash on her temple from hitting the window with her skull, and I guess even if he wasn't feeling as hungry since drinking Nicole's blood, he still liked the smell of it.

I pocketed my cell phone. "They'll be here any minute."

Mara shook her head while we waited, spouting curses at us in the training camp field. It wasn't like we had a shack or intimidating dungeon to get information out of her in, so the eerie night air had to do.

"When Alpha Jones finds out what you've done—he'll find you and kill all of you."

"Aw, is Shifter Barbie sad to be away from her boyfriend?" Juniper taunted, marching over to where we were, with Nicole and General Minifred following closely behind her. I assumed Bee was probably still sulking in Nicole's bedroom about Corbin.

Mara's eyes widened for a fraction of a second, and then she glared at Nicole. "You *bitch*. You ruined every-thing! *You will release me!!*"

Nicole waltzed up to me, all the confidence in the world, as she wrapped her arm around my middle. "Nice to see you too, Mara. By the way, we all have anti-compul-sion and protection spells in place, so don't bother."

Cristian moved to stand on my other side.

Juniper kept snapping her fingers, making a tiny blue flame appear. "Can we torture her now? I really want to burn her eyebrows off."

"Maybe give her a truth spell? Will you need more pubes for that June?" Nicole asked.

I snorted. At this rate, everyone at camp would have a Brazilian.

"I can, but she's pretty powerful. She'll be able to resist some, but it'll loosen her lips a bit."

Juniper started mumbling words to herself, and I watched in curiosity as her eyes rolled back in her head. She wiggled her fingers and then pointed at Mara.

A violet spark shot out of her index finger and floated over to Mara, caressing her lips before sliding down her throat.

Mara screamed, her veins bulging in her neck. "You have no idea who you're messing with!"

"Maybe not," Nicole said while cocking her head to the side. "But we know who *you've* been messing with. Sleeping with Alpha Jones, Mara? I didn't think even you would stoop that low."

Instead of looking ashamed or even embarrassed, Mara preened. "What can I say? Powerful men are drawn to me."

"Disgusting," I spat. "Tell me what my father is planning, or I'll let Juniper throw whatever spells she has in her arsenal at you."

Mara tipped her head back and laughed. "You can't hurt me. You *won't* hurt me."

I tipped my chin up. "You think so? Let's start at the

beginning, shall we? You put the camera in Nicole's dorm room. How'd you pull it off?"

I already knew it was her, even if we didn't have solid proof. She was the one who shared the video and mocked my mate while doing it.

Mara released an evil laugh. "I compelled her RA to let me in. Almost got caught, too. You showed up just as I was leaving. Nice show, by the way. Though Nicole was kind of underwhelming, don't you think? I can give you some pointers if you'd like. I know just how to make the Koenig men *heel*."

"Gross." Nicole's face twisted up in disgust.

"Why'd you do it?" I asked, pressing her for more information.

She shrugged, giving me a demure smile. "I always do what my alpha asks me to."

"So my father was behind it." I stroked my chin. "Why did you share it though? You know my father's feelings on human-shifter relationships. It hurt his image."

A flash of fear crossed Mara's expression. "I did that on my own. Believe me, I paid for my insubordination."

I knew with complete certainty that whatever punishment my father doled out was brutal. I refused to feel sorry for her though.

Nicole, who was too empathetic for her own good, spoke. "Did he hurt you, Mara? Is this relationship something you... want?"

Mara chewed on her lip for a brief moment before

speaking. "Of course I want it. He's alpha and the most powerful man in our community. He can give me everything I've ever wanted."

Nicole didn't look convinced. "Mara, if you're not safe—"

"Mind your own fucking business, cunt. You're just jealous because I'm on track to have more than you could even fathom. Alpha Jones *will* find you and kill you, Alexei." She paused to stare at me. "And when he does, I'll be the most important woman in the pack."

I scoffed. "Everyone in the pack loves my mother. He wouldn't—"

"I don't have to marry him, Alexei. In fact, we had everything planned out until you went and fucking *ruined everything* for some human pussy."

I took a step closer. "And what *plan* was that?"

She looked around, seemingly realizing that she'd said too much.

"Tell us." General Minifred stepped forward. He had been mostly silent during the exchange, letting me take the lead. "What is Alpha Jones planning? Where did he take those children?"

Mara shrugged. "I don't know."

I clenched my fist. "Yes. You do. Be decent for once in your fucking life, Mara. Tell us where the children are or else."

"Or else what, Alexei? You can't hurt me."

I eyed Juniper, who had a ball of fire the size of a base-ball in her fist. "Tell us, or Juniper will *make* you tell us."

Mara's eyes widened, and she started squirming in her seat. "Alexei, just wait a second."

Juniper walked over to Mara, a snarl on her face. "I'm going to enjoy this."

Mara shrieked, the piercing sounds cutting through the air. "Wait!" The flames danced across her skin, casting shadows on her tear-stained face. "Alexei, you can't hurt me because—" She let out another choked cry.

"Because *why*, Mara?" I pressed.

She looked around the field and then shouted something I never expected. "Because I'm pregnant!"

Juniper's ball of fire extinguished, and she took a step back, as if pregnancy was a contagious disease.

"What?" Nicole hissed.

"I'm pregnant, okay!" She heaved, her chest rising and falling as she looked around at each of us. "Alpha Jones's entire goal was to get me pregnant so that he could start over with a new heir. He forced Alexei to propose to me so that he could kill you off and tell everyone I'm carrying *your* baby."

I stood there in shocked silence. I knew my father wanted to get rid of me, but I never expected *this*.

"That's what he's been gunning for this whole time? Is that why he was taunting me into challenging him?"

She sighed. "Partly. But if you didn't challenge him, he

had a backup plan. I don't know the details, but I know it was going to look like an accident."

"Juniper, is there a way to make sure she's telling the truth about the baby?" Nicole asked.

The witch gave her an incredulous look. "I don't just carry pregnancy tests with me everywhere, Nicole. I know how to wrap that shit up."

My mate shook her head. "I meant with magic."

Juniper let out a little *ohhh* as she realized what Nicole was asking. "I mean... there are some spells, but they're really tricky and time consuming. It would be faster if one of us went to the local pharmacy."

Mara grunted. "I'm not lying, you assholes. Did you forget about the little truth spell you forced on me against my will? Speaking of... I thought witches were big fans of consent. What the hell happened to that?"

"Desperate times," June offered with a shrug.

General Minifred cleared his throat. "If she's pregnant with Alpha Jones's baby, then I need to talk to some of my team at the base. Let me know if she says anything else."

I looked at him. "You have a *team*?"

How many more secrets was this guy going to drop in my lap?

"The military is *very* involved in supernatural politics, Alexei." He nodded once at Nicole before marching back toward the house.

"So you're pregnant?" I asked Mara while dragging my palm down the side of my face.

She sat up in her seat in indignation. "I am. With your *sibling*. With Corbin's niece or nephew. You might hate me, but you aren't going to hurt this baby."

Juniper sighed. "Yeah, I don't torture pregnant women. There are just some karmic lines I won't cross."

"Mara," I said, trying to squeeze one last bit of information out of her. "Where did my father take those children? We want to save them. You're about to be a mother; you have to understand these kids don't deserve whatever he's doing to them."

Corbin's lead was a bust, so we were back to square one with finding this facility. A long moment passed, and I wondered if this power-hungry woman even had a heart.

Mara swallowed and shifted slightly in her seat before looking down at her stomach. "They're closer than you think."

I took a step closer. "Are they on campus?"

She snapped her gaze to me and looked me in the eye. "I'm done talking. If I were you, I'd start preparing for battle."

I scoffed. "What is that supposed to mean?"

She smirked condescendingly. "Alpha Jones knows his baby is in my belly. Once he realizes I'm missing, he'll burn the fucking world down to get me back. I suggest you gear up, Alexei. Looks like you'll be challenging him sooner than you thought."

CHAPTER
TWENTY-SIX

Nicole

I woke up before dawn. Alexei took the night shift patrolling the woods as he was too anxious after our meeting with Mara to trust anyone else with our safety. I had a feeling he'd be walking those woods until he collapsed from exhaustion. I knew in my gut that Alpha Jones would come for us eventually, I just had to hope we were hidden enough to buy ourselves some time.

Today was my birthday, but I didn't bother telling anyone. Turning nineteen didn't warrant a celebration when my father was still captured and we were all trying to stay alive. I knew Bee probably wasn't in a party mood either, since Corbin was still acting as a double agent for Alpha Jones. She worried incessantly, understandably so.

Besides, nineteen wasn't that big of a deal. It wasn't a milestone birthday, and I didn't really feel like eating cake. I just wanted Alexei and my loved ones safe, and something told me blowing out candles wouldn't grant that wish for me.

A wave of vertigo washed over me when I sat up. My vision blurred, and I cradled my head in my hand as my pulse seemed to buzz.

"Shit," I croaked while shifting my legs over the edge of the mattress so I could plant them firmly on the ground.

I blinked a couple of times, then stared at my palms, which felt hot.

"Nicole? You awake?" Juniper didn't knock but instead barged into the room, an excited look on her face. "Oh my gosh, shifters are going nuts! I couldn't wait any longer to tell you."

Damn, she was *really* energetic for six in the morning.

I shook my head and braced my hands against the mattress. "Is everything okay?" My exhaustion bled through my tone.

"Mates. Mates *everywhere*."

"What?"

"Sometime around midnight, shifters started mating like crazy. People are finding their fated bonds and going haywire. It's on all the major supernatural news sites. There are practically orgies in the streets. It's insane and if you ask me, really freaking hot. Ivan is going to be mad he missed it. He's headed back, by the way. I told him to stay in Brazil where it's safe, but he's worried about me."

I nodded while trying to decipher her rushed words. Fated bonds were popping up? But wasn't that rare? "Do you think Alpha Jones had anything to do with this?"

She shrugged. "I'm not sure. He certainly doesn't have the power to meddle with fate, and there isn't a witch alive with a spell capable of that. It's like a switch flipped." I rubbed my temples, drawing her gaze. She suddenly seemed to realize I wasn't feeling well. "Hey. Are you okay?"

I shook my head. "I think I'm coming down with something. The flu, maybe?"

She took a step back. "Oh no. We can't have a virus spreading through camp. I'm going to grab some fae ear wax and make you a remedy right away."

A wave of nausea rolled up my throat, and I clamped my mouth shut. I wasn't sure if it was the sickness or the ear wax that made me sick.

"Thanks, June."

She placed a hand over her mouth and backed away. "Don't leave this room until I get you that tonic, okay? We don't need everyone getting sick."

I nodded and lay back in bed, all too happy to spend the day resting since I was feeling like shit. The moment June shut the bedroom door, I closed my eyes and tried to calm my racing pulse. It was a weird feeling. Like the air was heavier and my body had an anxious current coursing through it. I wasn't tired, per se, but it was like I could feel the earth rotating. It was like lying in bed after a day in the ocean, you could still feel the waves moving your body if you focused hard enough.

My phone started ringing, and I answered it without opening my eyes to check the caller ID. "Hello?"

"Nicole, where are you?" Dr. Viden rushed out.

I cracked open one eye and stared at the ceiling. I trusted Dr. Viden—Cammie—but wasn't sure if the line was compromised. I couldn't risk exposing the camp. "Safe. Is my father okay?"

"He's fine. Nicole, it's not safe to talk on the phone right now. I need you to find me immediately. You're in a lot of danger."

I opened my other eye and slowly sat up. "What? No, I'm safe here—"

"You *aren't*," Cammie insisted. "Listen, I promised your mother—"

"My mother?" My heart started to race at her words, and my palms grew impossibly hot. "Ouch!"

"Nicole? Are you okay?" Her voice was full of worry.

I inspected my fingertips before responding. "I'm... fine. Just think I have a fever."

Or... you know, maybe my blood was on fire.

Cammie started breathing heavily. I could hear the familiar click of her heels on the tile. "Nicole, I promised your mother I'd keep you safe. There is so much you don't know, and we need to discuss it. Please, I'm begging you, come to campus so I can talk to you."

"What are you talking about?" I asked. "You knew my mother?"

"Yes, and I will explain everything. I promise. But I need to see you in person."

I tried getting out of bed, but a wave of vertigo hit me like a brick. "Whoa."

"What's happening?" Cammie asked.

I started shaking my head but stopped when it made the dizziness worse. "I'm not feeling too well."

The fae's sigh on the other end of the line came through loud and clear. "I was afraid this would happen. You're not prepared."

"Prepared for *what*?"

"Please, Nicole. Meet me. Or I'll come to you. Whichever you prefer."

"Let me talk to Juniper, and I'll get back to you."

I couldn't think of any safe way to coordinate a meeting right now without a little magical assistance. I hung up the phone and managed to make it into a standing position without puking. Somehow, I even managed to throw some joggers on and one of Alexei's hoodies. My inner fashionista would just have to deal with the ultra-casual vibe I had going on. I left my room in search of my witchy friend, finding her in the sorority's potion room.

"Nicole!" Juniper startled when I stepped into the small space. "What are you doing out of bed?"

"Dr. Viden called," I explained. "She said she *needs* to meet. It sounded pretty important. I thought maybe you could help with that whole witchy travel thing you have access to."

She nodded. "Sure. Let's get Alexei and we can—"

"It'll be fine, Juniper. I don't want to pull him away from his patrol."

"I don't know…" June nibbled her lip in concentration. "Normally, I'm all for being a girl boss, but…"

"Will it make you feel better if you came along? We can meet Dr. Viden, hear what she has to say, and get out of there. I just want to get this over with so I can go back to bed."

"May I suggest an alternative?"

"Of course," I replied.

"How about I magically zip to the professor and bring her back here?" she suggested. "Don't take this the wrong way, Nicole, but you don't look great. I really think you should get back in bed."

"That's not a bad idea." I pulled my phone out of my sweats and texted Cammie. "But I really think I need some fresh air. Maybe I'll go sit out back while I wait for your return."

The witches were really big on being one with nature, so when they moved the Kappa Zeta house into the middle of a forest, they ensured all their outdoor furniture came along for the ride. There was a thickly padded lounger on the back deck calling my name.

"Good call." Juniper pointed to my phone. "Find out where the lovely professor is, and I'll meet up with her. As a fae, she can technically teleport herself, but it'd be really tricky if she didn't know your exact location."

"Thank you, June."

"My magic is your magic, Nicole." She smiled. "The second I get back, I'm going to make you some of my grandmother's special tea. And when I say *I*, I really mean Mitsy, since that damn woman would tell me I'm doing it all wrong, anyway."

I smiled, thinking of our cantankerous yet surprisingly nurturing house-elf. According to June, Mitsy was grumpier than ever with all the extra house guests. Most of our new additions had set up camp out back, but they came in and out of the house throughout the day.

As I made my way out to the back porch, my feet seemed to drag. The swirling feeling in my head made it impossible to keep my vision straight. Whatever was wrong with me made me incredibly weak. Maybe I *did* need Alexei. Was this part of the mate bond...

Or was it something else?

My raging thoughts were hard to sort through, but Cammie's words played through my delirious mind on repeat. She knew my mother, and she was trying to protect me, but from what? And what did she mean I wasn't prepared?

The sudden influx of mate bonds and my strange symptoms was certainly a coincidence, right?

I sat on the lounger and closed my eyes, the sun warming my skin as I waited. I think I may have fallen asleep, because the next thing I knew, Juniper magically popped into existence with Cammie at her side.

"Nicole!" Dr. Viden exclaimed.

My lashes fluttered as I stared at my professor, frowning when my vision doubled. "I feel sick," I slurred.

She bent down to press her palm to my forehead. "It's the surge of power. You're like an open tap right now, and your body isn't used to it."

"Power?"

Juniper sat down beside me. "Do you know what's wrong with her?"

Cammie nodded. "Nicole needs to come with me. I can get her the help she needs."

"Where?" I asked.

Juniper and Cammie started talking to one another, but their words got muddled in my mind. I couldn't tell who was saying what or what their jumble of sentences even meant.

"It's impossible."

"We need to get her out of here now."

"Alpha Jones is coming for her..."

Juniper eyed me. "Shit, Nicole. Alexei is going to kill me, but we don't have time."

A burst of magic wrapped around my body, and I was

lifted off the lounge. My body levitated above the deck, my limbs limp.

Cammie pointed to the left. "I can set up a portal just over in that clearing."

They walked beside me as I tried to make sense of everything. "Portal?"

Juniper opened her mouth to explain, but a loud boom blasted my eardrums and the ground shook. Whatever magic was holding me sent me crashing to the ground as Cammie and Juniper went flying.

Growls could be heard in the distance, and a wave of vampires started darting between the trees.

My senses rang in confusion.

Training Camp was under attack.

And I was helpless to defend myself.

Alexei

There was a shift in the air this morning. I couldn't quite put my finger on it, but my instincts were telling me to go back to Nicole. The tether we shared was burning brightly in my soul, and I wasn't sure if it was because we were finally on the right path to being together or if something was wrong.

I let out a sigh while peering at the magic boundary Juniper had established, feeling tired and wanting nothing more than to crawl back into bed with my mate. I was just about to check the time for the next watch shift when a loud boom sent me flying through the air.

I landed against the hard trunk of a tree, and my spine cracked as bark scattered on impact. The groaning willow practically bent as wind whipped around me. I forced myself to stand up and stared at the boundary as snarling shifters sprinted through a crack in our defenses.

"Shit."

I didn't have time to do much of anything but shift. I let out a quick exhale, and my bones twisted. My hands morphed into paws, and fur grew all over my body. The moment I was in my wolf form, I snapped at the army invading us.

It bothered me to fight my pack, but I had to defend my mate.

A wolf with white fur sprinted toward me, and with a leap, he collided with my middle, sending me to the ground. The moment the other wolf was on top of me, I reached up to dig my teeth into its neck, sending a burst of hot blood into my mouth. The wolf made a choking sound as it died, and I rolled over, knocking the limp body off of me.

Dozens of shifters continued to pour in, some of them with their eyes trained on me. I knew I needed to get to Nicole. I took off at full speed, running toward the Kappa Zeta house. It wasn't my nature to run from a fight, but I could feel Nicole's distress as if it were my own. I ran with blinders on as chaos erupted all around me. Saving my mate was my *only* priority right now. Everything else could be dealt with after I got her away from this madness.

My paws pummeled the thick brush as I weaved my

way in between trees so fast they were practically a blur. My enhanced hearing in this form picked up Nicole's anguished cry in the distance, making me run even faster, impossible as that seemed. The moment I spotted her, I was equal parts relieved, concerned, and confused. Juniper and the fae professor stood in a small clearing, while Nicole's prone body was lying on the ground next to them.

What the hell?

My hackles rose as Dr. Viden waved her hand in a counterclockwise circle right before a shimmery green disturbance in the air formed.

Oh, fuck no.

There was no doubt in my mind what that was. What I *didn't* know was why the fuck the professor had summoned it. She turned toward my mate, scooping her into her arms before turning back toward the open portal. I was still at least fifty feet away, so I picked up my pace.

What was she doing? Why wasn't June stopping her?

I barked in warning, but no one paid me any attention.

As the professor carried Nicole toward the gateway to another dimension, my mate's barely cognizant gaze met mine.

It looked like it took considerable effort for her to reach out her hand as she whispered, "Alexei."

My transformation back into my human form came on so suddenly and against my will; my bones felt like they were grinding against each other. I was in agony as I continued running while shifting, my muscles, joints, and nerves screaming in protest as they attempted to find their rightful place. Just as my snout disappeared and my mouth fell into place so I could speak, the professor took another step, crossing the threshold. I yelled Nicole's name, but it was too late. The professor had taken my mate into the portal, *all three* women and the gateway disappearing into thin air the moment they passed through. The world around me seemed to disappear as my nude body fell to the ground, completely spent. I panted from the exertion, playing the last few moments in my head over and over. I had no idea what the fuck had just happened, but there were two things I knew for sure.

I had failed my mate yet again.

And *nothing* would stop me from getting her back.

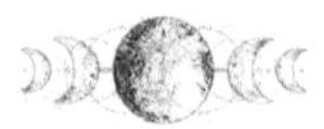

TO BE CONCLUDED in To Claim a Mate...

ANOTHER CLIFFHANGER?! SERIOUSLY?! Yeah, yeah, we hear you, but we promise this is the last one. (In this trilogy, anyway.) The good news is that we've formed an emotional support group for readers just like you! Come yell at us on Facebook @Poppy Ireland's Little Witchlings

xoxo, Poppy

About the Author

Poppy Ireland writes paranormal and fantasy romance. She is the brainchild of two longtime friends and *USA Today* Bestselling Authors who like to use their freaky mind melding powers to write spicy romantasy stories that will keep you on the edge of your seat.

To stay up to date on all the latest news, sign up for Poppy's newsletter at: https://www.subscribepage.com/poppyirelandbooks

You can also find her on social media:
Facebook: @poppyirelandbooks
Instagram: @poppyirelandbooks
TikTok: @poppyirelandbooks
Goodreads: @poppyirelandbooks
BookBub: @poppyirelandbooks

www.ingramcontent.com/pod-product-compliance
Lightning Source LLC
Chambersburg PA
CBHW062111290726
48975CB00001B/191